THE TREE OF LIFE

Ordering information:
Quantity sales. Special discounts are available on quantity purchases by corporations, associations, and others. For details, contact the publisher at the e-mail address below.

Printed in the United States of America
First Printing, 2015
ISBN 978-1-942306-16-0

Justin Stumvoll
1805 Hilltop Dr. Suite 203
Redding, CA
96003
info@StumvollConsulting.com
www.JustinStumvoll.com

Cover design and illustrations by Noah Elias:
www.NoahFineArt.com

Edited by Blair Reynolds.

Page layout by Ellyn Davis:
www.DoublePortionPublishing.com

THIS BOOK IS DEDICATED TO THOSE WHO ARE WILLING
TO CHASE THEIR DREAM NO MATTER THE COST.
TO YOU, I LEAVE ONE SIMPLE TRUTH I HAVE LEARNED:
FEAR IS THE GATEWAY BETWEEN US AND
THE DESTINY OF WHO WE ARE CREATED TO BE.

CONTENTS

PREFACE

One of the greatest gifts ever given to me was a divine interlude when life suddenly hit a pause, a pause that no matter how uncomfortable, frustrating, or painful things became, I could not push play. It was as though my life was frozen in time as the world passed me by. The uniqueness of my pause left no room for escape. I couldn't get lost in friends, family, entertainment, or hobbies.

As a young man driven by being productive, like much of the world around me, this season of life was borderline maddening. It forced me to stop everything and face the reality that I had been living life hiding behind a wall built from finely woven fears.

Prior to this timeout the chattering and distractions of life kept me in an out-of-body experience, distant from many of my real feelings. Hiding from the reality of my fears, insecurities, and shortcomings also kept me hidden and disconnected from all of the joy, peace, and life that equally existed inside of my heart.

As I chose to embrace this life pause I had to traverse a mountain of scary emotions and beliefs that had been lying dormant, buried by all the busyness. What I discovered in this journey is that I wasn't so fragile. The pain that I had avoided for all those years was not some monster that would easily swallow me alive, even if it felt that way at times.

Through choosing to face these hibernating fears and pains, the dreams of a child that had died long ago, because of hopelessness, were resurrected and birthed again by hope.

The Tree of Life is an allegory five years in the making. Interwoven in this allegory are the hidden nuggets of gold that were mined during this divine pause. This book is not meant to be devoured by those who would hunger for cheap entertainment. It is not a quick book to simply read for enjoyment and move on, though it is enjoyable. It is a story that is meant to be experienced. The book demands that you, the reader, stop just pushing on for the next moment of a story, and choose to be present with the moment in front of you.

I have come to believe that the fullness of my life is found only in understanding the people who make up the tapestry of relationships before me. It is their stories, who they are, and the love that they have to give that has shaped and continues to shape my life. With that, I say that no character in this book is without purpose and it is my dream that their stories and experiences not only shape who Oakie is, but you as well.

As you begin reading I want to leave you with this: *The Tree of Life* is not just a children's book, it is a cross-generational experience.

For the adult reading this book; there is an invitation to resurrect the child within. This opportunity comes through returning to a childlike innocence. This place of newfound innocence is where your imaginations are not hindered by the pain and beliefs that you've collected along the pathway of life.

To the child who would read *The Tree of Life*; this is a playful and strategic road map. This colorful map includes footprints to follow that will guide you into a life of depth, adventure, and love. You won't fully understand what you've learned until a time far in your future- when the lessons from this book will suddenly reveal themselves in your own story.

-Justin Stumvoll

THE TREE OF LIFE

CHAPTER
1

SERENDIPITY

1

Although there are countless types of trees that make this world special, each so uniquely designed, there is only one tree I know of worth telling a story about. Through a simple act of destiny, the course of one acorns fate was forever changed. This is that acorn's story—the story of Oakie the Apple Tree.

Now let us begin.

Under the blanket of a blue sky, stood a field filled with a family of oak trees. During this time of year, the giant oak trees gave birth to the tiniest acorn babies you've ever seen. If you didn't know better, you'd never believe anything that big and magnificent came from anything that small and insignificant. But looks can be deceiving.

Baby acorns lay scattered throughout the forest. As the acorns found their way to the ground, forgetful, bushy-tailed squirrels scurried along and gathered every acorn in sight. As quickly as possible they buried the acorns for food during the cold winter. Fortunately for many of the acorns, these forgetful squirrels could never remember *where* they hid their delicious treats.

Hanging high above the romp of the squirrels, Oakie the Acorn investigated the astonishing process. In his innocence, he longed to fall to the ground, hoping to get buried by the squirrels like all the other acorns. He spent days dreaming of the moment when it would be his turn.

One warm afternoon, while quietly relaxing in the refreshing breeze, Oakie was startled by the sound of a crickety-crackety, snippity-snap. Without warning Oakie plummeted to the ground and there was nothing he could do.

But he didn't have to.

As fate would have it, an adventurer known as Wild-Eyed Otis, a tiny-tailed squirrel, was impatiently running in circles below. Luckily for Otis, he had a rather thick noggin that broke Oakie's fall.

After a brief tango of dancing around dazed and confused, Otis realized his extraordinary find.

"Eureka!" Otis shouted. "Oooh baby, I found me an acorn!"

"Hey guys," Otis called to all the other squirrels, "I *told* you I'd get one. I told you this would be my day!"

In all his excitement, Otis launched into the air and did a back flip, followed by a brief touchdown dance, which left Oakie rather nauseous.

The other squirrels laughed at Otis. Otis wasn't called "Wild-Eyed" for nothin'. Because of his dramatic eye twitch and high-pitched voice, he had been declared "crazy" by all the squirrels in the forest. And let's be honest—he wasn't the best at gathering acorns. As long as Otis had lived, he had never gathered acorns—not a single one!

Otis was an adventurer at heart. While all the other squirrels gathered acorns, he was busy running around and exploring unknown parts of the forest that no one had ever seen, or even cared to see. Besides seeming weird, and not being good at squirrel stuff, Otis was smaller than the rest of the squirrels, and didn't have the same bushy tail the rest of them did. This made him the brunt of several of the other squirrels' jokes.

"You didn't find no acorn, you goofy-lookin' clown!" one of them hollered. "You can't even find your tail!"

All the squirrels laughed.

"Yeah! The only way you could find an acorn is if it found you," proclaimed another.

The antagonistic squirrels passed high-fives around their circle.

Otis rubbed the bump on his head.

"No it didn't! *I* found *it!*" retorted Otis.

"Then show us your acorn that you found," demanded one of Otis's accusers.

Boldly holding his head high and squaring his shoulders like an army general, Otis thrust Oakie into the air for all to see. A shimmer of light reflected off Oakie's head.

Shock washed the words from the other squirrels' mouths.

As the shock lifted, one of Otis's harassers came up with an evil idea. "Hey fellas! I'll give five acorns to the squirrel who can take that *one*, from Otis." He chuckled devilishly and rubbed his hands together.

Without hesitation, a barrage of hungry squirrels started an all-out sprint for the trophy.

Otis's moment of glory was over and Oakie was in for the ride of his life! Without warning, Otis thrust Oakie into the brown, worn satchel at his side.

In a twist of fate, Otis's days of explorations became the trampoline that would shoot him well out of the reach of those looking to steal his prize.

Barreling through the woods, leaping over stumps, dashing under logs and plowing through piles of leaves, Otis zigged and zagged, left and right, until there was nothing but a cloud of dust and leaves whipping through the air behind him.

After losing the mob of acorn pirates, Otis came to a standstill and Oakie released a giant sigh of relief. But, before Oakie could get too comfortable, Otis started up again. Spinning in circles, frantically looking up and down and all around, Otis hunted until he discovered a suitable place to bury his first and only acorn. With intense tenacity, he shot shards of dirt sailing into the air as he dug wildly into the earth.

All Oakie knew was that acorns got buried, and the day that he had dreamed about for so long had finally come! Joy swelled as he imagined what the dirt might hold for him.

Otis whipped his head left and right in one final scan for any treacherous bandits. Then, with decisive confidence, he flopped Oakie into the freshly dug hole.

Oakie squinted as the afternoon sky quickly faded and dirt piled atop his head. With a sense of wonderment, he waited expectantly for what would come next.

CHAPTER

2

THE GRASS ISN'T ALWAYS GREENER

2

This once-appealing pit, perceived as the realization of all of Oakie's dreams, now seemed silent and still.

After every raindrop of light had dried up and the patter of Otis's feet faded, Oakie quickly found himself rethinking his desire to be buried like the other acorns.

"Now that I'm finally here, what's next?" he asked himself aloud.

Sadly, there was no response.

"Hey is anybody else down here?" he asked the surrounding dirt.

The dirt had no reply either.

Without much to do, Oakie drifted away into daydreams. He thought about all the things that might happen. Maybe another acorn would get buried next to him and they would become best friends. Maybe Otis would come back and take him on adventures to far-away forests. Maybe Verstand the Eagle Owl would come looking for him and bring him back to his branch.

"Ahhhhh, the branch. I miss my branch," he sighed.

You see, sometimes, it's easy to think that grass is greener on the other side, and that's just what Oakie did. Before long he began to reminisce about all the wonderful things life had to offer before being buried.

During the evenings, he would sit for hours and watch Verstand; she was his favorite part of the forest. She embodied beauty. She had piercing blue eyes illuminated by the shimmering white feathers that wrapped her from head to toe. As the sun faded she would blaze silently through the sky and in the most majestic fashion land in the neighboring tree. There she would meticulously tend to the beautiful eagle's nest she had found, which had long ago been abandoned.

Before long, her nest was filled with adorable owlets. They grew as quickly as weeds, and soon were entertaining Oakie as they took flying lessons. One after another, they leapt from their nest and flopped like turkeys all the way to the ground. Oakie cackled aloud as he watched them take their turns.

Each time, with great patience and without hesitation, Verstand swooped down and checked them over to assure they had not been hurt.

She stood by their side, giving them her full attention, until they could take flight from the ground.

There was something so warm and inviting about her. Oakie couldn't help but be drawn to her as he witnessed her gaze at her children. She held each one of them with the loving embrace of her eyes.

When Verstand looked at him, he felt like one of her own. Her gaze spoke to him of unconditional love, acceptance, and a sense of hope. There was nothing that rivaled the enjoyment he had from being around Verstand. Oakie could do without many things, but the presence of Verstand didn't seem to be one of them.

Besides Verstand and her owlets, Oakie loved the magical light shows the stars put on when they came out at night to dance with the moon. Occasionally, a star would jump out of the sky and take off on its own journey. Sometimes Oakie was lucky enough to watch an entire family take the dive. They looked like beavers jumping into the pond.

As Oakie reminisced while buried snugly in the ground, a funny memory passed through his mind.

One day, while he was admiring all the beautiful colors of fall, Oakie watched a prank go sour. But to him, it was all so very sweet. Below, a mischievous band of jokester jackrabbits named The Three Amigos, who were notorious for their pranks in the forest, plotted out a devilish plan to scare someone for fun.

Oakie listened to their scheming from above. Their idea was to hide behind a couple of trees. When the next passerby crossed their path, they would leap out wearing scary masks made from grass and mud.

The plan was simple yet highly entertaining. After a bit of time impatiently hiding in their spots, an unsuspecting victim clamored down the beaten path. On cue, as planned, they sprung from their hiding places onto their victim. Unfortunately for them they met face to face with Mary, the forest's neighborhood skunk.

Oakie's face wrinkled as he remembered the terrible smell of the cloud Mary left behind as she bolted out of the forest. For weeks The Three Amigos smelled too terrible to sneak up on anyone.

Oakie chuckled to himself. *Yeah, those were the days*, he thought, as he continued to go through the list of things he missed before being left all alone with nothing to do and no one to do nothing with.

As Oakie lay fantasizing about the past and wishing for better times, minutes stretched into hours. Hours morphed into days. The days multiplied into months. Oakie was alone and lost in nothingness.

Poor little acorn. After spending so much time hunting for comfort in what he didn't have anymore, the only thing he found was despair and hopelessness, as there was no way to return to the things he had once so enjoyed. Thinking about happier times was torture.

"Why?" Oakie shouted at the top of his lungs. "Why am I here? What's the point of this? Isn't there something more! Is *anybody* out there? Anybody ... please. Someone please hear me!" Oakie shouted over and over until his little acorn lungs nearly dried up.

With a hoarse voice and tears flying down his face, he begged and pleaded with the absent audience, "Please! Please do something. Please change things. Please. Please. Please ... somebody ... please help me ..."

In all his pain, he worked himself into complete exhaustion. The begging and pleading subsided, and little Oakie fell asleep.

CHAPTER

3

HOPE FOR TOMORROW

3

The sound of chirping startled Oakie. A soft gust of wind rocked him gently like a baby in a crib. The smell of wild lilacs tickled his nose. The patter of deer hooves, trotting through leaves, flooded his ears. A scene long forgotten illuminated his eyes.

Squinting tightly, he peered through the blinding sunlight. Verstand stood perched by her nest with the most dignified of looks. She toted a small trout in her mouth. Three owlets, crying for food, filled the nest to the brim. Verstand leaned over and fed the babies their meal.

Oakie found himself so very confused. Verstand's owlets had long left the nest and were much larger than what he was now seeing. Had she had more babies?

"Miss Verstand!" Oakie yelled.

She didn't even turn her head.

Maybe she didn't hear him. Once more Oakie shouted. "Miss Verstand!"

Nothing. The babies didn't notice him either.

Along Verstand's nest crawled the fattest, hairiest caterpillar Oakie had ever seen. But what made this caterpillar stand out was neither its size nor its ungroomed body hair. What made this caterpillar the center of attention was the wondrous orchestra of colors enveloping it. Shades of red, orange, yellow, blue, green, indigo, and violet were present, accompanied by colors Oakie had never dreamed of. With every undulation of its body, the colors moved as if they themselves were alive.

While the owlets gobbled up their delicious dinner, Verstand stared intently, as if hypnotized by the caterpillar. Without warning, momma thrust out her wings, demanding the attention of her babies. Frozen stiff, they waited for insight into what was happening. Verstand turned their gaze toward the strangely beautiful guest. With a gentle, yet serious tone, she began to share a story.

"Each and every caterpillar must crawl," she began. "For many, their life seems very limited. They watch the birds of the air and dream of what it would be like to see what we see. Occasionally, they find a tree like this one and get a better view. For the few that climb all the way up here a holy dissatisfaction takes over their hearts. Something begins to grow deep within them. They know they can't go back to crawling on the ground, but they also can't seem to discover an alternative.

"Many lose hope and crawl back down the tree, remembering the voices of all those that told them it was a caterpillar's life to crawl. But a few refuse to stop believing, and those few soon find themselves doing something they've never done before."

Verstand gazed into her children's innocent eyes. As only a wise mother would, she asked, "What do you think they do, my darlings?"

The owlets looked at one another and shrugged their wings.

"I know! I know!" Oakie shook up and down on his branch, desperately trying to get Verstand's attention.

Verstand grinned proudly at her children, then she continued.

"As the caterpillars hang upside down from a branch, all the anticipation and excitement builds up while dreaming begins to pour out. It creates a cocoon around them. Their world suddenly becomes dark, and for what seems like an eternity, they are left alone, wondering how all their grandiose dreams got them there.

As time passes and all their worries fade away, when they are left only to trust that there is something more, a magnificent breakthrough happens. Light begins to pour in as an unknown force breaks out. Emerging, they find they now have wings and their real journey begins."

With that, the caterpillar with spellbinding colors

climbed out onto a branch and began releasing its cocoon.

A large smile stretched across Oakie's face. It was the most beautiful story he had ever heard.

Without warning, a familiar sound disrupted the moment. *Crickety-crackety, snippity-snappity!* And with that, he began to fall ...

CHAPTER

4

A SETTLED SOUL

SETTLED SOUL

4

O akie startled himself out of his own dream. The darkness still surrounded him, but the magic of what he had just experienced made everything brighter.

Peace began to flood his heart. He thought of Verstand's wisdom as he replayed the dream in his mind. With each remembrance, the peace was stoked like a tiny ember, setting his heart ablaze. Although he had no clue where in the world a dream like that came from, he also knew someone, or something, had heard his cries.

Sometimes it just takes one moment, one simple change in our perspective, to change our worst circumstances into our greatest opportunities. And thus it was for Oakie.

His damp, dark hole didn't have to be the end. There could be so much more! Imagining the possibilities built hope and expectation. As he pictured that magnificent caterpillar over and over again, he dared to dream that this hole was nothing more than his cocoon. The warmth of seeing Verstand again brought such comfort.

Suddenly, he realized this wasn't the end! Suddenly this seemed like it could actually be the beginning of something greater. Oakie was finally finding satisfaction in the dark, damp hole. No matter how long it took, he was determined to be content and enjoy this moment of time, knowing it wasn't going to last forever.

Oakie's change of heart was put to the test as fate took its time. Moments of doubt leapt at him like grasshoppers. Fears he didn't know he possessed stalked him like wolves. Sadness occasionally wrapped itself around him like a snake. But, with each challenge, Oakie held tight to his dream. With every stand Oakie took, the grasshoppers jumped less and less. With every charge forward, the wolves ran farther and farther away. With each struggle Oakie made, the snake's grip loosened more and more. In time the grasshoppers, wolves, and snake had all but retreated. His battle seemed to have been won.

Lying in his hole, during what he imagined might be a warm, relaxing afternoon above him, Oakie hummed a tune the beavers used to sing that went something like:

Fun and play,
Fun and play!
We work all day,
But it's nothing more
Than fun and play!

While happily daydreaming of the beavers building their dam in Mother Pond, something shifted. Without warning, water engulfed Oakie. Startled by the sudden change, he stopped humming. Feelings he had never experienced before churned inside his belly. His entire face felt ready to explode! The pressure was so much that he thought that this would be his last moment. Without any effort at all, the pressure popped and Oakie burst through the dirt.

The sudden change in light left him temporarily blinded. Raindrops drizzled down on his face. The smell of the fresh rain was intoxicating.

Oakie took a deep breath and savored it before releasing it and gulping another. The second sent shivers throughout his being. As his sight came into focus, a stunning view lay before him. He found himself smack dab in the middle of the most exquisite trees, holding what seemed to be the most gigantic red acorns he'd ever laid eyes on. Scattered on the ground all around him were more of the giant red acorns.

"Wow! Oh, man! This is the *best* thing in the whole wide forest! This must be where all the acorns go! How did they all get so huge? Hey everyone, it's me, Oakie!"

He was filled with uncontainable excitement. While doing a little acorn jitterbug, something seized his attention.

Jolted by the sight, he began to holler, "I'm green! Why am I green? I'm green and I'm stuck in the ground! Why am I green and stuck in the ground?" Caterpillars received wings ... and Oakie had turned green.

CHAPTER
5

UNEXPECTED EXPECTATIONS

5

Amid all the confusion of this transformation, some-thing like a tornado whipped in and spun erratic circles around our little Oakie. Stopping on a dime, the whirlwind disappeared. There before him was a giant furry nose dripping with snot and tickling his face with whiskers.

"Ugh! Ahhh!" Oakie yelled. "Get outta my face!" His moment of awe and wonder had been disrupted, but before him stood an unlikely surprise. As the annoyance dissipated, a familiar face came into focus.

"Where's my acorn?" demanded Wild-Eyed Otis.

"*Your* acorn?" Oakie shot back. "First off, I'm not your acorn. Second, where have you been?"

"Who are you?"

"Who am *I*? I'm Oakie. I'm the acorn you threw in here a really *loooong* time ago."

"No, you're a plant. An acorn is a little brown nut-looking thing. I put it right here for the winter." Otis scratched his noggin. "Err, maybe there, or there, or there, or there or there or there!" Otis started pointing in all different directions while curling his lip and squinting one eye.

"No, this is where you buried me. I know because I haven't gone anywhere since then," Oakie shot back with a glare.

"Well if you're *the* acorn that I buried here, tell me how you got here!"

"It pretty much went like this. I fell out of my tree onto your head. You claimed you found me."

Otis stood contemplating Oakie's defense.

"Then a bunch of your punk friends chased you down."

"Those weren't my friends," retorted Otis. "But go on."

"Go on? What do you mean go on? Then you shoved me

in this hole. What else is there to say?"

"Yeah." Otis said, rubbing his chin. "That sounds about right, except ..."

"Except what?"

"Except, I didn't *claim* to find you, I *did* find you," exclaimed Otis.

"Sorry, you *found* me." Oakie rolled his eyes.

A reflection from one of the giant red acorns pierced Otis's eye. Otis shot to it like a flash of lighting. The wind trailing behind him spun Oakie's tiny, fragile body around.

After settling for a moment, Oakie muttered, "I think I'm gonna puke."

Meanwhile, Otis had already piled a stack of those big red acorns in his arms so high that they looked as though they had grown the feet of a squirrel and become a wild monster. Giving his best balancing act, Otis made his return to Oakie.

"Hey Otis, what are you doing with all those giant acorns?" Oakie yelped. "Are you burying them too?"

"Acorns?" Otis reached out with his right foot and pinched the stem of another one between his toes. "These ain't acorns."

He tossed the apple up in the air to the top of the pile, "*These* are apples."

Oakie squinted funnily.

The apple landed on top, knocking the entire pile to the ground. The last of the falling apples bonked Otis on the head, sending him into a dazed tailspin until he finally crash-landed at Oakie's stem.

"Otis?"

No response.

"Otis, you okay?"

"Cows should never be married to chickens because bananas hate being peeled."

Speechless, Oakie stared down at Otis wondering if this is what happens right before someone dies.

Otis sat straight up. Pulling tightly on the end of his ears, he declared at the top of his lungs, "I am the greatest sea monkey that ever swam the seven seas!" And then he immediately fell over on his back and flopped around like a fish out of water.

Oakie watched with concern as Otis went limp.

Then, with one last burst of life, Otis shouted at the top of his lungs, "*Freeeeedooooom!*"

Finally the drama seemed to be over. Oakie wondered if he should mourn somehow ... maybe say a prayer, sing a sad song, or at least shed a tear?

But there was no need. As quickly as Otis's life seemed to have ended, it returned. He bounced to his feet, catching an apple on the way up, and began to ravenously devour it.

With a seamless transition, he began again. "Apples are the greatest invention ever!" Otis's mouth overflowed. Chunks of apple shot into Oakie's face.

Oakie tried, but couldn't shield himself from the barrage of debris catapulting his direction.

"Because of these hot little babies I don't have to spend my life gathering and burying acorns like all those other saps. I just explore this endless world and discover all of its mysterious—"

Otis continued to babble, going on a seemingly never-ending rant.

The gears turned in Oakie's mind until a stick of dynamite exploded. "OTIS! You big meathead!"

Otis froze. The apple plummeted out of his mouth to the ground.

"If you didn't need to gather and bury acorns, then why in all the forest did you have to throw me in that pit and leave me?"

"Caaaaaause ..." Otis chose his words carefully, "I'm a squirrel ...?"

"You're a squirrel?" Oakie shouted, startling Otis so badly that he spit the remainder of his treat back in Oakie's face. "What is that supposed to mean?" Oakie demanded while wiping apple off of his face with his tiny leaf.

"Well, it means that everyone keeps telling me that I'm a squirrel and that I need to quit playing around and gather acorns like everybody else." Otis backed away a bit just to keep a safe distance between him and the green goblin.

Fortunately for Otis, Oakie's most significant lesson concerning life was about to drop by and save Otis's life. After taking a deep breath, Oakie calmed down as he remembered the dream about the caterpillar and the promise that it held for him. Suddenly, it didn't matter *why* it had happened; he simply remembered that great things *would* happen because of it. Besides, it was over now. It didn't last forever.

Oakie noticed Otis bracing himself a bit, still holding the core of the apple. To lighten things up, Oakie decided to ask him a few questions.

"So, that's an apple?" Oakie asked.

"Yeah," Otis said hesitantly.

"How do you get apples?"

"Well, you see, apples grow on those trees right up there," he pointed out.

Oakie followed his finger, looking at never-ending rows of trees full of apples all around him.

"Around the same time each year they start falling down here," Otis pointed to the ground. "Then peoples start appearing out of nowhere and pick them up." Otis pointed in all directions.

"Peoples?"

"Peoples. They're these big things, kind of like squirrels, but no fur, and sadly no tails." Otis happily stroked his own tail. "They come in a few different colors and a lot of different shapes and sizes. They kind of walk like this—" Otis perched on his hind legs and began walking like a zombie.

Oakie giggled.

Otis ran up close to his face. Looking around to see if anyone was listening, he whispered, "Between you and me, they smell worse than dung beetles." Otis curled his nose. "It's the smallest ones ya gotta watch out for."

"Why?" Oakie whispered.

"Cause they'll chase you down and if they catch you," Otis whipped both his arms around Oakie, "they'll squeeze ya like this and shake you around until your eyeballs pop outta your head."

Otis squeezed and shook Oakie till he looked darn near sick. "And they won't quit until a big one pulls you outta their arms and throws you to the ground screaming at the top of their lungs." Otis paused, then leaned in again. "Don't get caught by the peoples, that's all I'm sayin'." He finally released his grip on Oakie.

Oakie gathered his thoughts once again and weighed the possibilities of asking another question.

So, would I ever have apples grow from me?"

Otis sat for a moment and built himself a hypothesis.

"Well, apples grow on these here trees. You're a plant. Trees grow from plants. You're growing in the middle of trees that grew from plants that now grow apples from their branches. Soooo, hmmm. Yes. Yes, you will one day grow apples after you grow into a tree." Everything seemed to work out pretty well in the equation.

So it was settled. Oakie was going to grow up like all the other trees and make apples that peoples would want. That seemed pretty great.

"Listen, I hate to eat and run, but I heard a colony of ants carried off William, an anteater, and hung him upside down by his tail from a tree. This is something I gotta see!"

"Will you come back and eat my apples and tell me about your adventures sometime?"

"Yes." Otis stood silently staring off into the distance for an awkward amount of time. Then without warning he took off sprinting, grabbing an apple as he exited.

Watching as Otis disappeared in the distance, Oakie began to dream of what it would be like one day when he himself would grow apples.

CHAPTER

6

INVADERS
FROM BEYOND

6

With Otis gone, the afternoon quickly approached. Oakie's new home in the apple orchard began to pulse with life. Everything was so like his old home, with the exception of apples.

He took a deep breath, as tranquility filled his heart. Then, without warning, a giant force smashed down in front of him, startling the breath right out of him. Something that sounded like a parade of wild boars rushed toward him.

What in the forest is going on now?

Being outside the hole sure didn't leave any dull moments for our new Oakie. A stampede that looked like hundreds of odd-looking hooves pounded down all around him, nearly smashing him right back down where he came from.

After a brief moment of disorientation, everything started to make sense.

It was the peoples Otis had talked about!

Peoples of all shapes and sizes. The smaller ones were running all over the place, grabbing apples and shoving them in their mouths. The large ones were yelling something at them about checking for worms. The medium-sized peoples were throwing apples back and forth. Some of them were even climbing trees like squirrels. Others were hanging from the trees like bats. And yet more of the large ones were pointing and yelling at the medium ones to get down. It was all so very odd and new.

The trees, which had been unaware of Oakie, the tiny sapling that had seemingly sprung up silently before them, all began to come alive with laughter. What first seemed like a full-scale war soon turned into a celebration. It was the wildest thing he'd ever witnessed.

"I love it when peoples climb me!" shouted one tree.

"Look at the short round one trying to climb me!" exclaimed another. All the trees erupted in more laughter as a cute, short, round little people tried his best to climb, but kept falling down and rolling around before getting up and trying again.

Some of the big peoples carried large wooden baskets. Setting them down below a tree of their choosing, a group of peoples would cluster around, pop apples off the branches and throw them into the baskets below. With every apple pulled, a giggle billowed out of the tree it came from.

"I never get used to that!" shouted a tree at the top of his lungs with the biggest smile Oakie had ever seen.

Oakie watched with wonder as the peoples romped about the orchard. Not one tree frowned. Not one tree complained. Not one tree despised the intrusion. The entire orchestration seemed to be what they were all made for.

As the sun made its way to bed, so did the peoples. Soon the last of the visitors vanished with the light. Fireflies surrounded Oakie, illuminating his face. Crickets began singing lullabies. Wolves howled their goodnights. The trees began to settle from all of the commotion. There was nothing uneventful about Oakie's first day—quite the contrary, in fact.

With the stars and the night came time to reflect on all that had happened. As Oakie stared at the glittering sky, he contemplated the new thing he had become. He sure wasn't an acorn anymore. Almost being smashed to pieces by the herd of peoples really made him think. He had become something that seemed so frail. He wasn't protected by a hard shell anymore. Now he felt exposed, and vulnerable in the form of this fragile plant—but in a weird way, it seemed freeing.

What Oakie didn't realize was that during the course of his life, he would truly discover how freeing this vulnerability could be.

Although he was small, Otis said he'd one day grow into one of the big apple trees. That gave him hope. He didn't know how long he would be like this, but he knew it wouldn't be forever. Beyond the dream of being big like all the other trees around him, he had the joy of knowing that in time he'd grow apples and peoples would come. By the looks of it, that's what made all the other trees happy.

As Oakie sat thinking, a star jumped out of the sky. A chill ran through him from the top of his little green head all the way to, well, to the dirt. Although this wasn't home, watching that star leap out of the sky made him feel like he was hanging from his branch again. He knew that Verstand and her owlets, which were now full grown, Mother Pond, Otis, and all the other friends in the forest had seen the same star. No matter where he was and no matter what he was doing, he knew he wasn't alone. A tear of joy grew from Oakie's eye and took its own journey to the ground. He wasn't alone, and there was so much more to his life than what he could see.

With that, Oakie snuggled down into the dirt and drifted off to sleep.

OUT OF THE MOUTH OF BABES

7

The surprises never seemed to end for Oakie.
"Ha, ha, ha!" Laughing himself awake, Oakie realized he wasn't alone.

A battalion of ants marched up his stem to the tune of their own chant.

Forward, forward,
Never left or right.
We will march,
Day and night.
Sound off, one two,
Sound off, three four!
We will march,
'Till our feet are sore!

The hundreds of little ant feet left Oakie in stitches.
"What are you doing?" Oakie burst out as he laughed.
His response startled the ant leading the pack.
"Company halt!" The abrasive command caused a pile-up all the way from the top of Oakie down to the ground and well off into the grass where the chain of ants disappeared.
"Who are you to ask me what I am doing?" demanded the commander.
"Well, I guess I'm the green plant you're marching up," Oakie said through giggles.
"State your name and rank, boy!"
"I'm, uh, Oakie. And ... I don't know my rank?"
"Well Uhoakie, I'm Commander Brick, and you're interfering with official army-ant business. Give me a reason why I shouldn't have your head on a stick for intruding on

my platoon's mission?"

"What's your mission?"

"That's classified! And don't answer a question with a question, boy. Now, answer me!"

A little confused and entertained by Commander Brick, Oakie took a moment to choose his words. "Putting my head on a stick would deviate you from your mission at hand?"

"Is that a question or a statement, boy?"

"A statement ...?" Surely this ant commander was a little more than crazy.

"That's a fine point, civilian. What are you doing up here?"

"I'm actually down there and I end up here."

"Are you getting smart with me? Because I don't tolerate smart civilians!"

"No sir, I'm not smart at all. With all due respect, Commander Brick, may I have permission to ask a question?" Oakie said with a smile, seeing where this game was going.

"Permission granted! And wipe that smile off your mug." Oakie took his leaf and wiped the smile away, trying his best not to laugh.

"Could you tell me a little bit more about your brave mission? You look very focused and determined to get somewhere."

"Classified!" The commander paused for a moment to scan his surroundings. "Civilian, I don't talk much to civilians. I have one purpose and that's to lead this army. It is my birthright. I was born a commander and I'll die a commander. These are my troops and I'm responsible for their wellbeing. Where I go, they go. What I say, they do. As long as they stay in that line and don't deviate from the mission, they will go unnoticed like any good soldier. If they step out of line, they will be disciplined for their own good. I *AM* the hand of discipline!"

Oakie's eyes began to grow wide, unable to take the commander seriously.

"We have a mission and a goal. Our mission is to march forward. Our goal is to do it well. Weakness will not be tolerated."

One of the soldiers down the line snickered loud enough

to catch Commander Brick's attention.

"Who was that? I'll have your head on a stick! This is no laughing matter! Utmost respect is demanded at all times."

Turning back to Oakie, the commander continued, "We will march without compromise. Those that are entrusted to me will find their greatness in obedience. Individualism will not be tolerated. It is the collective effort of the entire army that produces results we can be proud of. Fearing me is not just *a* way—it is the *only* way. A lack of fear toward me shows rebellion. And we can't have rebellion, now can we troops?"

"No, sir!" echoed through out the orchard as the army simultaneously agreed.

"What about you, Uhoakie? Rebellion can't be tolerated, can it?"

Oakie determined that not only had the commander lost his mind, but this was the funniest game he had played in a long time. "No, sir!"

"Do you fear me, boy?"

Looking at the commander, who talked much bigger than he was, only provoked more laughter to fill Oakie's tank. So much that he didn't know if he could handle any more. "Sir. Yes, sir!"

"Good, and it best stay that way."

"Sir, may I be permitted to speak freely?"

"As long as it does not conflict with anything that I have said, civilian."

"Well it sounds to me like you have a mission to march, but it doesn't seem like you're going anywhere specific. That seems kind of boring and pointless to me."

Anger swelled in the commander's eyes.

"And you have all these great soldiers," Oakie continued. "I'll bet they all have really good ideas you haven't thought of. Maybe instead of disciplining them, you could ask them questions and get some new ideas. 'Cause with an army this big, you could do all sorts of stuff besides just march."

The commander's anger grew like a balloon ready to pop.

"And maybe instead of having one line you could have a bunch of lines with other commanders and you could all be doing different things that were really cool," Oakie went on. "Or instead of lines you could have groups of ants that—"

In Oakie's innocence and curiosity he had unknowingly broken the final thread of Commander Brick's patience.

"No more! I will not tolerate this absurd thought and questioning. Boy, if you weren't a civilian you'd be scrubbing mold off a tree stump for the rest of your existence!

"I AM the first and last say-so. I am the ONLY commander. There will be no others. One line for all and that's final!"

Turning to the platoon the commander barked, "It's time to move out, troops. We've done enough lollygagging here. Back down we go! Now march!"

With that, the line retreated down Oakie. The tickling of their feet was too much. Oakie broke in laughter.

Turning to Oakie, Commander Brick made one last declaration.

"I will not be mocked. Laugh to your heart's content, civilian, because you'll never be part of this great army."

Oakie watched as the army made its way through the brush toward an unknown destination. Oddly enough, that strange little Commander Brick had brightened his day.

CHAPTER

8

VIVA LA REVOLUCION

8

Not only had the commander left Oakie with a good laugh, but it seemed as though he had also left a straggler.

From behind a rock, a solitary ant popped his head up high enough for Oakie to notice him. His head bobbed up and down like a yo-yo as he took a moment to ensure the entire army was gone.

"Pssst! Greenie! Greenie Dude, over here!" Motioning for Oakie's attention, the ant continued to bob up and down, shooting his eyes left and right to check for any scouts that could be looking for him.

"Are you all right?" Oakie asked.

"Are they gone, bro?"

"The army?"

"No, the giant rock monsters."

Puzzled, Oakie took a moment to look around. "I don't think there are any giant—"

"The army, dude. The army, are they gone?"

"I can't see 'em anywhere."

"Good." Cautiously tip-toeing from behind the rock, the ant made his way toward Oakie.

"Duuuuuude! The Duke is for sure not going back there. Commander Crazy is *waaaaay* too intense for The Duke, bro. It's like his panties are in a perma-wedgie. You got any bread crumbs, bro?"

Oakie stood for a moment just observing the interesting visitor.

"You know what, bro, don't sweat it. The Duke's got his own stash right here. Snagged it from the chow wagon a couple of nights ago."

"What's your name?" Oakie asked.

The ant began scarfing down his crumbs. Through a mouth full of food he responded, "Bro, what you said to the commander, that was, that was like—I can't even wrap my brain around how awesome that was, bro."

Oakie smiled. "Do you have a name?"

"Oh yeah, for sure bro, everyone has a name. Did you see the look on his face?" Mocking the commander, the ant began pulling on his antennae and making a monster face. " 'Don't talk back to me, green dude. I am the greatest commander since ever!' "

Oakie giggled. "I'm Oakie."

"Bro, The Duke says you're officially a legend as of right now."

A crunching rang out nearby. Without hesitation, Oakie's admirer barrel rolled behind some leaves and disappeared.

Oakie looked around, wondering what was going on.

"Umm ... Who's The Duke?" he asked.

"Shhhh, I am. Now keep it down." The Duke, still invisible, responded. Like a detective, he peered from around the side of a leaf to investigate the noise.

"*Cacaw cacaw! Cacaw cacaw!*" the ant called.

"What are you doing?"

Slightly irritated, The Duke responded, "Dude, bro, with all due respect, you're blowing The Duke's cover."

"Your cover is the sound of a sick bird?"

Jumping out from behind the leaf, The Duke retorted, "Look, bro, that is not a sick bird. That is the hunger call of a treacherous carnivorous ant-eating ghoul."

"A what? It sounds a lot like a—"

"Bro, the questions, seriously! The Duke knows what you think it sounded like and The Duke knows what it was. Trust me, if they came back for The Duke, he'd send 'em running for their mommies. Furthermore, dude, how did you come up with that stuff? It was like you drilled a hole right into The Duke's skull and sucked my thoughts out with a straw!"

Oakie beamed.

The Duke continued as he gripped his own face and

squeezed it around like clay, "You are wise like a bandicoot, bro! *Viva La Revolución!* Come on, are you with me, man?"

"Yeah! *La Revolución!*" Oakie had no idea what it meant but it seemed to be the appropriate response.

"The Duke and you, bro, we're going to set this place ablaze!"

A fire seemed like a bit of a bad idea, as Oakie and the surrounding trees were—well, trees. "A fire?"

"Yeah, but not just any fire—a fire more intense than the noonday sun!" The Duke stared at the sky, briefly blinding himself, then stumbled around rubbing his eyes. "I can see millions of ants all gathered around, drinking this brain juice of ours. It's going to be beautiful, bro. No more conforming to The Man. It's time for free thought. No more endless lines. No more shutting our mouths for fear of having our heads on sticks. No more—"

Frozen in mid-sentence, The Duke looked like a finely chiseled statue. Oakie was once more baffled and entertained. He got no response as he waved his leaves in front of the ant's face. Leaning down, Oakie abruptly took a different approach.

"*Rarrrr!*"

Still nothing.

Maybe something a little scarier would snap Oakie's new friend out of it.

"*Cacaw, Cacaw!*" he cried.

Oakie paused for a moment but did not receive so much as a blink. Minutes rolled into hours. Countless attempts later, nothing more than a petrified ant sat before Oakie.

The morning stretched into late afternoon, and the sound of apple trees chattering back and forth filled the air. Convinced there was nothing more to do for The Duke, Oakie began replaying what he had said to Commander Brick.

Was it really all that amazing? It all seemed so simple to him. Oakie knew he wasn't an ant, but following someone in a line going nowhere seemed pointless. Even more than pointless, it seemed so boring. Reflecting on the face of each soldier, Oakie began to realize that not one of them seemed excited about what they were doing. All the ants marched with a stone-cold look on their faces as if their brains had been washed of all thoughts and their hearts drained of all feelings. A sapling could say they almost looked … lifeless. There must have been at least a million ants marching in that line, and each one probably felt so alone, as if no one else was there except for the voice yelling, "March, march, march!"

A hint of sadness swept over Oakie. Sure, there weren't a million other green little Oakies all around him, and he couldn't move from where he was in order to see new sights, but he still felt alive. Even when he was angry and sad about being buried in the ground, he felt something more than what the whole group of ants seemed to feel. Everything inside Oakie hoped for the best for all those ants. But before he could feel any worse for them, The Duke picked up where he'd left off.

"—being just another ant doing the same thing day after day!"

"What happened to you? Are you okay?" Oakie asked.

"What happened to The Duke is you, bro. I've never been better. Smell the air green, dude." The Duke took a great big whiff of the fresh orchard air. "That right there is the smell of freedom, bro."

"And *revolución!*" Oakie shouted for fun.

"Exactly, bro! A new dawn is at our fingertips and all we have to do is grab it with our hands, squeeze tight and wrestle that bad mama to the ground." The Duke grabbed a big handful of air and wrestled the nothingness into the dirt.

"What if it fights back?"

"You can count on it fighting back, compadre. The question isn't will it fight back. The question is, will you let it go?"

This new dawn, a fresh unexpected opportunity, appeared in seemingly thin air, and though it was ripe for the taking, it would not be The Duke's without a strong resolve to battle for it. The Duke's new dawn had come, but Oakie's hid in the distance.

"Not a chance!" Oakie huffed, "So I'm curious …"

Oakie paused, waiting for a reply.

"Yeah, bro?"

"Earlier this morning, you just kind of quit talking and stood there frozen for most of the day. What was that all about?"

The Duke stared at Oakie so long he began to think it had happened again.

"The things The Duke has seen, bro," the ant finally responded. "No words could describe the things The Duke has seen."

With that, The Duke raised his fist high in the air. "To the new dawn, greenie dude! When The Duke returns, behind him, beside him, and before him will be an ocean of freedom bandits for as far as the eye can see! This day marks a new beginning."

With that The Duke began to march into his new destiny. Although that didn't make a lot of sense, Oakie was happy and excited that The Duke seemed full of life and purpose.

"*Viva la revolución*, bro!" The Duke shouted as he disappeared into the grass.

"*Cacaw, cacaw!*" Oakie shouted back, giggling.

What an amazing day.

CHAPTER

9

PROPER INTRODUCTIONS

9

Days passed quickly after Oakie's encounter with Commander Brick and The Duke. The surrounding trees were slowly noticing Oakie's presence in the orchard. Without his knowing it, a buzz began between the trees about the newcomer. And for good reason. Sure he was cute and all, but he didn't look like all the other apple tree saplings they had seen before. Something was different about this one.

Boy oh boy, were they ever right! And one day they would discover what really set this sapling apart.

Not far from Oakie, a cluster of purple lilacs sprang forth. As peoples came and went, Oakie was so caught up in daydreaming about apples that he didn't even notice the lilacs growing. It was almost as if they had magically appeared before his eyes.

Without warning, a mischievous skunk named Caleb blazed past Oakie, chased by a small people Caleb had carefully baited for his enjoyment. Most of the large peoples dropped their baskets, threw smaller peoples over their shoulders or tucked them under their arms, and frantically ran away. Oakie and the rest of the trees laughed and gagged as the vile stench trailing Caleb filled the orchard, clearing it of its guests.

"Caleb!" a tree shouted through a violent fit of coughing, shaking apples loose that showered down around Oakie. Oakie dodged back and forth, doing a dance to avoid being crushed.

"It's not funny anymore, Caleb. I hope you get trapped by a hunter and skinned alive!" the young tree continued to shout while coughing and shaking apples loose.

"Hey, what are you trying to do, kill me?" Oakie glared

at the tree. It tree looked down.

"Chill out!" The tree worked up a cough and shook a branch, shooting another apple toward Oakie.

Barely dodging it, Oakie stood, shocked, for a moment.

"You did that on purpose didn't you?" Oakie pierced the tree with scornful eyes.

Nonchalantly, the tree looked around and ignored Oakie's reprimand.

"Hey knothead, I'm talking to you," Oakie fired at the tree. It cracked a mischievous smile and continued ignoring the little green weed below him.

Feeling powerless, Oakie became infuriated. Bending over, he scooped up a leaf full of dirt and tossed it at the tree. The few specks of dirt didn't even come close to hitting a root.

The tree roared with laughter.

Again and again, over and over, Oakie winged leaves full of dirt at his harasser.

With each feeble throw, the tree only laughed harder, until a barrage of apples shook loose and hailed down around Oakie. Oakie curled up in a ball and covered his head with his leaves. The last of the apples bounced around and rolled to a stop. Oakie didn't dare move.

"Dakota, stop," a larger, older-looking tree demanded in his deep and powerful, yet calming voice.

"Come on, Dad. I'm just playing around with him."

"You're being mean, now apologize."

Dakota rolled his eyes.

"*Fiiiine.* I'm sorry you can't take a joke."

"Not an apology. Try again," the larger tree reprimanded Dakota.

Dakota looked at Oakie, who hadn't moved in the slightest. The sapling seemed scared; Dakota began to feel a bit remorseful.

"Hey ... are you all right?" Dakota asked, genuinely concerned. Oakie stayed curled up on the ground in fetal position.

"Listen, I'm really sorry."

Oakie went limp and stretched out across the ground.

Dakota tensed up, realizing he might have accidentally hit the little sapling, wounding it badly, or even worse, killing it.

"Dakota! What did you do to him?"

"Nothing, I swear, I don't even think I hit him. I was just playing around." Dakota became frightened. The neighboring trees began to shake their heads in disgust. "I'm so sorry, little guy. Wake up. Please, just wake up." Dakota's fear intensified. He was a murderer and everyone knew it! He couldn't take it back. Tears filled his eyes as he stared at the innocent sapling lying lifeless before him.

"Gotcha!" Oakie shouted as he sat up and pointed a leaf at Dakota.

Dakota shook his head, relieved, and feeling stupid for being played by a little kid tree.

A humbling experience for a sarcastic jokester and a lesson that if you poke at someone long enough, they poke back. Just one of the many lessons Dakota would learn in Oakie's presence.

The neighboring trees erupted in laughter.

"Serves you right Dakota," shouted one tree.

"Looks like you're not the only court jester around here anymore," chimed in another.

Dakota hung his branches.

The trees billowed with laughter until Dakota's father stepped in.

"All right everyone, let's just calm down and give Dakota a break."

One by one the trees collected themselves.

After a moment of silence, he added, "We don't want him to turn into a weeping willow!" Dakota's father exploded into a riot of laughter and all the other trees joined in again.

Oakie stood below, basking in his brilliance as he watched the orchard celebrate his prank. Grinning from ear to ear, he suddenly felt much bigger than he was.

"Fair enough, you win." Dakota surrendered. "Job well done. Now, what's your name?"

Oakie crossed his leaves and held his head up high. "Oakie."

"Well, Oakie, I'm Dakota and this is my dad Morgan, who clearly loves you more than me."

"Dakota, it's not that I love him more than you; it's that I don't love you at all." Morgan said with a mischievous, sarcastic smirk.

"Shut up," Dakota said playfully and shook his head. "Hello, Oakie, it's very nice to meet you." Morgan greeted Oakie with the loving grin of a father.

"Nice to meet you too, sir."

"No need for 'sir,' Oakie, Morgan will do just fine."

"You're pretty quick for a little weed," Dakota poked.

"Well, you're pretty quick for a giant stump." Oakie reveled in his wit.

"I'm not a stump."

"You are compared to the trees back in my forest."

Dakota frowned.

"You are a bit stumpy," Morgan added.

Dakota frowned harder.

"What's this you say about a forest, young fella?" Morgan asked.

"Oh, the forest where I hung before Otis buried me here."

"Before Otis buried you here?"

"Yeah, it was so crazy. Otis is the wildest squirrel alive!"

"Squirrel, huh? So you were just a cute little acorn not all that long ago?"

"He's not cute anymore. That's for sure." Dakota chuckled to himself as he showed Oakie who was the top knot in this orchard.

Morgan and Oakie turned to Dakota and glared.

"Fine, I get it. Fun's over. Pay no attention to me. I'll keep myself entertained by watching this moss grow below me."

Morgan and Oakie turned back to each other and continued.

"So you were an acorn?"

"Yep. Now I'm not sure what I am, but Otis says I'll be just like the rest of you one day and I'll make lots of apples. I can't wait." Oakie's smile wrapped from one side of his face clear around to the other.

Morgan hesitated for a moment, choosing his next words

wisely. "Every tree is unique and beautiful in its own way. No matter what you're like, it'll be perfect for you."

Oakie thought Morgan's response seemed a bit odd, but continued on nonetheless, "I catch myself daydreaming about peoples climbing me and picking my apples. It looks like all of you have so much fun when they come around."

"We sure do, little guy. You know what I dream of?" Morgan looked off into the distance.

"What's that?"

"Seeing what's out there beyond the orchard again. I was the first tree here before all the rest of these. I used to watch sunsets; it was my favorite thing to do. Some nights, as the sun sank below the hills, the most elegant oranges, purples, pinks, and blues would paint a magnificent picture. No two were the same."

Oakie thought of all the sunsets he had watched as an acorn from high in the tree where he had hung. An appreciation for them that he had never had before rose up from within.

"Soon my family began to spring up all around me, and before long, the days watching sunsets became nothing more than a memory."

"Do you ever wish all the other trees were gone so you could see it again?" Oakie asked.

"No, I love this orchard with all my heart. I would trade a million beautiful sunsets for just one of these trees. What I do wish, however, is that I would have enjoyed them more while they lasted. I spent my entire life before these trees grew wishing things were different, dreaming about what could be or would be, instead of loving what was."

"I do that a lot."

"Do what?" Morgan smiled.

"Well, I'm always thinking about what's going to happen and what it's going to be like one day. When I was in the tree hanging, I thought about being buried all the time. When I was buried I was thinking about getting out and what it was like before I was buried. It seems lately all I can think about is what it's going to be like when I make apples."

"Does that make you happy?"

"Does what make me happy?"

"Always wanting something else."

"I don't know. Sometimes it makes me sad."

"Speaking as the oldest tree here I've learned one thing." Morgan paused for a moment, marinating in his thought. Something about Morgan intrigued Oakie in such a way that made him feel like he could listen to him talk forever.

"What's that?" Oakie pulled for the answer.

"Life is a collection of moments. Each and every moment has to be enjoyed and experienced for what it is. Otherwise ..." Morgan paused again.

"Otherwise?" Oakie prompted.

"Otherwise happiness can never be truly found."

The words were strong and struck Oakie.

Something about Morgan's demeanor and words of advice sounded like something Verstand would have said, yet in a unique way that Oakie couldn't grasp yet. But like I say, *with patience and time comes understanding.*

As Oakie weighed what Morgan had said, a herd of peoples stampeded into the orchard. A rather large one jumped onto Morgan and started climbing.

"We'll talk some more later, little guy. Great things lie in store for you—great things are in store right now." Morgan howled with laughter as the people made its way out onto one of his branches. Dangling like a monkey from one hand and holding an apple in its free hand, the people shouted and swung about.

Morgan's words echoed in Oakie's mind as he watched peoples climb the other trees. Although he wasn't big enough for them to climb on him, he could at least be in the moment and enjoy watching as they climbed others.

The day passed but Morgan's words stayed with Oakie. As his time in the orchard went on, a love for his new friends took root. With every passing day, the orchard felt more and more like family.

One early morning, while watching a turtle play hide-and-seek with a rabbit, the swooping silhouette of a bird soaring amidst the clouds caught Oakie's attention. Angelic in nature, the bird danced in the clouds. It reminded him of all the times he used to daydream about Verstand picking him from his branch and carrying him away. He had shared with her his secret wish to have his own wings so that he could see the fantastic sights she told him about before he fell asleep at night.

Verstand had kindly reassured him that he would never grow wings, but promised to one day take him for a flight that he wouldn't forget. Oakie thought to himself, *I might even trade making apples just to take an unforgettable stroll through the sky with my best friend.*

Oakie's thoughts were abruptly interrupted in classic Dakota style.

"Hey weed!"

Oakie looked up with a frown.

"Watchya doin'?"

"I'm not a weed, I'm a blossoming apple tree." Oakie puffed up his chest.

"Sure, if you say so. So what are you doing?"

"Standing here thinking."

"About what?"

"About how ugly you are."

"People say I have my father's looks. You should take it up with him."

Morgan glanced over at Dakota for a second before deciding to mind his business and ignore the two altogether.

"Seriously though, what are you thinking about?"

"My friend Verstand."

"What about?"

"Well ..." Oakie hesitated. "You'll just make fun of me."

"At some point in the near future I probably will," Dakota said mischievously, "but I promise I won't make fun of you about this." Dakota looked at Oakie with sincerity.

"Well, I was thinking about her promise to take me flying some day."

"I take it she's a bird."

"A cow."

"I deserved that. Please continue."

"I was so excited about being like all the other acorns that I didn't realize that once I was buried, I would never get a chance to fly with Verstand." Oakie looked at the ground and hung his head as he grieved the thought.

"Who says you can't?"

"What do you mean who says I can't? I'm stuck in the ground." Oakie pointed at the ground with his leaf.

"I know it sounds stupid, but unlikely surprises are around every corner. You just have to believe." Dakota proclaimed encouragingly.

Oakie rolled his eyes.

"So I suppose that if I believe enough I will somehow grow wings," Oakie said facetiously.

"I know it sounds like I have some holes in this theory—"

"Some?"

"All right, you're probably not going to sprout wings, but when you want something bad enough, and are willing to look like a fool for believing it, things start to happen! It might not happen the way you think it will, but—"

"OK," Oakie cut in. "I'm willing to try anything. If it works, I get to go flying with Verstand. If it doesn't, you look like a fool for telling me to do this."

"I am fool. There's no denying that."

"Fine, you're a bigger fool if it doesn't work."

"Fair enough." Dakota grinned.

"You're not that bad of a tree. You're kind of crazy, but you're not that bad."

"I can be sincere when I want to."

"A sincere pain in the knot." Oakie poked at Dakota.

"You know what? You're kind of like the little brother I never wanted, but somehow got stuck with."

"You're welcome." Oakie raised his head high.

"Promise me one thing."

"What's that?"

"You'll come back and tell me about all the incredible things you get to see. I've never been beyond this orchard."

"If ..."

"When," Dakota corrected.

"*When* I get to fly with Verstand, I promise to come back and tell you about everything I see."

"Deal." With satisfaction, Dakota agreed.

Oakie looked up into the sky. Was Dakota actually right?

Was it possible? It seemed rather stupid to even consider. For the sake of humoring his friend, Oakie took a moment and thought, *One day I'm going to soar in the clouds with Verstand. I don't know how, but it's going to happen.* As he let the words run though his mind, he drifted off and began to imagine what it would feel like to not be tied down. The wind, the clouds, the endless sky.

"I'm glad you're here." Dakota interrupted Oakie's thoughts.

Oakie sprang back to reality.

"Why, because now you have someone to pick on?"

"I have plenty of trees to pick on." The neighboring trees glared at Dakota. "But they're already sick of me."

The trees nodded their heads in agreement.

"I'm glad you're here because you make this place better. Just thought you should know."

Oakie was stunned. He hadn't done anything to make it better. Perhaps Dakota was just being nice, but it felt good nonetheless. At that, Oakie awkwardly nodded his head and smiled.

Little did Oakie realize just how tangible Dakota's absurd notion could really become.

CHAPTER

—— 10 ——

AN UNEXPECTED JOURNEY

10

Days had passed since Oakie and Dakota's conversation. Mesmerized, Oakie sat staring at a spider as it meticulously wove its web inside a log that lay on its side. Each of the strings was beautifully knit to the others in a tapestry of the most intricate detail.

While admiring the art on display, a moth looking to explore the hollow log veered into the web. The spider hurried to the unfortunate passerby. The grace and beauty of what the spider had created was in no way lessened by the harsh reality of what was in store for the moth. Like a wild cowboy would rope a bull, so the spider spun its silk around the moth until it was nothing more than a mummy.

Though the sight may have seemed brutal to some, Oakie knew from watching Verstand feed her owlets that such was the glorious cycle of life.

"Oooooakie! Ooooakie!" an unknown invader shouted.

Spinning his head around, Oakie could see the green brush whipping wildly in the distance.

"Oooooakie!" The voice shouted again as the invader drew near, kicking leaves high in the air.

Oakie waited intensely as the mysterious voice grew closer.

"Ooooakie! Where are ya, buddy?" Zig-zagging left and right, the movement came to sporadic stops, then began again. Birds scattered every direction, fearful of the train that seemed to be off its track.

"You gotta see this! Oakie! Oakie!" The voice was all too familiar.

Oakie shouted back, hoping it was who he thought it was, "I'm over here!"

"Over where?" The movement veered hard to the left and stopped.

"Over here!"

Dashing forward and then to the right, the voice hollered again, "You are gonna love this!" Springing forth from atop a log and pouncing down in front of Oakie stood none other than Otis.

"Otis!" Oakie shouted gleefully.

Running in circles around Oakie, Otis made his declaration. "You're coming with me, no ifs, ands, or—"

"But—"

"—buts about it. This is so awesome and mind-blowing I could get a nose bleed just talking about it!" Otis shot his hands high in the air and shook his head back and forth. "I tasted the unknown and it is like sweet maple syrup, my friend!"

"But—"

"Ah, ah, ah!" Otis waved his finger in Oakie's face. "What did I say? Listen, buddy boy, the sight you are about to see is tongue-tyingly splendorous."

Morgan peered down at the commotion, smirking with pleasure at the afternoon interlude.

"Calm down. Breathe for a second." Oakie's plea for sanity went, not surprisingly, unnoticed.

"Jumping jackrabbits, man!" Otis leaped atop a rock. "This is what it's all about, for as far as the eye can see!" Otis swiped his hand through the air above him.

"What are you talking about?"

Otis sprang from the rock and charged at Oakie.

Pulling himself back as far as he could, Oakie was unable to evade Otis's grasp.

Clenching Oakie's face, Otis pulled his head to his own, squishing their noses together.

"The promised land, baby, and it's all ours! You're coming with me 'cause I gotta share this with a friend."

"I … can't … breathe! You're squishing … my face." Oakie muttered, muffled by Otis's nose, which now looked as though it was one with Oakie's face.

"Ooops!" Otis released Oakie, sending him whooshing

back like a slingshot.

While Otis jumped up and down doing back flips, Oakie grabbed his own head between his leaves and tried to settle his brain from the whiplash. "What do you mean by 'friend?' " Oakie didn't really think of them as friends.

"What do you mean, 'What do you mean by "friend"?' You know exactly what I mean." Otis's excitement began to crumble.

Oakie, being the sensitive sapling that he was, noticed the droop in Otis's demeanor. Before Otis could lose all his thunder, Oakie continued, "Well, all I'm saying is I'm sure you have friends who you are much closer to who would be disappointed if they missed out on such an opportunity."

Otis hung his shoulders and his tail. "Um ... they're all kinda busy. You know ... doing things and stuff ..." Otis looked at the ground and dusted the dirt with his foot.

Oakie began to get the feeling that Otis was short on friends.

"You see ... actually ... well, since I'm always exploring and doing non-squirrel stuff ... I kinda don't have any friends ..." Otis kept his head down.

Oakie realized he couldn't turn down the invitation without really hurting Otis's feelings. "Well ... sure, I suppose. But there's one probl-"

"Woohoo! I wasn't gonna take 'no' for an answer anyways. You're coming with me!" Otis beamed with joy.

"All right, all right already. How am I supposed to come with you then?"

"Houston, we have a go!" Otis charged Oakie, grabbed his leaf, and took off on a dead sprint. Coming to the end of a rope, Otis's feet flew out from under him, sending him sailing across the ground. Tumbling end over end he came to a stop below Morgan.

Morgan, Dakota, and the other trees erupted with hearty laughter. Truly it was more comical than any peoples they had ever seen.

All the motion had Oakie feeling rather green to his stomach, much greener than he looked.

A hush fell over the trees. They paused and watched

Otis intently as he lay stiff on the ground.

"Is he dead?" one tree asked in a whisper.

"Dazed and confused," another responded, holding back his laughter."

Without warning, Otis shot back to his feet. Facing away from Oakie, he stated the obvious.

"We have a problem." Hustling back to Oakie, Otis quickly began problem-solving.

"Yeah, I think I'm going to puke."

"No, that's not it." Otis scratched his chin. "You're stuck in the ground. When did this happen?"

Oakie dismissed the absurd question.

"When a squirrel buried me here."

"They're always burying things, but we can fix this." Otis started to circle below Oakie with his face near the ground. "I've got it!"

Oakie became very apprehensive.

"If a squirrel buried you, surely a squirrel can unbury you!" Without time for a retort from Oakie the dirt began flying. Otis dug furiously.

For Oakie, there was a strong sense of *déjà vu.* There was no stopping this tornado.

The trees looked at each other, unable to believe what they were seeing. For a brief moment, Morgan thought about stopping the whole ordeal, but he was too curious to see if it would actually work.

Oakie began coughing uncontrollably as dirt shrapnel from the squirrel bomb blew up in his face.

"Otis. Otis. *Ooootis!*" It was too late; a small mountain of dirt lay all about Oakie.

Frozen, Otis looked up at Oakie with a dirt-filled grin. "You're in for a ride my friend." Otis plunged his arm deep into the satchel strapped to his side and retrieved an adventurer's rope. In an instant Otis had Oakie lassoed. Backing up to Oakie, so the two of them were standing back to back, Otis spun a web of rope around them until Oakie was tightly fastened to Otis's back. "If you have to go to the bathroom, you best do it now or forever hold it!"

"Go to the bathroom?" Oakie looked puzzled.

"Adios amigos and amigas!" Otis shouted at the top of his lungs, and burst off running.

Bouncing up and down and all around, Oakie watched as the sight of the apple trees waving goodbye quickly went out of focus and disappeared altogether.

Since poor Oakie was strapped to Otis's back, he couldn't see what was ahead of him, only what was left behind. To say he had motion sickness would be an understatement. A blur of twigs, leaves, and various woodland creatures rocketed past Oakie as Otis flew through the trees.

"Hold on tight, little buddy!" Otis kicked into overdrive.

Taking a sharp turn straight upward, the two travelers began their bumpy ascent up a large tree. Otis leaped from branch to branch, lunging without hesitation.

"You almost took my head off! Pay attention, you goof!" Oakie shouted at the top of his lungs, after almost losing his head to a branch.

"You're going to need that for the rest of your life! I suggest you protect it at all costs," Otis replied in a serious tone, darting dangerously between a cluster of leaves.

"What I need is squirrel insurance to protect me from deranged squirrels that put me in dangerous situations!"

"Don't worry about it. You stick with me and I'll protect you from them, little buddy."

"It's not them I'm worried about!"

"Good. Fear is a bear trap you'll get caught in every time."

Otis leaped with all his strength to the highest branch on the tree, then came to an abrupt stop. The driving force left him balancing like a tightrope walker before he gained stability.

"Magnificent ... simply magnificent!"

Oakie's words were few. There was nothing to adequately describe the freedom Oakie felt atop this tree. Nothing hindered his line of sight. The view was vast and endless. Birds of all types roamed the air. In the distance, a mountain range stood with kingly dignity. The tops of the trees looked like a lush green bed suitable for a giant.

"This is amazing, Otis! I'm so thankful you brought me here. It's well worth the ride."

Gazing through his two front paws, which formed something like binoculars, Otis responded, "Glad you enjoy it, but this isn't what I have to show you. It gets better—exponentially!"

"What? How could it get better? This is breathtaking!"

"This, my friend, is just a lookout to help me navigate where we are going."

"Where *are* we going?"

Otis spun around one hundred and eighty degrees so Oakie could get a better view of where they were headed. "Now look straight in front of you as far as your eyes can see. What do you see?"

"An endless ocean of trees."

"Just beyond that—that's where we are going."

Oakie's eyes stretched wide open. The journey ahead was quite an undertaking.

"How are we going to get there?"

"How did we get here?" Otis replied.

Nausea set in. Oakie's stomach bubbled and grumbled at the thought of the ride ahead of him.

"I suggest you hold on." Without warning, Otis leapt from the top of the tree and spread his arms.

To Oakie's surprise, they didn't plummet to their deaths, but instead floated on an updraft of wind across the tops of the trees. Otis wasn't just any ordinary squirrel. Nope, he was a flying squirrel—something he had failed to mention to Oakie.

Riding the current of wind, they quickly covered a great distance.

"How are you holding up back there, buddy?" Otis shouted as the wind stretched the skin on his face all the way to the back of his neck.

"This is AAAAWESOME!" Oakie yelled at the top of his lungs while wildly shaking his head and leaves.

"Oh it gets better, mucho better!"

"It can't get *better!*"

"Good. That means you're going to be pleasantly surprised."

Oakie's dream of soaring with Verstand felt so real. This

must have been what it was like for her. This was the dream he'd had over and over ... finally, it was happening!

Otis descended through the trees as the updraft faded. Like a spaceship navigating a meteor shower, he dodged through the debris of branches, leaves, and bird nests.

Oakie's excitement began to dissipate as Otis barreled through the maze of foliage that endangered his future. "Hey! I'm still strapped to your back! Be careful!"

"Wooohoo! Yeah, baby!"

Oakie's plea went unnoticed, as Otis got lost in the excitement of his favorite part of every descent, the landing. "Prepare for landing!"

Oakie had little control over preparation, so rather than worry about the landing, he simply braced for it.

In a very fashionable manner, Otis performed a beautiful barrel roll any gymnast would be proud of.

Unfortunately for Oakie, Otis didn't take into account that there was still a sapling strapped to his back.

"Now that is first class travel, my friend." Otis declared while brushing himself off.

Oakie coughed up a mist of dirt from his lungs and did his best to shake the sediment from his face.

Without pause, Otis took off sprinting, leaping over rocks, dodging trees, and diving under logs.

"Otis! Stop! Stop! Stop! OOOOOTIS!"

Breaking on a dime, Otis came to a halt.

"What is wrong with you?" Oakie shook his head in frustration.

Otis, forgetting that Oakie was strapped to his back, spun around to face his accuser. "What do you mean what is wrong with me?"

"You're crazy! You're crazy and you're going to kill me."

Otis spun around again. "No, I'm not! Quit being a baby. You're alive aren't you?"

"Yeah, but I'm not sure for how long."

Otis spun yet again, pointing his finger in the air like an all-knowing guru. "No one is sure for how long! That's the surprising mystery of life."

"Well, I don't need you ending my life before the surprising mystery takes its natural course."

Again Otis spun.

"Quit nagging and being a whiner. Learn to embrace fun."

"I am embracing fun, just not death!"

And again Otis spun around and retorted, "No, you're scared and worried and you're being a real drain on things. If you die, at least you die doing something no other plant in this forest has ever done or will ever do. Why don't you just learn to be thankful? No more complaining the rest of the trip or I'll bury you smack dab in the middle of a briar patch!"

Oakie's temper subsided as he began to feel the reality of what Otis had just said.

"Fine."

Spinning again, Otis demanded an answer. "Do you mean it? Are you fine, or are we going to be burying you five minutes from now?"

"I said it and I meant it, *fine!*" Oakie crossed his leaves as Otis spun again.

Before speaking, Otis took a brief pause to gather his thoughts and feelings. "I'm sorry for not being more careful. I'm just really excited for you to see this."

"I'm not a drain," Oakie said sadly.

Otis turned again, this time with sympathy and a genuine apology in his heart.

"No, you're not. I didn't mean that. I was just angry. I'm really sorry for saying that and getting mad at you. I would never bury you in a briar patch."

Oakie took a moment to gather his thoughts and feelings as well. "I'm sorry for nagging you and worrying about everything. Honestly, I kind of wish I was more like you."

Slowly turning with a bit of embarrassment, Otis responded, "How so?" Oakie had moved Otis' heart.

"Well, you're adventurous and fun and you don't care what anybody says about you."

Otis's eyebrow perked up. He whipped around again. "I'm being talked about?"

"I don't think you're crazy at all."

A little offended, Otis spun again. "Who says I'm crazy?"

"And I love your playfulness and I am so thankful that

you took me on this journey. I'm thankful you wouldn't let me say 'no.' I'm thankful that you did everything you could to bring me along."

Otis began to tear up.

"You're brave and strong and smart."

A tear made its way to Otis's chin.

"You are and you do what others only dream of. In a way ... you're kind of my hero."

Clenching his quivering bottom lip with his teeth, trying his best not to break down crying, Otis turned once again. Quickly and quietly he choked out, "Thank you."

"How did you do that?"

"Do what?"

"Fly."

"I was born with squirrel wings." Otis lifted his arms and gestured to the wings he had glided on. "But I can't just fly when I want to, like birds."

"Why not?"

"Because if I could fly whenever I wanted to I wouldn't know how special it was when I did fly. I guess flying just wouldn't be as much fun and the gift would be kind of a curse. At least that's what my new friend Isaiah said. I think it's because I haven't figured out how to do it yet."

Otis rubbed his chin for a moment while Oakie took time to let Isaiah's advice marinate in his mind. It seemed to make sense, but he knew there was much more to it than he actually understood. With that, Oakie reached his leaf over Otis's back and extended a peace treaty.

"Friends again?"

Otis thought for a moment, then reached back and shook Oakie's leaf.

"Friends forever."

Oakie grinned with joy in his eyes. "Let's get moving you crazy rodent!"

"I'm rethinking the briar patch scenario," Otis said with a mischievous smile.

"Who's Isaiah, by the way?"

"The guy who's going to turn your world upside down." And with that they were off.

As evening approached, Otis searched for a good spot to bed down for the night. Under the arms of a maple tree, he dug a small hole to set Oakie comfortably in for the evening. After getting Oakie settled, Otis trekked to a nearby river where he gathered some water to quench Oakie's thirst, then Otis pulled two small rocks from his satchel and started a fire to warm himself for the evening.

Although Oakie enjoyed the warmth of the fire, he couldn't help but feel a little awkward watching the wood burn, knowing where it had come from. The irony was admittedly a bit funny.

"Tomorrow's going to be a fantastic day. Get your rest; you won't want to be sleepy when you see what I have in store for you."

Otis smiled with anticipation. In his fervor to share something wonderful with a friend, he never could have imagined that he was about to fulfill one of Oakie's greatest dreams.

CHAPTER

— 11 —

A BUMPY RIDE

11

A light drizzle during the night whet the appetite of the woods. A bobcat sat lapping up water in a nearby puddle. The sound of her drinking startled Otis from his rest. A moment passed before his sight focused clearly. To say Otis was shocked would be a large understatement, and for a good reason: Bobcats were well known for dining on squirrels.

In the quietest of manners, Otis attempted to snag Oakie's attention.

"Psssst. Psssst. Ooooakie ... psssst, Oakie."

Oakie sat motionless, in a deep sleep. Otis knew if this kitty caught wind of him, his next exploration would be the inside of a belly. Crouching down, Otis crawled to a nearby pile of stones. Taking careful aim, he began to gently sling stones in Oakie's direction. The first few landed at Oakie's base, but there was not so much as a yawn from him. Checking over his shoulder to assure himself that the kitty was still occupied with her morning drink, he took aim again and launched another stone, this time nailing his target between the eyes.

A bit bewildered, Oakie shook back and forth.

"Aaah, what the heck ...? Otis what are you—"

Otis dropped to the ground and quickly waved his paws back and forth, gesturing toward his lips and making a zipper motion.

The bobcat perked up to see what the disturbance was all about. Fortunately, Otis was out of her view.

Oakie sat frozen, realizing what Otis had been attempting to communicate.

Assured that nothing was wrong, the bobcat went about her business.

Crawling commando-style on his belly, Otis continued the trek toward Oakie. Otis veered to the left of a pile of leaves, effectively navigating past the danger. Before jumping to a crouching position, he checked carefully to be sure he was out the bobcat's sight. He was clear. He sprang to his feet and sprinted to Oakie, hunched over to avoid notice. Looking over his shoulder, he took another glance to ensure there was no sign of the cat.

Unfortunately for Otis, the missing danger behind him didn't mean there wasn't danger in front of him. While turned around, a pine tree had somehow sprung up in front of him. Swinging his head forward, he came face-to-face with this mysterious, immovable obstacle. The tree won the collision, sending Otis sailing onto his back. The force of the impact was enough to shake a few pinecones loose, capturing the cat's attention.

Otis lay on the ground, trying to make sense out of where he was. His vision was blurry and something blocked his sight. Behind him the bobcat stepped away from her puddle in order to investigate the clamor.

Oakie sat as quietly as possible, trembling, yet trying not to laugh at Otis's predicament.

The bobcat carefully scanned the area with her eyes and listened with her ears.

Meanwhile, Otis lay still until he could collect his thoughts. His forehead began to throb fiercely. Reaching up, he realized the thing blocking his sight was an extremely large bump growing from his forehead.

Behind Otis, the bobcat continued surveying the area. Sniffing the air, she carefully catalogued all she sensed.

Clenching his mouth tightly in his hands, Otis did everything he could to keep from screaming at the top of his lungs.

Fortunately for Otis, he was downwind from the cat, whose nose knew *everything*. Happy with her assessment of the situation, the kitty strutted back to her dish and continued lapping water with enjoyment.

This was it! With her back to him, Otis was in the perfect position. Struggling to his feet, he grabbed hold of his satchel, which he'd lost in the wreck. Before sprinting to

Oakie, he reached into the satchel and grabbed his rope. Rubbing his new lump, he looked over his shoulder again, making sure the bobcat still had her back to him.

With all his agility and speed, Otis made a run for it. Like a poorly trained ballerina, he danced back and forth, fighting to keep his balance as the effects of the crash wore off. Like a modern-day cowboy, he twirled the rope through the air and lassoed Oakie.

Oakie braced himself. Rather than make a fuss, he chose to be quiet and trust Otis to get them out of this sticky situation.

Spinning a cocoon around the two of them with the rope, Otis strapped Oakie to his back and shot up the nearest tree. Reaching a safe distance above the ground, Otis paused to divulge his makeshift plans.

"We're alive," he whispered.

"I noticed."

"I have an idea."

"A good one?"

"*Great* ... it's a *great* one." Otis bobbed his head up and down. Fixing his hands together like a pair of binoculars, he looked carefully at the bobcat far below. "Do you think flying is fun?"

"Of course."

"How about riding?"

"Riding?"

"Attention passengers," Otis said, giving his best imitation of a flight attendant. "This is your flight crew. Please fasten your safety belts and keep quiet for the remainder of this flight."

"This flight?"

Without warning, Otis leapt from the branch and spread his arms. Diving like a bomb, he lasered in on the bobcat.

As they jetted downward, a thought shot through Oakie's head. This is it! *This is what life is all about!*

Pouncing on the cat, Otis gripped her ears and wrapped his feet around her neck. "Passengers, this is your flight crew again, please hold on tight!" he shouted. "We're about to experience some strong turbulence!"

Familiar ... all too familiar to Oakie, yet welcomed like never before.

"Woo hoo! Get 'er Otis!" Oakie cheered at the top of his lungs.

Jumping and whipping around in circles like a regular ol' rodeo bull, the bobcat was not about to be tamed without a fight.

Pulling back hard on the ear reins only seemed to infuriate the cat more. Leaping high in the air, she did her best to buck the riders off.

With great confidence, Otis assured Oakie mid-jump, "I got everything under control. Don't worry little buddy."

"This is control?"

"She's wearin' down. Just keep holding on," Otis assured Oakie as the bobcat began galloping through the woods.

Oakie shouted sarcastic encouragement at the top of his lungs. "I think you got her right where you want her."

"She's putty in my hands." Otis pulled hard on the cat's right ear, steering her up a tree like a bolt of lighting as she leaped from branch to branch. "It's the scenic tour. This will cost you extra, buddy."

"I think I'm already paying too much," Oakie shot back.

"Too much, my hiney. This is priceless!" Otis shouted, steering the cat from a tree to a giant boulder.

While climbing boulder after boulder, good ol' little Oakie suddenly had a revelation of sorts. Something began to click. Our young and insightful acorn realized how scared he had been his entire life.

He realized the difference between Otis and all the other squirrels was *fear*. The reason Otis explored on his own was because he didn't listen to fear. He didn't worry about where food would come from. He didn't worry about where he would rest his head at night. He didn't worry about whether he would live or die. He simply chose to experience life free from the voices of fear and worry. That's why no one understood him. That's why he was alone: No one else knew how to live life free from the voices of fear and worry—including Oakie.

One thing was for sure: No matter how splendid the surprise was that lay ahead, this trip had already surpassed Oakie's greatest expectations.

Cresting the top of the hill, Otis loosened his grip on the cat's neck. Like a surfer preparing to catch a big wave, he gathered his feet under his haunches, then shouted, "Get ready!"

"For what?"

And without hesitation, Otis released his grip, sprang into the air, and grabbed hold of a branch, watching their mount race off into the wild blue yonder alone.

"Well, enough hanging around. We got sights ta see." Otis dropped from the branch and made his way for a clearing up ahead.

"That was incredible!"

"What would really be incredible is riding a bear—backwards and blindfolded!" Otis proclaimed while staring off in a trance. "Anyways, that was nothing compared to what's ahead."

"It was the best thing that's ever happened. Ever, ever, ever! The best ever!"

"Never say 'ever,' my friend." With that, Otis stepped into the clearing and spun around so Oakie could see for himself.

Oakie's eyes bulged from his head. Before him was a sight he had never *ever* seen before, so beautiful it defied description.

Otis dropped into a reverential whisper.

"That," he said softly, "is the Valley of Eagles."

CHAPTER

12

DREAMS FULFILLED

12

Vast, open, and never-ending, the valley stretched as far as the eye could see. All around it, rivers emptied as waterfalls, flowing to the lake in the center. Trees and foliage blanketed the entire scene. Fields of lilacs, daisies, and daffodils, colored in pinks, reds, yellows, purples, and white scattered the landscape, giving the valley a magnificent vibrancy. A herd of elk gathered by a stream for an afternoon drink. A goat leaped down rocks, descending from the hills to the valley floor. A pack of wolves stalked through a cluster of thickets, targeting a moose whose head barely showed above the towering grass. A badger invaded a rabbit's den, driving the occupants out to make room for herself. It was a scene almost too majestic for me to even describe.

The vegetation and wildlife was very familiar to that of Oakie's first home. Other than the waterfalls, which set this valley apart from anything Oakie had ever seen, giant trees were scattered about. Atop these towering trees, perched above this lively orchestra of beauty, sat wonderfully sculpted nests. And not just any nests; these were *giant* nests.

"You see those nests on top of the giant trees?" Otis said, pointing. "Those are bald eagle nests, homes for the most powerful, magnificent birds I have ever seen. There's probably two or three bald eaglets packed tightly together in each one."

Oakie scoured the valley for nests. There were far too many to count.

"The real sight is above you. Take a look." Otis pointed toward the sky.

Above the valley soared the real miracle. Not just dozens, but rather hundreds of majestic bald eagles filled the sky. Diving, darting, swooping and sailing, the valley was theirs. Though many other creatures clearly lived here, this belonged to the eagles, and they politely shared it with the rest of the residents.

Oakie had never seen eagles. The sight was almost overwhelming. Tongue-tying, as Otis said it would be. Oakie simply stared, soaking up the sight. He watched as an eagle ascended so high that it simply vanished. The sight at that height must have been astonishing. "I don't know what to say," Oakie murmured through his awe.

"*Riiiight?*" Otis nodded and began to unstrap Oakie from his back.

"I never could have dreamed of something so ... so ..."

"I know. It's everything I said it would be, and more!"

"Uh-huh." Oakie felt like he could stay here forever. This could be his home. Every day, he could sit peacefully and study the beauty of this valley.

"The best is yet to come." Otis began re-strapping Oakie to his chest.

Oakie took a moment to respond, a bit overwhelmed at the thought of something more. "Otis, I don't know how to thank you. And yet again, I sure don't know how this could get any better."

Otis finished locking Oakie snugly in. Reaching into his satchel, he dug out a red cloth, which he clenched tightly and swung wildly above his head. "Wouldn't it be amazing to see what they see?" he asked with a grin.

"It's something I've always dreamed of. Verstand promised me she'd take me flying someday. When you flew from the tree, it's the closest I've ever come to seeing what she always talked about."

"Who's Verstand?"

"A beautiful owl from the forest where I first dropped to the ground."

"The one with the owlets?"

"There wasn't any other that I knew of."

Otis looked over his shoulder, then turned around and gave one more pull to double-check the knot he had tied. "You don't have to dream about it anymore," he said.

"What do you mean?" Oakie responded, confused,

Otis looked over his shoulder. "Hold on!" And with that, the two travelers were once again flying through the air.

Oakie twisted his head back, only to see the talons of a bald eagle wrapped around Otis's shoulders.

"Isaiah, you rock my face off!" Otis shouted at the top of his lungs to the eagle who held them securely. Apparently, they were friends.

It was happening! It wasn't a dream; it wasn't in Oakie's mind. It was real!

Veering left and right as he navigated through the eagles' air traffic,, Isaiah shot Otis a big smile.

"Aaaaaah! Oh my tree! This is aaaaaamaaazing!" Oakie screamed.

"Ready for some real fun?" Isaiah asked with the voice of a wild daredevil.

"What are you asking for? Just do it!" Otis shouted with a smile.

"Hold on!" Isaiah replied.

With nothing to hold on to, good ol' Otis finally realized the folly of this statement that he had made so many times before to Oakie.

Pumping his wings with all his might, Isaiah gripped his passengers tightly as he climbed toward the clouds clustered far above. Like a bullet bursting from a gun, they shattered the thick cottony cluster. "Only the strongest come here," Isaiah boasted.

"I take it you're one of the strongest," Oakie smirked.

"I take it you're one of the smartest," Isaiah shot back.

"Aren't eagles supposed to be dangerous to your health, Otis?" Oakie asked.

Both Isaiah and Otis looked at each other and in perfect synchronization responded, "Yes."

"Shut up and enjoy the flight," Otis said, giving Oakie a wink.

They continued to climb higher and higher. The sun seemed only a leaf's reach away, as though Oakie could pluck it from the sky and bring it back to earth with him. Only the sound of the wind and the wings were audible up here. Everything else was silent in a way Oakie only remembered from when he was buried. Yet this time, the silence came with such freedom and never-ending possibilities.

Oakie observed the horizon as they climbed. At this height, the earth looked much more round than flat. Below, the clouds looked like large puffs of fresh snow. Further below, the other birds looked like a swarm of flies hovering over the seemingly vast and unending Valley of Eagles.

The travelers transitioned seamlessly from climbing to floating. Gravity appeared to have no power over them as they drifted calmly through the air.

Oakie took a deep breath, inhaling. "I could take a nap," he said, Zen-like peace on his face.

"Is it *that* boring?" asked Isaiah sarcastically.

Oakie simply looked at Isaiah and rolled his eyes. While the two exchanged sentiment, Otis made binoculars with his paws to get a better look below.

Isaiah noticed Otis scanning the scenery and asked curiously, "What are you doing, Otis?"

Otis continued surveying the land below.

"Otis, what are you looking at?" Isaiah asked, but still nothing. Isaiah exchanged glances with Oakie, hoping to prepare him for what was to come.

Now, let it be known that as majestic as Isaiah looked, he was as playful and wild as the crazy squirrel he was carrying in his talons.

Using a more effective tactic, Isaiah jolted his passenger by quickly tipping to the left, then to the right.

Shocked by the sudden jerking, Otis yelled, "Whoa there, pilgrim! Don't be a turkey! Easy with the turbulence. You've got precious cargo aboard this bird!" Otis shot Isaiah a perturbed look.

"No harm, no foul," Isaiah said with a mischievous grin, winking at Oakie.

Oakie winked back. "So what are you looking at down there?"

"I'm strategizing for my next exploration," Otis said. "Beyond the valley, it looks to me to be barren land."

Isaiah grimaced a bit.

"Yeah ..." Isaiah shook his head, trying to discourage Otis. "I don't think you want to go there."

"Why's that?" Otis demanded.

"It's not safe. That's all."

Otis's ears perked up with excitement.

"What's not safe about it?"

"They call it Vulture Desert. I don't know of any who have gone there, besides eagles of course, and returned."

"Are you saying I wouldn't return if I went there?" Otis exclaimed, feeling challenged.

Oakie usually knew when to keep his mouth closed. This was one of those times he knew to listen to his intuition.

"All I'm saying is that what is out there is unknown, and there are vast legends of travelers who have never returned," Isaiah continued.

Otis's eyes sparkled with interest.

"Besides, only one stream that I know of flows through there, and it comes from The Valley of Eagles. Since there isn't any other water source, there's mostly only cacti growing and crazy reptiles that have had their brains fried by the sun. And of course, the countless vultures who feast on the bones of any weak, or better yet, *dead* travelers," Isaiah added. "It seems like it could be a pretty boring journey for so much danger."

Otis started to jump into one of his customary back flips before realizing there was no ground to push off from. Judo-chopping the air instead, he retorted, "Bite your tongue, Bird! Where there is danger boredom has no place! I welcome you, Danger, to step into my judo chops of fury!"

Oakie started sweating. The ground below didn't seem very welcoming at this height.

"I'm no traveler, no simple-minded nomad. I am an adventurer, an explorer extraordinaire!" Otis pointed into the air.

Isaiah listened, more amused than ever before.

"The Unknown quivers at its knees and begs for mercy as my name is carried about by the wind. 'Otis, Otis, Otis!'" Otis shouted "Danger knows my name and cowers in a corner, hiding from my presence. The claws of fear retract, and the paw that carries them scampers away at the sound of my approach."

Oakie and Isaiah looked at one another, less amused, and growing slightly tired of Otis's proclamations.

"The ages will reminisce as the suspenseful tales are told of the brave, the bold, the daring, the debonaire squirrel known as—"

Oakie suddenly wrapped his leaves around Otis's mouth, muffling his ravings. Assured that Otis was finished, eventually Oakie relinquished his grip.

"The voice of courage will not be silenced!" Otis shouted. Oakie covered his mouth again.

Now, in my opinion, you can't silence the rantings of a lunatic—you can only hope to contain them. But Isaiah was quite the crafty bird, and in all his wisdom he carried a few unconventional methods for dealing with a chatterbox like Otis.

Deciding that it was the perfect time for a lesson in shutting up, Isaiah signaled to Oakie with a big, bold, bald eagle smile that he was about to do something, and then let loose. Breaking from the casual afternoon drift, Isaiah pulled his wings snugly to his side and shot like an arrow toward the earth. As the three plummeted, Otis shrieked at the top of his lungs until he grew purple in the face. Before Otis could catch his breath, Isaiah released his wings and swooped upward, looping over and over again through the sky. Otis shouted in terror under the cage of Oakie's leaves.

Diving again, Isaiah went into a barrel roll, spinning in circles. Oakie lost a bit of his grip on Otis's mouth, giving him a chance to be heard. "We're gonna die! I don't wanna die!"

Breaking the roll, Isaiah revisited the loopty-loops, this time horizontally, then vertically. Then he came to a sudden stop, followed by a drop. The rollercoaster plummeted downward and exploded through the clouds.

"I stole Melinda's first acorn when I was five years old! I'm sorry, God!" Otis revealed his most troubling secret before what seemed to be his last seconds on earth.

Just before Oakie was about to become a potted plant, Isaiah pulled up, skimming lightly just above the river. Oakie reached out his leaves and dipped them in the water.

Jerking back, Isaiah ascended again, giving his friends a better look at the valley before returning them to the launching pad from which he had snagged them.

Otis covered his eyes with this paws ... and then, everything stopped. There was no motion, no wind, nothing. He had died; he was sure of it. Then, looking to see what the afterlife had in store for him, he realized they had landed safely where they had begun.

In a flash, Otis slammed himself flat on the ground and began kissing the dirt until he was unrecognizably covered with it, forgetting that Oakie was still strapped to his chest.

"Otis, I'm not meant to eat dirt. I'm meant to be planted in it!" Oakie yelled. "Otis! You meathead, get off of me and untie me!"

Masked by the dirt that now covered his face, Otis paused long enough to feel his stomach catch up with him. Thrusting his hand in his satchel, he whipped out a sharpened rock and cut Oakie loose before covering his mouth with his hand and making for the heavy brush, where he would get a good look at what he had eaten for breakfast.

Oakie lay in silence on the ground briefly before sitting up.

"Not *completely* fearless," Isaiah said, shrugging.

"I thought he was going to cry," Oakie said, shaking the dirt off his face.

"He's going to do it."

"Puke?" Oakie inquired.

"Yes, but no. He's going to explore Vulture Desert."

"You think so?"

"Absolutely. I fully believe he's the one to do it."

"How so?"

Isaiah looked to see if Otis was returning before he continued.

"Humility. He has fear, but he's not controlled by it. If he didn't have fear at all I'd say he was arrogant, ignorant, and foolish, therefore more likely to get himself killed."

"What's arrogant, ignorant, and foolish about not having fear?"

"Nothing at all. The problem is I've never met someone without any fear whatsoever. I've just met arrogant beings that pretend they have no fear. In their arrogance, so as to appear brave, they ignore the caution within their hearts because that caution looks similar to fear. This puts themselves and others in danger," Isaiah explained.

"Otis has fear and he's aware of it. Because of his humility, he has that awareness and can choose wisely between fear and the healthy voice of caution in his heart. His humility is what keeps him from worrying about what others think, and that is truly a virtue. Humility has granted him the ability to discern between fear and caution, and that has liberated him to battle actual fear. Thus, he is able to see all of his dreams come true."

Oakie stared, mesmerized and perplexed by this kung fu ninja of wisdom. Then, thinking aloud with concern for Otis, he said, "That doesn't mean he's indestructible, though. He could still die if it's as dangerous as you say it is."

"I didn't say he's indestructible," Isaiah said. "I also didn't say he wouldn't die. I simply said he's the one to do it. He has all the qualities needed to be great. He has a tender heart full of love and caring. He is brave and bold. He's humble, but confident. He's strong, yet weak. He's honest, yet imperfect in all his ways ..."

Rumbling through the brush Otis made his way back, wiping his chin.

Isaiah looked toward him. "Enough for now," he said softly to Oakie.

Oakie nodded in agreement.

"If I had pants to pee, they would be soaking wet right now! I love you and hate you for it all at the same time," Otis hollered as he approached.

"Was it better than last time?" Isaiah asked, knowing the answer.

"Better? It was okay," Otis answered nonchalantly.

"I guess I'm going to have to try harder next time, then," Isaiah replied, provoking Otis.

Waving his arms around, Otis shot back, "Whoa there, now don't get hasty. What I meant to say was—it doesn't get better than that!" He jabbed the air with his arm.

"And the truth shall set you free," Isaiah laughed. "I

have to be off. If you need me later, you know how to get a hold of me. Oakie, you're an exquisite young tree. I do hope we will get to chat more."

"You're right, I am." Oakie and Isaiah chuckled to themselves and exchanged warm smiles as though they were old acquaintances.

Isaiah turned, and as quickly as he had appeared, vanished into the mix of eagles circling the valley.

"I need a nap." Otis dropped to the ground and curled up in a patch of thick grass.

"Good idea," Oakie whole-heartedly agreed, exhausted from all the commotion.

What our little sapling didn't know was that he would need his rest—because he was about to be forced to make the hardest decision of his short life.

CHAPTER

13

THERE'S MORE TO LIFE

13

"*Hi-ya! Whaaa! Yyyyaaa! Whaaacha!*" Otis screamed mightily, as he launched a roundhouse kick into the air, which unfortunately landed him on his back. Dirt flew everywhere.

Oakie woke slowly, no longer fazed by Otis and all of his unexpected commotion.

"*Ya, ya, ya!*" Otis sent his fists flying into nothingness. Oakie stretched his leaves and yawned. He rubbed his eyes and said, "Get 'em Otis! Get 'em good!"

"Get who?" Otis asked, perplexed.

"Crouching mongoose, hidden snake!" Oakie shouted and burst into laughter from the deepest places of his belly.

Otis dropped his arms, staring at Oakie in confusion and shaking his head.

Wiping laughter tears from his eyes, Oakie continued, "Watch out! It's about to strike!" He laughed even harder.

This reminded Otis very much of his father, who was always the only one "in" on his "inside" jokes.

"Hey! Shut up, you garden vegetable," he said. "I'm preparing for my destiny."

Oakie broke his own laughter long enough to raise his leaves in the air like a praying mantis and flex his face like a vampire ready to strike. "Rarrr!" Oakie yelled, and continued squealing with laughter.

"I'm glad you amuse yourself so well." Otis shifted his stance and centered his mind.

Oakie calmed himself enough to speak.

"Seriously though," he said. "What are you doing?"

"Getting ready to unleash sweet, sweet terror on some unsuspecting vultures. These instruments of destruction," Otis raised his hands in the air, "Are going to release a melee of death on any adversary that stands in the way of me and my explorations."

Lingering for a moment, Oakie stared at Otis. Then he erupted in laughter again.

"Bwaa ha ha ha!" He curled over, grabbing his belly as he lost all composure.

In three swift moves, Otis flipped over a nearby rock, tucked and rolled across the ground. Then he lunged into air and landed before Oakie, sending his fists through the air over and over again, faster than lightning, purposely missing Oakie's face by less than a hair.

"*Wa, wa, wa, wa, wa, wa! Ya-chaaaa! Woooo!* A thousand fists of fury, and every one of them could have killed you before you hit the ground, dying a thousand deaths all at once!"

Oakie laughed harder.

"Stop laughing!" Otis shouted lightheartedly. "I'm serious."

Exhausting himself fairly well, Oakie began to ease out of his reckless laughter.

"All right, all right. I can see this is mostly one-sided. So what are you doing?"

Holding his head up high, Otis said again, "Strategically preparing for my journey into Vulture Desert."

"Didn't you hear what Isaiah said?" Oakie asked.

"What I heard Isaiah say was that *he's* only heard legends of travelers who haven't returned. Other people may have heard about those who have. Besides, Otis hasn't been there yet," he said, pointing to himself. "So that means the best hasn't taken on the challenge."

Oakie smiled, loving Otis's confident heroism.

"So what's with fighting invisible foes?" Oakie chuckled.

"Training. Not only will I fight off the vultures, but I plan on capturing one, taming it, and riding it like a pony back to The Valley of Eagles for all to see." Otis stood triumphantly, as though he had already done so.

Beyond all of Oakie's laughing and joking, a force of inspiration grew within him. Otis's boldness, courage, and strength made Oakie feel life had endless possibilities.

"You're really going, huh?"

"How could I not? I was made for this. This is who I am. I'm an adventurer."

"You're more than an adventurer." Oakie looked at Otis and thought about all that he was, what Isaiah said he was, and most importantly, the fact that he was Oakie's friend.

"You're right!" Otis pointed to Oakie. "I'm a hero, too. Now I just need me a damsel in distress."

They smiled at each other.

"I was thinking while you were getting your beauty sleep, which is much needed, as well as a good teeth brushing—" Oakie blew his breath into his leaf and waved it back into his face, smelling what Otis was saying.

"Did you have the most amazing time here?" Otis asked.

"Did I ever!"

"Is this the most magnificent thing you've ever seen?"

"Without question."

"Would you love to stay here forever?"

"What I would give for that!" Oakie grinned.

"Then so be it."

Oakie questioned Otis with a look.

"I'll leave you buried right here on this mountaintop all by yourself, overlooking the valley. You can make your apples here. You never have to leave. It's all yours. All day, every day."

Surprisingly, Oakie didn't say a word. He just stood there.

"So great of an offer you're speechless, huh?"

"I just need a moment, Otis."

Oakie reflected on the orchard where he had become this new green thing that he was. He thought about Morgan and Dakota, and all they had said. He remembered all the other trees he had begun to befriend before the trip. Although Oakie loved this valley and it seemed like a dream come true, there was something about the orchard that felt like ... like it was becoming his family.

Suddenly Oakie realized that for the first time in his life, he felt as though he belonged to something bigger than himself. He didn't feel alone. He was *actually* enjoying life for the first time. Although he might never see this valley again, he would always have the memory of it. It was an

amazing experience he could never forget, but it wasn't …
home. Besides, maybe all of this was simply about fulfilling
Verstand's promise in a roundabout way, and this beautiful
valley was just the dessert to a gourmet meal.

"I know this is going to sound strange—" he began.

Otis snapped out of the trance he'd fallen into while watching two spiders battle it out for world domination below.

"What's going to sound strange?"

"I need you to take me back."

For whatever reason, Otis had already known what Oakie's decision would be. Without hesitation, he dove his arm
into his satchel and pulled out a blue cloth. Like a bullet,
an eagle broke loose from the swarm of eagles hovering over
the valley.

"What's happening?" Oakie asked.

"I'm taking you home. Well, not *me* exactly." In the blink
of an eye a giant eagle, much like Isaiah, stood next to Otis.
Otis leaned over and whispered into his ear before introducing him to Oakie.

"This is Bob."

"Bob?"

"Bob."

"Bob?"

"Yes, Bob, also known as Bullet Bob. Not a fancy name,
I know, but he doesn't need one. Bob doesn't talk much,
so don't bother. He's great at what he does, which is flying
fast. He'll have you back before you can cry for your mother, which is easy to do with Bob because it can be a little
scary. Right, Bob?" Otis looked at Bob; Bob nodded.

"Aren't you coming with?" Oakie asked. Otis sent another
roundhouse through the air, this time landing it smoothly.

"Not today, Junior. Like I said, Vulture Desert is my
destiny." Otis grabbed Oakie from the ground where he
sat and walked him over to Bob. "He's all yours. Take good
care of him."

"Will I ever see you again?"

"Do squirrels eat nuts?"

"All except for you, Confucius."

"Well, since *most* do, let that be a *yes to your question*."

Otis smiled.

"Hey, aren't you curious as to why I'm not staying?"

"Deep down inside, it feels right. Anything else I should know?"

"No."

"Have a good trip and I'll see you soon, my friend."

Otis backed up as Bob grasped Oakie in his claws and took flight. Ever so quickly, Otis became a tiny blot on the ground, waving his paw. Oakie felt the loss, hoping it wouldn't be forever.

That afternoon, Bob delivered Oakie to the Orchard where the journey began. He successfully replanted Oakie, packing the dirt in around him the best he could with his beak. As Otis had pointed out, Bob was not much of a conversationalist, and he left without so much as a goodbye. Although Oakie thought he heard Bob mutter something about that squirrel owing him one.

That evening, the orchard buzzed with excitement over Oakie's return. The nearby trees listened intently as Oakie told the story to Dakota as he had promised, with intensity, passion, and joy.

As Oakie shared the decision he had made to return to the orchard, Morgan's eyes sparkled. The entire orchard could see his pride in Oakie—and in my opinion, Morgan had good reason.

Oakie carried wisdom and heart beyond that of most older trees. I believe Oakie not only made a good decision, but the best decision. Though he couldn't see it in the moment, it was a decision that would alter not only the course of his own life, but many others.

CHAPTER

14

ONE OF THE FAMILY

———— **14** ————

After Oakie's return from The Valley of Eagles, he became what I would call downright popular. He wasn't
just Oakie any longer, he was *Oakie*. He had made himself a
name without even meaning to. *Everyone* knew about Oakie and loved him. Seemingly overnight, he went from that
odd-looking sapling that no one really noticed to something
much bigger—quite literally.

In a miraculous feat, our little sapling had a sudden
and explosive growth spurt. I'd say that all the love and
attention showered on him from his new family worked like
some sort of fantastic miracle-grow serum: Oakie was now
so large that peoples were making sport out of climbing him
just as much as they did the other trees.

Running full-speed down a beaten path, a short, round
red-headed people made his way for Oakie. Dressed in brown
shorts and a red-and-brown striped shirt, the boy looked rather funny. Mice, frogs, butterflies, birds, and everything else
that could move scattered out of his way to save their lives.

Dakota leaned over to Morgan and pointed out the obvious. "This looks like it's going to be painful."

"Oakie's much larger than he looks. He'll be fine," Morgan replied.

"That people is much larger than *he* looks," Dakota retorted with a smile.

"Dakota, you're right. You should probably suggest a
helpful idea to Oakie before this gets too ugly."

Dakota nodded.

"Oakie!"

Oakie snapped out of the daydream he was in. "What's
going on Dakota?"

"I got a riddle for you."

"All right, go ahead."

"What did the rabbit say just before the bear tripped and fell on him?"

"I don't know, what?"

"This is going to be *beary* painful!" Dakota laughed hysterically to himself.

Morgan rolled his eyes as Oakie sat confused. He reveled in the fact that both Dakota and Oakie were so similarly "unfunny" at times. If Morgan didn't know better, he would swear they were brothers.

"Oakie," Morgan said calmly. "You are about to experience the pain a mother wolverine has when she gives birth."

Oakie's eyes widened.

"I suggest you shake your branches as wildly as possible in hopes of knocking him out before he climbs too high."

"He?" Oakie questioned.

And in one lobbing bound, Oakie had his answer. Throwing himself forcefully onto Oakie's base, the large and awkward youth made his climb.

Oakie and the onlookers flinched as the boy thrashed his arms around, grabbing anything he could get his hands on. Branch after branch snipped and snapped in two. With every thrust the boy made upward, a shower of leaves made its way downward.

"Get it off of me!" Oakie wailed in a deep booming voice.

"Shake him loose, Oakie. Buck like a wild bronco! He'll drop like a fly!" Morgan shouted.

"He means a two-ton gorilla!" Dakota blurted out with a laugh.

Oakie shook and shook. This people had an iron grip.

Sweat poured like a shower in the rainy season from the boy's head. He gave every bit of strength he had to climb up Oakie, and giving up was not an option.

"I am not an ice-cream cone! Get off of me!" Oakie hollered again.

The commotion had everyone's attention. A crowd of creatures gathered below to get a front-row view of the spectacle. Among them stood Caleb the skunk and his partner in crime, a porcupine named Frederick, watching as they plotted their next strike. Not far down the trail a small crowd of peoples watched and laughed with each other.

Oakie gave it his all, whipping every last branch he had back and forth.

The boy climbed even harder, with great tenacity.

The forest filled with a chant. "Oa-*kie*, Oa-*kie!*" Louder and louder. "Oa-*kie*, Oa-*kie!*" The orchard's chant became a boom. "OA-*KIE*, OA-*KIE!*"

The boy declared loudly as he approached the top, "I'm gonna make it! I'm gonna make it! I told you guys I could do it!"

The crowd of peoples exploded in laughter.

Oakie shook harder, the orchard chanted louder, the boy pushed farther. With all his might, he jumped for the second branch from the top. Everything stopped in one moment. Frozen in time, the entire orchard watched as the branch between that one single people and his victory broke. Everyone braced themselves as the boy sailed downward ... straight through every branch that stood in his way. For once, his size seemed to pay off as the extra cushioning in his backside took the brunt of the needles from Frederick, who was waiting excitedly below.

Oh my! Just telling the story makes my backside cringe.

Flailing around and shrieking loudly in pain, the boy rocketed back up into the air and came crashing down face-first in a pile of dirt where Caleb greeted him with an evil smile on his face.

The foul stench pierced the orchard and drove everyone out of the area at lightning speed, including the peoples who had been rolling on the ground laughing wildly.

The boy lay motionless, defeated and traumatized, almost as if he had died the most embarrassing death imaginable.

Morgan cringed at the sight of both Oakie and the red-headed boy on the ground.

"You think that it's all right?" Dakota asked Morgan. Wincing, Oakie barked at Dakota, "Forget him! What about me? I just had a mini-elephant climb me."

Laughing, Dakota returned, "You'll grow back. He won't."

"I certainly hope he doesn't, for your sake! I'm sending him your direction if he does," Oakie said in agony.

Dakota laughed again.

"You think this is funny?" Oakie's irritation was growing.

Morgan kindly silenced them. "Quiet down, both of you, and pay attention. I think he's moving."

The two stopped their squabble and took a look at the people. "And to answer your question, Oakie, yes. Yes, this is hilarious." Morgan bellowed a hearty laugh filled with love.

Oakie knew he was right. Had that boy done the same to Dakota, Oakie would still be laughing hysterically. Oakie lightened up and turned his attention back to the boy on the ground.

The boy was covered in dirt; leaves and small twigs were meshed in his hair. His arms and legs were wrapped with in scratches. Worst of all, hundreds of needles sprouted from his butt. Frederick had unquestionably won this round. Reaching back, the boy began plucking quills. He squealed like a pig with the removal of each one.

Oakie, Morgan, Dakota, and the rest of the onlookers winced in pain as they imagined how bad it must feel.

"Joshua! Joshua!" The voice of a frantic mother echoed through the orchard. "Joshua, where are you?! Answer me now or you're going to be in big trouble, mister!"

Joshua perked up quickly.

"You better not be making a mess of your new clothes!" Joshua leaped to his feet and brushed his clothes off in less time than it took him to fall from atop Oakie.

"What's the big deal?" Oakie said, looking toward Morgan.

"Angry, scared mother. That's the big deal. Even badgers know to stay out of their way. That boy is done for," Morgan replied.

"I don't think you could really mess those clothes up. Personally I think it's a bit of an improvement," Dakota responded.

Bursting forth from the trees and foliage, something that looked like an angry bear came stampeding their direction.

"What are you doing, young man? Look at you!" she scolded him. "Your new shorts and shirt are just ruined. You are beyond me. Were you climbing trees again?" Slamming to an abrupt stop, the mother clasped her nose with her hands. "Oh, dear Jesus! Did you get sprayed by a skunk?"

Joshua lowered his head and stared at his feet.

"That is horrible!" The mother coughed and pulled back a bit. "What did I tell you about climbing trees?"

Oakie covered his face with his branches. Somehow he felt a little responsible.

Morgan and Dakota looked away, also feeling awkward as Joshua's mother scolded him.

"I wasn't climbing trees, Mom." Joshua continued to stare at the ground.

"Then what were you doing?"

"I was climbing that *one* tree. Just *one*, Mom."

Only matadors ever see nostrils flair that wide. Maybe one day Joshua would be a bullfighter. In my opinion, it looked as though he had plenty of experience.

"Yeah, and what happened? You fell out, didn't you?"

"Mom, I'm okay."

"I told you this would happen. I told you that you would fall and get hurt. Why don't you listen to me when I tell you not to do something? When we get home you're in big trouble."

"For what?" Joshua demanded.

"For ruining your clothes, disobeying me, and getting smart with me."

"Mom, I'm not getting smart with you I'm just—"

"March. Now!" Keeping her hand tightly clenched around her nose and mouth, Joshua's mother grabbed him by the back of the neck and forced him in the direction from which she had come.

As Joshua made his way out of the orchard, he turned and looked at Oakie with determination in his eyes.

It was a look I've seen many times myself—heck, it's a look I've even given. And the truth is, not even the wrath of that boy's mother was going to stop him from finishing what he had started.

His new nemesis would be conquered.

CHAPTER

15

GROWING PAINS

15

Flashes of lightning illuminated the midnight sky. Giant gusts of wind whipped wildly through the trees. Leaves swirled about in clusters like swarms of bees. The rain rode the wind, which blew whatever direction it saw fit. Every animal and insect that could found shelter. Those that weren't as lucky braved the storm, directionless and lost. Lightning pounded the ground, leaving its mark like a bull-whip throughout the orchard.

"What do we do?" Oakie shouted at the top of his lungs to Dakota.

"We just have to hope for the best and wait it out," Dakota shouted back, then turned frantically to his father. "As long as I've lived, I've never seen a storm this intense, Dad. Are we going to be okay?"

Just then, a nearby tree was sliced in two by the most fascinating and terrifying bolt of lightning any of them had ever seen. All the trees shrieked in unison at the booming sound and jarring sight.

"I don't want to die! I still haven't made apples!" Oakie yelled.

"Dakota! Oakie! Look at me!" Morgan shouted. "This is not a time to get scared." Without warning, a great crack-bang grabbed their attention. Off in the distance, an avocado tree came crashing down, crushing the smaller trees around it. The wind howled louder and blew stronger.

"If not now, then when?" Dakota screamed. Morgan stood strong in his heart like only a tree with decades of experience, wisdom, and truth could.

"Listen closely, everyone!" Morgan commanded the attention of the orchard. "Pay no attention to the lightning and thunder. You cannot control it. It will do what it wills. If you can focus closely on what I say, you will become stronger than you could ever imagine."

The torrential downpour of rain made rushing rivers throughout the orchard, sweeping away the smaller creatures that didn't have the strength or power to hold on. A young apple tree, not nearly big enough for a squirrel to climb, lost root in the ground and was taken prisoner by the monster winds and treacherous river, never to be seen again.

Oakie watched in horror.

"Oakie, look at me! Keep your eyes on me, and me alone. Everyone! Right now the ground is extremely soft. We can either lose root and be knocked over, or we can do something that was previously impossible."

The orchard held tight to every word, pushing in for Morgan's direction.

"SINK YOUR ROOTS IN! Sink them deep! This is a gift for all of you, if you'll accept it. Allow yourself to grow. The ground can't stop you. There's nothing in your way. Don't miss this opportunity by being afraid of everything that is going on around you. This storm is *for* you. It's *not* against you. NOW GROW! SINK YOUR ROOTS!"

The orchard accepted the challenge. For some, the doubts and fears were greater than the storm itself. The doubt and fear stole the critical attention needed to sink their roots into the earth. They began to uproot and tilt over.

Others forgot the storm altogether, hearing only Morgan's words over and over in their minds. They began growing their roots. To their amazement, it was even easier than Morgan had said. Years and years of pushing through the hard soil seemed pointless and strenuous compared to this one brief moment of time.

Oakie stared, frightened for those that began tipping over. Fear overwhelmed him. "I can't do it, Morgan!" A gust of wind punched Oakie hard in the side, knocking him back and loosening some roots.

"Oakie! Did you not hear me? This is a gift for you. Keep your eyes on me," Morgan demanded.

Oakie watched Morgan closely and began to focus on

growing. At first it seemed hopeless, but soon he felt the movement downward. "It's happening, Morgan. I feel it!" Oakie continued to gaze deep into Morgan's eyes. More roots expanded and stretched. "It's really happening!"

"Don't give up!" Dakota cheered.

A bolt of lighting struck nearby.

Oakie glanced away from Morgan. Another bolt struck, then another. Like the grand finale at a fireworks show, the sky went wild. Oakie tipped backward, more than before.

"Oakie! Look at us!" Dakota shouted again.

"I can't do it! It's too hard. I'm not going to make it." Oakie became completely hopeless.

"That's a lie. You can do it, Oakie it's so easy. You were already doing it," Dakota pleaded.

More lightning billowed from the clouds. Oakie shot his eyes at Dakota, then Morgan, then the lightning. Over and over again he scanned the scene. Some of the trees in the orchard stood strong, many were giving up, and others had lost the battle altogether.

Dakota continued to beg Oakie.

"Dakota!" Morgan shouted firmly. "It's his choice. He knows the truth. He has to decide for himself. Begging him won't change anything at this point."

"Trust," Morgan proclaimed. "Trust that he'll choose life. He's got it in him, Son. Besides, focusing on what Oakie isn't doing or can't do will only take focus away from your own roots."

Dakota knew his father was right. It was Dakota's time to go deeper, and he couldn't afford to miss this opportunity. Worrying about Oakie wouldn't help him. Oakie had to choose for himself.

The storm blazed louder and stronger. Oakie tilted back farther. Suddenly he was in the ground again, buried and alone. His hopes, his dreams—he remembered them all. Otis, Verstand, Isaiah, Bullet Bob, The Valley of the Eagles, The Duke, Dakota, Morgan. His life was so rich, so great, so worth it. Oakie had come so far and experienced so much. He couldn't quit now.

Staring into Morgan's eyes once again, Oakie fought

against all that was around him and gave way to growing. "I won't give up!" he screamed. A rush of life jolted through every root and plunged them deeper into the ground than any other trees in the orchard.

And then something magical happened that not even Morgan had ever seen: The roots not only went deeper, but Oakie grew taller and rounder. Every part of him expanded. It was an indescribable growth spurt.

"I will live!" Oakie hollered over and over again. The phrase echoed throughout the orchard, drowning out the sound of the storm.

Other trees heard the cry of life and followed suit, screaming at the top of their lungs, "I will live! I will live! I will live!" The orchard began a storm of its own. Trees that had almost completely toppled over began to rise. Their roots sank in. None of the orchard was too far gone.

Without meaning to, Oakie had started something magnificent. He had started a fire of life, and it couldn't be put out. All he had to do was choose.

UNBRIDLED
IMAGINATION

16

Days came and went after the devastating storm marched through the orchard, trampling all that stood in its way. Boy, oh boy, was it ever a mess. The farmers that tended the orchard spent those days clearing the area of all the destruction that was left behind.

Many of the trees that survived no longer had apples. Their branches had been picked clean by the winds. The farmers gathered what they could from the ground and harvested what was left from the trees. The orchard sure was barren, and kind of lonely, if I do say so myself. This time of the year should be filled with the laughter and play of peoples. Instead, it remained silent and motionless. Although there had been great triumph, there was still great loss. In the silence of the days that passed, the orchard took time to grieve all that had changed and adjust to the new season.

Morgan was right. Those that heeded his wisdom were stronger than ever. Not only were their roots deeper, but they felt there was nothing left to fear. The worst that could happen had come and gone, yet they still stood.

Hopefulness bubbled into Morgan's soul. Looking around, he took inventory of all that was left. One of Morgan's greatest gifts was that he could always see the goodness and abundance in any situation. Seeing his family still standing brought him much joy and gratitude. The loss was minimal in comparison to all that was gained.

The transformation that Oakie had undergone left Morgan in awe. Oakie had at least doubled in size; he now towered above the orchard. Even Morgan could not have foreseen what his words could do when Oakie embraced them. In one moment, Oakie was transformed from the wavering little sapling that lived in the orchard's heart to the mighty oak that now loomed above them. It wasn't just size that made Oakie so grand. It was something much greater.

Oakie felt the change. He wasn't just surviving in the wake of the storm—he was thriving. Standing against the greatest opposition he had ever experienced, and seeing so many survive because of his bravery, solidified a triumphant confidence and assurance in his heart.

Looking down, Oakie caught Dakota staring at him. "What are you looking at, Dakota?" Oakie asked.

"The penguin flying above you," Dakota retorted. "What do you think I'm looking at? My trunk is getting sore just trying to look up at you. You're huge!"

"Thank you," Oakie replied.

"That wasn't a compliment. It was an observation."

"Okay, so what's the deal?"

"The deal is that this is amazing. How do you feel?"

"Besides tall?"

Oakie and Dakota both giggled.

Morgan shook his head and rolled his eyes as he listened to their silly banter.

"I don't know how I feel. Maybe powerful? I feel like a new tree, but not. You know what I mean?"

Dakota looked at Oakie blankly, not understanding. "No. I don't know what you mean."

"Hmmm. Well, let's see. I know I'm me. I am still Oakie and all, but I feel bigger."

Dakota shook his head and laughed. "Yeah, of course you're bigger, you knothead. That's clear to the whole orchard."

Oakie became a bit irritated. "Aaaah!" he yelled, throwing his branches in the air. "Dakota. I know I'm physically bigger. I'm trying to say I feel bigger on the inside. I don't feel small. I don't feel scared on the inside. I don't feel worried about anything. I'm not sad. I feel like only great things can happen. I feel like nothing can push me over."

"Well that's because you're so big. Duuuuh," Dakota smirked.

Oakie gritted his teeth. "Whatever. Forget it."

Morgan laughed and decided it was time to step in. "Oakie, I completely understand everything you are talking about."

"You do?"

"I do. In fact, quite frankly, I'm amazed."

Dakota grew tired of trying to understand what Oakie was talking about and couldn't follow Morgan, who seemed to already know. Losing interest in the conversation altogether, he directed his attention to two deer locking horns and battling in the meadow.

Morgan continued, "It took me the majority of my time in this orchard to become what you became almost overnight."

"Is this it, then? Is this how it will be forever?"

"No, it gets better. It's still changing, even for me." Morgan smiled.

"Is that possible?"

"It's what we call living life, and you're at the beginning of it. Unfortunately for most trees, it takes their entire lives to start living it."

Oakie stood in silence, taking time to think about what Morgan was saying.

Suddenly, the two bucks froze and stopped their sparring. An unsettling sound ripped through the trees and drove them off. Morgan, Dakota, and Oakie all turned at once toward the commotion. A familiar freckled face appeared, huffing and puffing.

Now, before we continue, I need to make a little confession: This story is not entirely about Oakie. Yep, I know I promised you I was going to tell you a story about Oakie the Apple Tree, and that's what I'm doing. But here's the thing: Sometimes the story of others' lives is just as important to understanding the story of our own. Thus it was with Oakie. What am I talking about? How about you just sit there and listen? Before I'm done it'll all make sense, I promise.

Now as I was saying, a familiar freckled face appeared, huffing and puffing. The pudgy red-headed people made his way into the orchard, running as fast as his stumpy little legs could carry him.

"Round Two, perhaps?" Morgan suggested.

Dakota looked at Oakie to see if he was bracing himself. Joshua's previous attempt at climbing to the top had left

Oakie pretty sore.

Oakie stood confidently, staring Joshua down. "He'll be lucky if he makes it to my first branch," he said firmly.

Howling at the top of his lungs, screaming like a Comanche warrior, Joshua charged, fearless and mighty. Unfortunately for him, the tiny stump in front of him wasn't moved by his war cry. Catching his foot, the stump threw him end over end, and he rolled to a stop behind none other than Caleb the skunk.

Caleb could not have been happier.

Dakota whipped his branches back and forth, trying to wave away the horrible smell. "Caleb! Stop doing that!" he shouted.

Caleb ignored Dakota's reprimand and scurried off to find Frederick to share this delightful story.

"If Caleb does that again, I'm convincing a badger to pay him a visit." Dakota was furious.

Oakie chuckled. Fortunately for him, the smell didn't reach his height.

"Stop laughing! It's horrible!"

Oakie found sweet satisfaction, watching Dakota's torment.

Joshua lay briefly on the ground, gagging from the smell and trying to collect himself. Sitting up, he shook the leaves out his hair and rubbed the pain out of his lower back. Flopping around like a turtle on its back, Joshua made his way to his feet.

The orchard couldn't help but giggle.

Looking over at the stump that had so easily thwarted his battle charge, Joshua puffed up his chest and unleashed a pitiful roundhouse kick on the stump.

Although it couldn't kick back, it didn't have to.

Joshua danced in a circle on one leg, holding his aching foot, until he fell over a second time.

Dakota couldn't keep quiet. "He reminds me of a very uncoordinated pink flamingo." Dakota and Oakie burst out laughing.

"Dakota, quit being mean," Morgan said sternly.

"I'm not being mean; I'm just making observations." Dakota said, still chuckling.

"Morgan's right. That's just rude. Pink flamingos don't deserve being compared to that," Oakie added, laughing harder. Morgan shook his head, knowing there wasn't much he could say to wrangle their behavior.

Joshua rolled around a bit longer before hopping to his feet once again. After taking a minute to gain composure, he looked around the orchard: He had come back for vengeance. He had lost the battle with Oakie last time, but had returned to win the war. His mother had warned him not to climb trees ever again, but what did she know? She was a thorn in his side that needed to be plucked. He was her precious porcelain doll. She kept him on a tight leash because in her world he was helpless and breakable.

But in Joshua's world, he was powerful and bold. Behind the pudgy exterior and goofy looks, he was a warrior who in one moment could change into a stealthy ninja assassin. In the next instant, he could morph into a mystical magician who controlled space and time. If something bigger than magic was needed, he could easily summon and take command of his pet dinosaurs. Nothing was too big or too scary for Joshua. If the dark powers of evil were too great for the ninja, magician and dinosaurs, he would simply strap his vibrant red cape around his neck and pummel his opponent with his super powers. Joshua was indestructible. In his world, he couldn't be stopped.

The orchard looked much different than before. But, that was a small hurdle easily overcome. Waving Caleb's smell from his nose, Joshua tapped the side of his forehead and turned on his electronic scanner eyes (E.S.E.s). With strength and assurance on his face, he scanned the orchard looking for his nemesis, Oakie. Multiple mice, two blue-bellied lizards, and a toad turned up on his Nemesis Detector Meter, or N.D.M, but no tree. With seismic trip bombs scattered throughout the orchard, like the one that had blown up and sent Joshua flying to the ground, he knew it wasn't safe to continue the search without protection. It was time to gear up and put on his hazard protection suit, or H.P.S. Opening up his chest core, Joshua pulled out his metallic tactical flak boots and strapped them on.

"Oh my leaves, what the skunk is he doing?" Dakota mumbled.

"I think he hit his head really hard when he tripped. We might need to get him help," Oakie replied with concern.

"Apparently, neither of you has any imagination. You really should ask him for tips. Then, you'd both be much less of a bore." Morgan shook his head, laughing.

The three continued poking fun at each other while Joshua finished gearing up.

Next, Joshua slipped his hands into his reaper gloves, which were covered in tiny spikes, perfect for climbing. Before closing his chest core and putting on his impact armor, he strapped his Translocating Molecule Splitter, or T.M.S., to his left thigh for quick access. In a moment of danger and at the press of a button, the T.M.S. could split him into a billion molecules, teleport him to safety, and reanimate him. To his right thigh, he strapped his pulse cannon, which could shoot shockwaves that would agitate an enemy's stomach so terribly as to render it powerless and cause it too ... well, poop itself. Joshua always wore a mischievous grin just before pulling the trigger.

After attaching a ripper blaster to his wrist, a small blaster that shoots spinning blades, he closed his chest core and strapped on his impact armor. Joshua was ready for battle. Forging ahead, he would stop at nothing until his nemesis was apprehended and conquered.

A heavy wind kicked up a large cloud of dust, much like a morning fog, swallowing the orchard. Joshua's E.S.E.s were useless in this mess. He would have to rely on instinct. Pushing through the cloud, he could sense something was stalking him. He spun around wildly, trying to protect himself.

"What is he doing now?" Dakota whispered to Morgan.

The three trees watched as Joshua spun in circles and judo-chopped the air.

Morgan knew Joshua was only playing—but *what* he was playing? Well, Morgan had no answer to that.

Houdini, a dusty gray rabbit, suddenly appeared between the trees. "Hey guys! Whatchya lookin' at?" he asked softly.

All three shrieked liked babies.

"Houdini!" Morgan protested. "I told you not to sneak up on me like that anymore."

"How about, 'Hi Houdini, how ya been? I haven't seen you in forever. Oh, and by the way, this giant tree that wasn't here before is so-and-so, and the crazy-looking people that's freaking you out is hopefully going to go away,'" Houdini countered.

"Houdini, this is Oakie. Oakie, this is Houdini." Morgan made the introduction.

"Nice to meet you, Houdini." Oakie grinned.

"The pleasure's all yours, I'm sure." Houdini bowed and winked. Then he turned to Dakota. "Dakota, you going to just stand there, or are you going to say 'Howdy' to your long-lost partner?"

Dakota rolled his eyes.

"I saw that!" Houdini threatened.

"You were supposed to!"

Dakota and Houdini locked eyes for a moment before busting into uproarious laughter.

"Good to see you, kid."

"You too you, old fart."

"Honestly guys, that kid is freaking me out." Houdini tugged at his ears and crossed his eyes.

"Welcome to being friends with you," Morgan retorted playfully.

"I'm gonna mess with him."

"Play nice," Morgan cautioned.

But Houdini had already vanished.

Joshua continued to spin in circles, blinded by the dust. Vines slowly began curling up and slithering across the ground like snakes toward him.

Wrapping itself tightly around his ankle, the first vine seized Joshua, tossing him to the ground.

Instinctively, with precision, Joshua fired a ripper blade and cut the vine. Without hesitation, he leaped to his feet. Dozens of vines burst from the dust cloud. Like a mystical ninja, Joshua began an onslaught. A fury of ripper blades sliced through the orchard, decimating his attackers.

Houdini bounced around, dodging the handfuls of rocks that Joshua was throwing everywhere.

"This kid is nuts! I love him!" Houdini shouted.

The vines were being diced to pieces but they kept coming. Joshua had no choice but to grab the T.M.S. from his thigh and transport out of there.

The rocks stopped flying.

Houdini sat still and watched as Joshua locked his arms tightly to his sides and ran awkwardly behind a tree. Holding his breath so not to give away his new location, Joshua popped his head out from behind the tree. He watched as the dust slowly settled. Teleporting away from the vines had saved his life.

Houdini had a brilliant idea. While Joshua scanned the area, he zipped through the trees.

All danger seemed to be eliminated. Wiping the sweat from his forehead, Joshua began to breathe quietly. He was safe, or so it seemed.

Without warning, Houdini launched out of the brush behind Joshua as he turned to search for his nemesis. Just as Houdini had hoped, Joshua shrieked at the top of his lungs in terror and took off running. Fleeing as fast as he could, he turned to see if his attacker was still in hot pursuit.

Unfortunately for Joshua, the problem wasn't behind him. Houdini cackled hysterically as Joshua slammed face-first into his nemesis and fell to the ground.

The impact shook some of Oakie's leaves loose. The entire orchard gritted its teeth with pain as Joshua crashed to the ground.

Dakota glanced around, looking for Caleb so he could yell at him. Luckily for everyone, Caleb was nowhere to be seen.

"Houdini, you haven't changed a bit, have you?" Morgan asked, shaking his head with a smile.

Houdini shrugged and disappeared.

"He sure enjoys the ground," Dakota mumbled.

Joshua lay dazed. His forehead felt as though it was ready to explode. Reaching up to rub the pain away, he discovered a giant lump the size of a baseball.

Houdini appeared, perched on a rock next to his victim's body.

"Hey guys, I think his brain is trying to escape." Houdini felt little remorseful.

Oakie peeked down.

"Oh! Oh, that's bad. Morgan, do you think he's going to die?" Oakie was worried.

"I hope not. Have you ever smelled a rotting carcass? It's worse than Caleb and stays forever," Dakota blurted without remorse.

"No, he's not going to die, Oakie. Have some compassion, Dakota. Houdini ..." Morgan looked at Houdini the way a father would to address a child who's just colored the walls with crayon.

"What?" Houdini raised his paws in innocence.

Morgan continued to stare.

"He should have been watching where he was going."

Morgan was relentless with his look.

"Okay ... okay, I get it. All right, I'm sorry. Maybe it wasn't the best idea."

Morgan's gaze didn't budge.

"It was a bad idea, okay?" Houdini looked down at Joshua, who was moaning as he continued to rub the apple on his forehead. He looked back up at Morgan and continued, "It is slightly amusing, though."

Dakota chuckled.

Like a laser beam, Morgan shot Dakota the same look, silencing his son. Then he refocused his attention on Houdini.

"Maybe not ... I think this is my cue to disappear." And Houdini did just that, before Morgan's eyes could burn a hole straight through him.

After collecting himself, Joshua opened his eyes. Squinting tightly, the blur in front of his face began to come into focus. Towering high above him stood his nemesis. He thought perhaps he still wasn't seeing very well. Joshua shook his head and hoped everything would adjust and return to normal size, the way he remembered it.

Not a chance. Oakie stood tall, a skyscraper in comparison to the puny nemesis that had given him a run for his money before. Squirming, Joshua collected himself and stood up. Leaves and dirt camouflaged him. Head cocked back, he stared intently at the top of Oakie, mesmerized by the towering tree. Breaking his moment of awe, a woodpecker dropped in and landed on the bump protruding from his head and began to peck. Joshua swung wildly at the bird and chased it away.

"I guess the woodpecker thinks he's kind of a knothead!" Dakota announced.

Oakie exploded with laughter.

Morgan wasn't amused, and it was clear that both of them knew it because they stopped laughing faster than they had started.

Joshua stumbled around in circles, rubbing his head until most of the pain was gone. Looking back toward Oakie, he could see the nearest branch to grab was at least two or three times higher than he could reach. This tree couldn't be his nemesis. Confused, Joshua examined the orchard around him. None of the other trees looked anything like the nemesis he had attempted to scale such a short time ago.

Baffled, Joshua retraced his steps and dug into the memory of his previous attempt at a climb. Everything he could think of placed his nemesis right where this giant tree now stood. This wasn't the nemesis he remembered. Joshua stared at Oakie, having second thoughts. Even King Kong would think twice about taking on this climb! This wasn't a time to quit, though. He knew there had to be a solution!

He paced back and forth for a minute or two until an idea struck him: If he could run fast enough, he might be able to run right up the side of Oakie and seize the first branch. On his own it would be impossible, but with his superhero speed-booster power boots, he could probably run as fast as a million miles per hour. With that kind of speed, he might just run all the way to the top of Oakie! Rummaging fiercely through his superhero suitcase, Joshua pulled out an old pair of flashy boots suited for only the greatest of heroes, and thrust them on.

"Why's he shoving branches in his shoes?" Dakota asked rhetorically.

"He's part people, part beaver," Oakie chimed in.

The two laughed.

Morgan observed quietly, very interested in Joshua's imagination.

After lacing the boots, Joshua bent down to get a good stretch. If he wasn't careful, running a million miles an hour would cause a pretty bad cramp. Touching the top of his knees with the tips of his fingers, he held the stretch while grunting loudly. Once satisfied, he backed up. Like an Olympian preparing for a hundred-yard dash, he got down into starting position. The sound of a gun echoed throughout the orchard.

Joshua exploded from the starting line. He was moving so fast that his heightened super-senses had to kick in so he could navigate. The world morphed into slow motion. Grasshoppers were scattered all about him, frozen mid-jump. Apples falling from the trees hung between heaven and earth, trapped in a single moment. An unsuspecting worm weaving itself through the grass lay paralyzed, awaiting the inevitable moment of becoming an afternoon treat for the blue jay reaching out to grasp for its head.

"Morgan, all jokes aside, I think there's really something wrong with that people." Oakie stared with concern as Joshua slowly inched toward him.

Each foot took its turn raising and lowering itself with care and detail, so as not to go too fast. Joshua looked like he was moving through molasses. Then, without warning, he sped up and barreled toward Oakie.

To his disappointment, Joshua made it no more than two steps up Oakie before he found himself clawing and scratching his way to nothing. The defeat tasted like a mouth full of bark.

He took a moment to calm down and spit out the wood chips that covered his teeth. It seemed that even the super-hero speed-booster power boots weren't a match for this behemoth tree. He needed something greater than cheap fancy tricks. He needed a new strategy. He needed a strategy that only the most brilliant mind on Planet Earth could devise.

Joshua grabbed his backpack and pulled out a giant

brain. Unlatching the top of his head, he tore out the smaller brain that was filling it and replaced it with this new superbrain. Latching the top of his head tightly back down, the brain-crunching began. Numbers and scenarios swirled about in his mind. A tornado of possibilities exploded.

"Standing cross-eyed with his finger drilled straight up his nose solidifies it for me—his head is broken. I want to blame it on Houdini, but I think there were problems long before he ran into Oakie. Maybe one of the trees could save him any further embarrassment and just fall over on him," Dakota said, pitying the little people.

"Dakota, stop. His head is not broken. He's a child that's using his imagination."

"I don't see other peoples acting crazy like that."

"Well, Dakota, most peoples don't use their imagination. They're just boring robots coming and going without thinking or feeling much. They pick their apples, fill their baskets, and then get on their way. Occasionally some of them have a bit of fun, but for the most part they're just boring. I rather enjoy this *odd* people. He's entertaining and quite refreshing. You don't see this every day, do you?"

"No, that's why he's crazy."

"That's where you're wrong, son. You don't see this every day because he's *different*."

"He sure is different."

"But not in a bad way. That little people is alive in his heart and his mind. If you understood the situation correctly, you would recognize the beautiful opportunity we are having at this very moment." Morgan gently prodded with his words.

Dakota looked at Oakie and rolled his eyes.

Oakie thought the little people was crazy just as much as Dakota did, but he knew Morgan was right. Morgan understood more about the world than the rest of the orchard put together. He always looked through eyes of love, and through that love was pure truth.

Joshua removed his finger from his nose. The bigger brain granted him instant access to a whole world of thought. He was going about this all the wrong way. He wasn't defeated—he was just delayed. There would have to be a different approach this time around. His nemesis wasn't what it had been in the beginning.

He twisted around. Pointing toward the way he had entered the orchard, he trotted off, hustling home to devise a plan. Following mischievously behind was Houdini. Before leaving the orchard's line of sight, Houdini turned back and winked at Oakie, Dakota, and Morgan.

"Remember, he's just an imaginative, innocent boy!" Morgan shouted, knowing it probably wouldn't do much good.

"You know, he's actually quite enjoyable, I really hope he survives Houdini. I think he'd make a great addition to the orchard," Oakie confessed. As he watched Joshua disappear, he couldn't help but feel as though his destiny was somehow intertwined with this imaginative, quirky little people.

If only Oakie knew how truly intertwined his destiny would become with this little boy, for the good and the bad ...

17

MISGUIDED JUDGMENT

—————— 17 ——————

Scaling the mountain of shelves before him, Joshua grunted and sweat as he dug through the boxes of his father's belongings that were stored deep beneath layers of dust, untouched for years. *Somewhere* buried in the mountain of knick-knacks stacked in his parents' garage had to be something that could help him conquer his nemesis.

Houdini schemed as Joshua dug ravenously through the debris.

Box after unopened box sailed to the ground, smashing open and scattering its contents about the garage. Joshua lunged from one shelf to the next, using his imaginary rock pick to anchor himself to the imaginary canyon wall before him. The climb was dangerous, but if he backed down now he'd never grasp victory. Piercing the next rock with his pick, he prepared to make a dangerous leap. Without warning, the rock crumbled from the canyon wall. Joshua nearly plummeted to his death. Like a bomb, the rock sailed toward the canyon floor, braking for nothing.

Upon impact, the rock sprang into the air and targeted Houdini. Leaping out of the way just in the nick of time, Houdini tucked and rolled under the blue Subaru sedan parked in the driveway.

Coming to rest, the battered bowling ball settled into the neighbor's yard.

Hidden behind the boxes sat a one-man workout trampoline—the culprit who fired the bowling ball at Houdini.

"Seek and ye shall find! Eureka!" the young explorer shouted at the top of his lungs.

Back in the orchard, Joshua climbed a rock near his nemesis. Licking his finger and waving it in the air, he determined the wind resistance and the exact spot in which to place the trampoline in order to jump up to the first branch.

Houdini popped out from behind the rock. "He's planning on killing you!" Houdini shouted. "RUN AWAY AS FAST AS YOU CAN!"

Oakie looked at his roots, then glared at Houdini. Houdini shrugged awkwardly. "Well, just so you know he's planning on killing you. Nice knowing you, kid."

"He's not planning on killing me, Houdini. How would he kill me?"

"He'd shoot a giant marble at you with that bouncy thing. That's how. I came back to warn you. He almost did me in."

Joshua adjusted the trampoline, then climbed the rock again.

Houdini fled the scene, hiding behind Morgan.

"What are you doing, Houdini?" Morgan asked.

Houdini popped his ears out from behind Morgan. "I cheated death once already today. I don't want my luck to run out. When that ogre topples over, I don't want to become a flapjack. Get it? I'm a jackrabbit and I would be flattened like a *pancaaay* ..."

No one laughed.

"Whatever, guys. Don't have a sense of humor about this; I sure don't."

Firing up from the rock like a NASA space shuttle, Joshua launched into the air toward the trampoline. Landing perfectly in the middle, the trampoline stretched tight, like a slingshot ready to be released. Then it ripped to shreds.

Joshua stood silently. His eyes were closed, and his arms at his sides, waiting for the instant propulsion the bowling ball had received. A second passed before he realized that he wasn't going anywhere.

Oakie, Dakota, and Morgan turned to Houdini and shook their heads.

"Thanks for the heads-up, Houdini." Oakie offered sarcastic gratitude.

Houdini huffed at the three.

Choosing not to wallow in grief at the minor setback, Joshua returned to his parent's garage to prepare for Round Three.

The solution to his problem *had* to be under the vast ocean of clutter. He knew if he looked long enough, somehow the answer would find him.

Springing from the door that led to the backyard was Joshua's obnoxious younger sister, Katie. Wielding a pogo stick, she bounced past, giving Joshua only enough attention to stick her tongue out at him before proceeding to hop into the driveway.

Houdini had returned to keep an eye on the strange people. Hiding under the car, he sat mesmerized and mildly jealous of the graceful hops this other people made. Not a single jackrabbit he had ever met was so graceful or elegant.

Joshua didn't see grace, or elegance, for that matter. He saw a glorious solution. Fortunately for him, Katie's behavior made his decision weigh little, if at all, on his conscience as he booted her off the pogo stick and sent her sailing into the bushes that lined the driveway.

"I'm telling Mom and Dad when they get home, you big jerk!" Katie wailed at the top of her lungs.

Joshua knew his idea was impervious to any setbacks. By the time Mom and Dad got home, he would have mounted the highest branch of his nemesis, come back down, been made king of his fifth-grade class and well on his way to becoming a nationally renowned adventurer. And all before dinner.

As Joshua hit the trail, fantasizing about how untouchable he would be, Houdini sprinted ahead to warn the orchard.

"Look, guys, you have to listen to me!" Houdini begged Morgan and the boys. "This thing has this contraption that makes him bounce like a super jackrabbit. He destroyed another people without even blinking. I'm telling you, he's going to infiltrate this entire orchard by secretly posing as a rabbit. Then he's going pluck each of us away quietly in the night, one by one. He'll take his pudgy little people fingers and scoop out our brains. He's a lunatic, I'm telling you. We have to do something!"

"Houdini, don't get your ears in a knot over this. He isn't

going to scoop anyone's brains out." Dakota rolled his eyes.

"Obviously that's not frightening to you, bub, but for the rest of us who have something to lose, it's an issue," Houdini retorted.

"Zing!" Oakie shouted and laughed.

Before Dakota could think of something witty to say, Joshua came barreling down the trail, carrying the pogo stick.

Houdini and the orchard trees braced themselves.

When Joshua reached pouncing distance, he lunged into the air and placed the stick between his legs. Landing on the ground, the spring in the stick smooshed together, creaking and howling.

The spring struck back.

Joshua shot into the air, then down, then up again, and then down again, gaining height and distance with each jump. This was it—this was his chance to shine!

With all the squeal it could muster, the pogo stick shouted at the top of its lungs before exploding like a jack-in-the-box. Its life was over and Joshua was back where he started. He picked himself up off of the ground, dusted himself off and returned to his parents' garage.

"Aaaah ... oooh," Oakie moaned like a zombie.

"Oh no! Please no! Dad! The monster scooped Oakie's brain out with his pudgy people fingers. We should have listened to Houdini! Why didn't we listen? WHY?" Dakota cried dramatically.

Houdini turned to Dakota and hissed like an angry cat before sprinting off to follow Joshua home.

"Did he just hiss at you?" Oakie chuckled to Dakota.

"Oh my tree ... he hissed at me like some kind of sick cat ..." Dakota laughed heartily.

Back at his parents' garage, Joshua stood speculating in the middle of the room, carefully studying the contents lying about. Realizing that he wasn't going to *find* anything that would help scale Oakie, he decided he would have to *create* something.

Rushing inside, he grabbed his father's white trench coat and returned. Science was needed here. Ingenuity that no mere mortal man could muster up was the solution.

Taking note of his father's workbench, Joshua seized the goggles hanging on the wall, put them on, and then proceeded to devise a plan.

Up until that point, his greatest problem was that he wasn't tall enough to reach the first branch. He could somehow create a concoction of food that might make him grow rapidly, but many of the ingredients, like horny-toad legs, needed for that type of miracle-grow serum weren't readily available.

He'd have to build his legs, not grow them. A crummy four-legged desk sitting in the corner that must have been older than his grandpa seemed perfect for his scientific cause. Grabbing a jagged-toothed saw from his dad's bench, Joshua unknowingly whaled away at the legs of his great-great-grandmother's antique table that had been passed down for four generations to his mother.

It was easy, just like watching his dad cut down the Christmas tree every year. Chopping wood from the corners of the table, Joshua was able to create planks to stand on that he nailed to the legs. A little bit more wood from the table, and he had made handles. Before long he had two perfectly crafted cybernetic leg extensions. He was going to be a freak of nature and a modern marvel all in the same bowl of soup.

From the step that led into the house he could mount the legs and take them for a spin.

Hiding in the corner of the garage behind an old coffee can, Houdini sat with his mouth wide open. The boy was a monster, towering high above everything. He could pluck birds right from their nests if he so desired. Houdini had to warn the orchard. If they didn't listen this time, it would surely be the end for everyone!

Joshua hobbled and wobbled back and forth, tip-tapping and tap-tipping his way atop the concrete in the garage. From this height he could reach past the highest shelf with little effort. Smiling from ear to ear, Joshua noticed his dad's "special" box, which previously had been well out of reach.

It was time to find out what Dad had been hiding. Inside was a pile of little cards. Each card had the picture of a man holding a big stick and a little white ball. One of the

cards had a name under the picture that read "Babe Ruth."
Sounded like a lady, but looked A LOT like a guy.

A door slammed behind Joshua, startling him. The entire
box dropped to the ground and the cards scattered everywhere.

"I'm telling Mom and Dad that you're doing stuff you
shouldn't be doing," Katie whined.

"Yeah, I know, and don't forget to tell them that I kicked
you off your pogo stick earlier—which, by the way, is a piece
of junk. It blew up after only three or four hops on it." Joshua laughed to himself and made for the driveway.

Katie's eyes boiled with anger. Her favorite toy was broken because her brother was a giant turd.

Joshua hobbled awkwardly toward the big garage door.

With the instincts of a wise serpent, Katie smashed the
door button, stuck out her tongue, and walked into the house.

Joshua couldn't stop. Before he knew what hit him, he
walked right into the closing door and flopped back onto
the ground.

After he conquered his nemesis, he swore to himself
that he would return for his sister.

Back at the orchard, Houdini nearly did back flips while
shouting and hollering about the giant monster that the
little people had become.

Even Morgan was beginning to miss the mischievous
Houdini who used to cause all the trouble, not the Houdini
who whimpered and whined about it.

Joshua reappeared, trucking down the path as fast
as he could move his feet while he carried the two long
poles. His white overcoat whipped viciously behind him. He
squinted, trying to see through his goggles as he forged on
to conquer his nemesis.

"Did you scoop your own brain out, Houdini? He's no
monster," Oakie said.

"He's going to transform into one, and when he does
it's *kahblammo* for this orchard!" Houdini said, waving his
hands back and forth like an explosion in front of his face.

"Houdini, what happened to your sense of humor? It's
seems to have *poof!* Disappeared," Morgan taunted Houdini.

"I cheated death, you dried-up stick of firewood. It's all

fun and games until the wabbit almost gets decapitated!"
Houdini sliced his thumb across his throat. "My sense of
humor was lost with that maniac's drive to murder me."

Morgan began, "He's just an innocent-"

"Innocent, my tail!" Houdini cut in. "If you won't do
something about this, then I will. I've got a trick or two up
my sleeve." With that, Houdini vanished.

"He's really dramatic," Dakota commented to Morgan.

"Almost as much as you," Morgan replied.

"I'm not dramatic! Am I dramatic, Oakie?" Dakota began
to ramble about not being dramatic, which only furthered
Morgan's point.

While Dakota went on, Joshua mounted the nearby
rock, using it as he had the stairs back in the garage. After
a few jumps, his cybernetic limbs were attached. He awkwardly danced around, trying to keep his balance as he
tripped on rocks and twigs. The orchard was proving much
more difficult to navigate than the smooth cement floor of
the garage. After a bit of stumbling around, he seemed to
get a better hang of it.

"He's pretty agile for a beefy kid," Dakota pointed out,
breaking from his rant.

The thick grass at the edge of the orchard began waving like an ocean. Three notorious tree-killers known as
The Stooges burst into the clearing. The evil beavers were
a well-trained force of wood chippers. Aiming for Joshua,
they stampeded like a herd of wild buffalo.

The trees in the orchard gasped and trembled with fear.
The Stooges had been banished long ago.

Riding atop the leader of the trio was none other than
Houdini. "Mush, my minions! MUSH!" Houdini shouted,
cracking his arm down like a whip.

The orchard sat paralyzed. The only thing more dangerous than beavers was fire.

Tugging a rope in the mouth of the lead beaver, Houdini
drove the pack toward Joshua as he hobbled toward Oakie.
"Feed your hunger!" Houdini raved. The beavers ravenously
devoured Joshua's stilts until he stood with his feet planted
firmly on the ground. Houdini dismounted his beast before

The Stooges fled back to the river from where they had come.

Joshua stood dumbfounded. He was left holding only the handles of his great invention.

Morgan's eyes flared up and his leaves began shaking wildly. "Houdini!" he shouted. "What are you doing?" The entire orchard went silent.

"Saving the orchard," Houdini replied proudly, crossing his arms. "The Stooges owed me a long-overdue favor."

"You didn't save anyone," Morgan pointed out.

"I did too, and you should thank me."

"Houdini, you listen here! You *didn't* save anyone! In fact, your fear endangered all the lives in this orchard. Furthermore, that fear stirred up a world of anxiety here. The Stooges spent years plucking away our innocent. In your fear and ignorance of something you don't fully understand, you endangered *everyone*." Oakie and Dakota exchanged glances, grateful they weren't Houdini in this moment.

"You can't just stand by when there's a threat like this," Houdini retorted.

"You didn't even seek to understand this people!" Morgan exclaimed.

"He's odd, not like any of the other peoples that come and go through here—or anywhere else, for that matter."

"That doesn't make him dangerous. However, your lack of desire to understand makes your choices dangerous. Your choices make you a danger to all of us. You've created an unrealistic reality out of thin air. This is the very reason wars have been waged and countless innocent lives have been lost. Animosity, bitterness, and hatred have been birthed out of sheer ignorance toward those we don't understand."

Houdini hung his ears, feeling ashamed.

Morgan realized the effect his weighty words were having on Houdini. While Joshua trudged home to strategize another plan, Morgan continued speaking in a much softer tone.

"Houdini, please look up at me," he asked gently.

Houdini lifted his head.

"Houdini, you're not bad and I'm not shaming you. I treasure every child in this orchard."

Oakie smiled. Even though he hadn't come from Morgan, he knew he was one of the children Morgan was talking about.

"My highest value is to protect all those I love, including you. I'm not mad at you. I'm angry at ignorance. Ignorance steals so many lives. Ignorance and lack of understanding destroys the very foundation of my core value, which is love."

The weight on Houdini's shoulder's lightened.

"I'm frustrated, but not with you. I'm frustrated with the fear you've agreed with. Fear cannot coexist in a loving and peaceful family. It will only bring destruction. It's either peace and love, or chaos and fear. I stand here in this orchard promoting and protecting the truth of peace and love. The truth is you didn't do long-term damage here, but fear could have."

Houdini looked down and scratched random drawings in the dirt with his foot.

"Houdini."

"Yes," Houdini replied, looking up from the mess he was making in the dirt.

"I love you," Morgan said warmly.

"I'm sorry, Morgan," Houdini said.

"I know you are, and I forgive you. Now why don't you hop along and find out what that people is up to. And don't forget to have fun—it's what you do best." Morgan smiled and shook some leaves onto Houdini.

"I still think he's nuts—not dangerous, but nuts." Houdini smiled charmingly and ran off.

Feeling a bit awkward about Morgan's kind scolding, Dakota chimed in, "Do you think those beavers might be of any help in the shedding of a few pounds of unneeded extra bark?" Dakota twisted about, looking at his trunk.

"You're going to need an army of beavers to accomplish a task that large," Oakie poked.

The neighboring trees giggled with relief and began to chat quietly once again amongst themselves.

Now, I don't know about you, but I feel like that little people, Joshua, keeps things rather interesting in the orchard and I think there's plenty of excitement to be had with this young boy, even for an old fella like me.

RELENTLESS FORTITUDE

18

Back at the garage, amidst the explosion of debris that had further accumulated during Joshua's search for an answer, sat a pudgy dreamer lost in thought.

Houdini rounded the corner of the garage and began snaking his way through the mess of junk littering the floor.

Without warning, Joshua leaped to his feet, tore a notepad and pencil from his front jacket pocket and began scribbling a drawing. In no time he dropped the pad and raced to the saw and the two-legged table sitting on its side.

Houdini crept quietly to the notepad as Joshua hacked away at his mother's antique. On the pad was a poor drawing of what seemed to be a tree. Houdini assumed it was Oakie. On the tree were steps that led all the way to the first branch. Houdini sat back and contemplated the genius of the idea. Simple, but brilliant.

Sawdust shot into the air and swirled around the room as Joshua continued hacking away. As the table slowly became a stack of boards, Joshua found himself at a crossroads. There was no way he could carry all of this by himself. Even if he took multiple trips, it would take him forever.

Houdini understood the dilemma. The last time he'd been in the garage, he had found a red wagon covered by boxes. He wasn't quite sure what this kid was up to, but Houdini knew he could always trust Morgan. Taking his advice, Houdini dashed to the corner of the garage where the red wagon lay buried under mindless clutter. Hopping up and down under the wagon, bouncing his head off the metal to make noise, Houdini summoned Joshua's attention.

The noise startled Joshua, but didn't scare him. Explorer scientists are never scared—they are intrigued. Following the noise, Joshua discovered the wagon as well as the source of the intrusion.

Houdini sat paralyzed, not sure what to do. Maybe if he stayed frozen the people would see right through him.

Joshua lunged down and swept Houdini off the ground. Squeezing him tightly between his hands, he spun Houdini in circles like a crazed tornado.

"What's luckier than a rabbit's foot?" Joshua shouted. "The whole rabbit!"

Joshua pulled Houdini in, gave him a big wet kiss on the forehead, then set him on the ground. He shoveled through the mess of boxes until the red rusty Radio Flyer wagon appeared.

Houdini lay on his side, holding onto the ground until the room stopped spinning.

Grabbing the black handle, Joshua dragged the wagon through all the clutter and delivered it next to the workbench. He loaded it up with nails and a hammer. Then he made his way to the pile of boards, stacking them as high as possible. Before heading back to the orchard, he remembered he had forgotten something.

Before Houdini could completely catch his bearings, he was abruptly whisked from the ground and soaring through the air again.

"I'm not going anywhere without my lucky rabbit and all four of his feet!" Joshua exclaimed, tucking Houdini under his arm like a football. Kissing him on the head again, he returned to the wagon and made his way to the orchard.

As always, back in the orchard Oakie and Dakota stood clowning with each other while Morgan shared the meaning of life with a toad. In the distance, a clacking, whacking, smacking sound began, building until Joshua appeared on the dusty trail dragging his red wagon in one hand and packing an agitated Houdini under his other arm.

"He took me prisoner and tasted my forehead—twice now!" Houdini shouted in a sarcastic tone to the three trees staring at them. "Before this day's over he'll have boiled me in a pot by the heat of your burning branches and feasted on my carcass!" Houdini smirked and winked at Morgan.

Morgan grinned.

Joshua parked the wagon below Oakie and pulled a stick from his pocket.

"I think it's time for a bit of magic," Joshua said, looking down at Houdini. Raising him high in the air with one hand, he waved the stick in his other hand.

"He's gonna make a shishkebab out of me!"

Dakota and Oakie shook their heads and laughed.

"Look me in the eyes, both of you!" Houdini demanded. "I hope this cute bunny face is forever etched into your mind. I hope it haunts you for the rest of your days after I go to my grave."

All the trees nearby lost their composure along with the boys as Joshua began to chant.

"Lucky rabbit to lucky man,
Alahkazoo alahkazaam!
Guardian of none
To guardian of all,
Grow like a weed
From short to tall.
Paws turn to feet,
Then take a stand.
Once you can walk,
Then you need a hand.
A defenseless bunny you were,
A defender you'll be!
Now transform in order to protect me!"

Joshua tapped Houdini on the head with his wand, spun around in a circle three times, then set him on the ground. Before Houdini could gather himself, Joshua grabbed a handful of dirt and threw it in the air. "You're much bigger than I expected," he marveled. "I dub thee Ox Warrior, for you are strong and powerful like an ox, yet stupid. Sorry I haven't perfected the magic quite yet."

Joshua looked around. He continued addressing Houdini. "This mystical forest is filled with evil mutated tarantulas and blood sucking bat-cows. YES, BAT-COWS!" Joshua exclaimed, pointing his finger in the air. "They're exactly what they sound like—part bat, part cow. A crazy farmer genetically engineered them. His land was filled with hidden treasure that was left by the ancient natives who once roamed his fields. In order to protect the secret treasures from land pirates, the crazed farmer created an army of bat-cows. Unfortunately, his experiment with nature turned terribly wrong. He was unable to control the bat-cows, and the crazed doctor was overtaken and destroyed by the very thing created to protect him."

Houdini had gained his composure while Joshua was ranting about bat-cows.

"Guys, what do I do? Should I bite him and sprint for the hills?"

"No, he's harmless. Let him finish. He'll be bothering Oakie soon enough." Morgan smirked at Oakie.

"Now the bat-cows roam thirstily through the mystical forest in search of blood to suck."

Houdini stared at Joshua, motionless.

"What about the evil mutated tarantulas, you ask? Well … they're just an unexplainable freak of nature that no one knows anything about, but they'll eat you if they see you!" Joshua waved his hands in the air. "Now go, mighty Ox Warrior, and cleanse this forest of all the dangers that might deter me from conquering my nemesis! Muha ha ha ha haha ha ha ha! Go, my little worker bee!"

Morgan looked down at Houdini.

"You might have been correct about him. You should run for you life," Morgan said playfully.

Joshua bent down and nudged Houdini. "Go ahead, buzz off." Joshua pushed Houdini harder.

Houdini looked up to Morgan. "This kid is all yours. Best of luck, guys." With that, Houdini disappeared.

Joshua returned to the wagon and tossed the wood out on the ground. After collecting all the nails and grabbing the hammer, he stood before Oakie, staring silently.

"I may be a wee bit regretful about how badly I heckled Houdini. This people is really starting to weird me out, Oakie confessed to Dakota. "Throw an apple at him or something, would ya, he's making me feel awkward."

Dakota shook his branch until a few apples broke loose and bumped Joshua on the noggin.

Joshua rubbed the top of his head, knelt down, grabbed an apple, then chucked it back at Dakota before returning to his stare.

"He's a little spitfire," Morgan noted.

"I will conquer you!" Joshua proclaimed. "I will conquer anything that gets in my way. I will not be defeated. Sooner or later I will finish this. They all laughed when I told them I could do it the first time. They laughed even harder when I didn't, but I won't quit. Not for them. I won't quit for me, and you won't stop me!" Joshua pointed his finger at Oakie and held it for dramatic effect.

"Did you do something offensive to this people before you were planted here?" Dakota asked.

Oakie shrugged his branches. "At least we're entertained."

"Now taste the wrath of my hammer and nails!" Joshua declared. Reaching into his coat pocket, Joshua grabbed the blueprints and examined them one last time before beginning. After selecting the first board, he stood in front of Oakie, awkwardly holding the step and nail in one hand and the hammer in his other. Cocking the hammer back in the air, Joshua brought it down on the nail lightning fast. Joshua successfully hammered the nail and his thumb. In celebration, and in pain, he danced a terrible reenactment of what looked like a native rain dance.

"Are you okay?" Dakota asked Oakie.

"I don't think I'm the one you should be asking that question." Oakie watched Joshua twirling about below him. "Too bad Houdini isn't here, I'm sure he would appreciate this."

"He would, and I do," Houdini shouted from some undisclosed location. "I wouldn't miss this for the world!"

The boys laughed.

Joshua settled down. His thumb was now big enough to plug a hole in a beaver dam, but he would live nonetheless. Back to the boards he went, taking extra care with each nail hammered. Soon the steps were as high as he could reach. Climbing the ladder one step at a time, he continued building. Before long Joshua's hair and shirt dripped with sweat from all the work it took climbing, hanging, and nailing. After an eternity of anticipation and failed attempts, he stood only one step away from reaching that prized first branch. With each swing to that final nail, Joshua's excitement grew to monumental proportions. He felt like his chest would explode if he didn't scream out soon.

At last he reached out, grabbed the branch and struggled about until he pulled himself up. Standing silently atop the branch, he contemplated everything it took to get there. Without the slightest thought, a scream rocketed from the deepest places of Joshua's belly.

"Aaaaaaaahhhhhhhhh!!!!!!" The scream was so loud it was as though he had broken the sound barrier.

Like confetti, the grandest flock of birds broke loose and scattered from the treetops all across the orchard. The birds blanketed the sky and blocked out the sun as they fled the scene.

Lost in the moment, Joshua leapt in the air. Unfortunately for him, the branch was a rather small landing pad. Missing it, he plummeted toward the ground.

Thinking quickly, Oakie whipped his branch around and caught the corner of Joshua's lab coat.

Squinting tightly, Joshua braced for the tough landing that never came. Dangling like a puppet from the coattail hanging at the end of Oakie's branch, Joshua swung back and forth, adrenaline pumping so heavily he felt lost in ecstasy.

"I'm invincible! I'm like Iron Man or The Hulk!" Joshua's belly jiggled about as he cackled aloud.

"Lucky for Iron Man he has someone looking out for him," Morgan offered to Oakie.

"Yeah, good catch, buddy, that was very ninja-like. Maybe even superhero of you," Dakota added.

"I'm no superhero, guys. Superheroes have special powers. I'm just a common tree being uncommonly AWESOME!"

The trees laughed heartily.

Joshua snapped the end of Oakie's branch by bouncing up and down, dropping the last foot to the ground.

"Ouch! That kind of smarted," Oakie whined.

"It's part of being a common tree that's uncommonly awesome. Suck it up," Morgan playfully shot at Oakie.

"Dad, I think Oakie and I might be rubbing off on you," Dakota observed.

Oakie nodded in agreement.

Morgan silently smirked at his sons.

Joshua's stomach rumbled as he picked himself up off the ground and dusted his coat. He needed to get going; it was definitely time for dinner and his work here was done for the day, but he would be back. He had plenty more to conquer before he was finished.

At that, Joshua grabbed his wagon and trucked off home.

CHAPTER

19

THE ASCENSION

—————— 19 ——————

Poor Joshua. The little guy just couldn't get a break. While Oakie was back in the orchard recovering from his broken branch, Joshua was at home doing hard time in his bedroom for his crimes against his sister, his great-great grandmother's antique table, and his dad's prized baseball card collection. But such is the cost of being an adventurer.

In adult time, a month was just a brief time-out. However, a month in kid time was a life sentence without parole. In my opinion it might have been a bit excessive, but I've never been very fond of antiques or baseball, or obnoxious kid sisters, for that matter. That's just my two cents.

Anyway, the orchard spent the majority of the first week waiting for Joshua's return. With the weeks that followed, life settled back into its routine and the time they had with Joshua became a fond memory, something to be laughed about and revisited for fun. Oakie remained decorated with Joshua's handiwork, an impression that would not be soon forgotten.

Just when life had returned to normal, an unexpected visitor trotted back down the beaten path. Roaring through the bushes, Houdini made tracks toward the fellas.

"Hey guys! Guess who's on his way here?" Houdini blurted with enthusiasm.

"Houdini, maybe you can answer a question for me. If not, maybe someone else around here has an explanation that would scratch my curiosity that has been itching," Oakie inquired, ignoring Houdini's question.

"I'll give you three guesses, and the first two don't count," Houdini replied.

"Inquiring minds want to know—mostly mine. Where

did you come from? Where do you go? Why do you random-ly always appear out of nowhere?" Oakie continued.

"He's back for more pain, and I'm ready to bring the thunder," Houdini said, pounding one paw into the other.

"Because you're a lot like one of the random characters Morgan uses to help his stories make more sense. They come out of nowhere, I have no idea how they relate to the story or what their purpose is, and then they just disappear without much being known about them."

"I actually didn't realize how much I missed that kid. I've been hanging around his house watching him stare grimly out the window at me. He kept opening it up and screaming random babble."

"That's not what they're for. They're there to help intro-duce a new perspective from someone else, and I suppose add some comic relief," Morgan replied while chuckling.

"Like I said, make more sense, and how exactly does that response help answer any of my questions?" Oakie asked Morgan.

"Well if it isn't my dimwitted mighty Ox Warrior," Joshua pointed accusingly at Houdini as he broke into the orchard wearing oversized hiking boots, a fishing vest, a safari hat, and a rope hanging around his chest. "My oppressors still stand unpunished for their unlawful imprisonment of your master, yet you do nothing. I begged and pleaded that you might do something. I devised a masterful plan that even the simplest of minds could have accomplished, yet you stared blankly as if to mock me and my misfortune." Josh-ua continued to point sternly at Houdini.

"This is what I'm talking about, guys. Every day while he was gone from here, he just opened the window and ranted relentlessly."

"I think it's kind of endearing," replied Oakie.

"You haven't been on the other end of his finger," inter-jected Houdini.

"And you!" Joshua shot his finger at Oakie.

"Yeah, less endearing than I thought, but still endear-ing," Oakie offered as sympathy to Houdini.

"I'm not finished with you, nemesis. I've only begun."

Whipping his finger back at Houdini, Joshua continued, "Now, I understand you are my handiwork, and for that I take responsibility. My spell needed some perfecting, which I had ample time to work on in my cell atop the tower." Joshua marched over to Houdini. Standing above him he pulled out a thick twig that had been tucked under his belt.

"Big muscles you had,
But no brain to be seen.
From dumb to smart,
You shall be somewhere in between.
When I'm finished here,
The pea you had will begin to grow.
What you did not understand,
You shall surely know!"

Joshua dipped down and grabbed a handful of dirt, hawked up the biggest loogie he could muster, then spit it into the dirt. After mixing it around, he bent over and smeared it all over Houdini's head.

The three trees exchanged glances of disgust.

"Eeeeeeew," Dakota moaned with sympathy.

"Is there a reason you let him do that?" Oakie asked Houdini.

Houdini sat frozen in disbelief. "He just signed his death warrant!" Houdini exclaimed.

"I give you a mind of your own, Mighty Ox Warrior. Now seek out my oppressors and avenge me!"

Houdini sat as the loogie-mixed mud dripped down his face and fell to the ground.

"This I command!"

Houdini boiled with anger.

"Houdini, promise me you won't be bringing back any beavers with you." Morgan knew Houdini was about to split and avenge someone, namely himself.

"I already learned that lesson," Houdini said solemnly.

Joshua knelt down and softly prodded Houdini to move him along. "Now scoot away, little guy." Joshua finally let Houdini be and turned his attention to Oakie.

Houdini vanished into the orchard.

"Our time for reckoning is here and now! I spent my days of solitude imagining this. The feeling of conquering you hounded my soul. Every day, I basked in the feeling of triumphantly standing atop your highest branch, nemesis. I've conquered you a thousand times in my mind, and the victory has only tasted sweeter with each thought. No matter how long I spent locked in that cell, I wouldn't let it break me. I'm here to finish what I started."

Joshua stormed toward Oakie and began his tenacious ascent. Like a mountaineer scaling the side of a treacherous cliff, he carefully reached for each step and grasped tightly, pulling himself up as though one wrong move could be his last.

A wind raged through the orchard, picking up the hat from Joshua's head. Pure explorer instinct caught the hat before it was lost to the wind. He shoved it tightly down; without it he was just another kid climbing a tree. But with it, he was a true explorer extraordinaire.

"He sure is persistent," Dakota mentioned.

"Like a hound dog headed down a badger hole," added Morgan.

"He sweats like a boar," Oakie noted as drops of sweat showered his bark.

Mounting the first branch, Joshua could taste the victory he previously had when he built the steps. Looming above him, just out of his fingers' reach, hung the next branch. Untying the rope around his chest, he took his mountaineer gear and hurled it over the obstacle. After tying his famous slipknot, something he was well known for in the Cub Scouts, he cinched the rope and started his Spiderman climb to the next branch.

Joshua struggled upward. Lying flat on his belly and hugging a branch tightly, he paused to catch his breath.

A familiar woodpecker landed on his safari hat and searched for a soft spot to chip away at.

"Get off me, bird! You don't know who you're messing with. I'm a well-respected explorer and author. I have a *New York Times* bestseller based on all my dangerous feats and explorations. I've searched and conquered seven of the eight wonders of the world. Furthermore, I was the one who discovered the eighth wonder. Now leave me alone so I can conquer it." Swatting away the bird, Joshua climbed to his feet and made for the next branch.

As you can imagine, there was nothing pretty about our little hero's struggle to conquer his nemesis. With little strength, he spent most of the afternoon flailing around while Oakie bore the brunt of the battle as Joshua snapped away at his lower branches.

While Joshua wrestled about, an oddly shaped bird, flying awkwardly, approached from the distance. As the blob neared, the three trees realized it wasn't a bird at all. A platoon of bats struggled toward Oakie, pulling what appeared to be a large anchor. It was Houdini, riding atop Caleb the skunk.

"Fear the stink of the Midnight Army!" Houdini shouted at Joshua.

Joshua continued to climb, unaware of Houdini and the trick up his sleeve.

"Feel our shock and awe as we rain down thunder and lightning!" Getting in position above Joshua's head, Houdini shouted the final order. "Release the Doomsday Device!"

Houdini rode Caleb like a wild stallion as the bats let go and they plummeted toward Joshua. The bomb was dropped and no one could escape its devastation. Nailing the target, Caleb wrapped himself tightly around Joshua's face and released his stench, smiling deviously from ear to ear. "Today you pay the piper!" Houdini howled, still clinging to Caleb's back.

Joshua whipped back and forth, trying to lose his attacker. The gang of bats swooped down and snagged Caleb from his victim. Sailing away with the Midnight Army, Houdini cackled devilishly. "Yours was the battle, mine was the war. Smell your defeat!"

"Banish them with the beavers! Please, please banish them with the beavers," Oakie pleaded with Morgan.

Staggering around, Joshua slipped off of the branch he stood on and plummeted like a baby bird from its nest. Luckily for Joshua, he had anchored himself securely with his rope to another branch. Swinging back and forth, he hung suspended in the air.

"It looks to me like you have a rotten apple, Oakie," Dakota taunted.

"It looks to me like you—" Oakie fumbled for some witty retort. "Shut up," he finally replied in defeat.

The same rascally woodpecker, watching from afar, swooped in to lend a helping hand to Joshua. After hacking away at the rope for a second or two, the woodpecker completed his mischievous task, leaving Joshua lying on the ground to recover from the fall.

Neither kids at school, nor his parents, his sister, a skunk, a porcupine, beavers, an obnoxious rabbit, nor the nemesis itself could keep Joshua from doing what he had set his mind to do. Failed attempts were just setbacks, and setbacks weren't failures. Quitting was the only failure, and Joshua refused to be a failure. He refused to believe there was something he couldn't have if he wanted it badly enough.

Being stubborn wasn't always a bad thing; in fact it was one of Joshua's greatest strengths. The kids said he was too fat to climb that tree. His mother said it was too dangerous. If it wasn't the tree, it would be sports. If it wasn't sports, it would be a school dance. If it wasn't a dance, it would be popularity. Everything and everyone told him what he couldn't do, who he wasn't and what he wouldn't be. And for a long time, he had agreed with their belittling voices.

On the day Joshua first introduced himself to the orchard, he had a momentous life experience on the bus ride home from school. As always, he was minding his own business and riding quietly in the front seat, reading his superhero comic book. He listened as a group of his classmates chattered about going to the apple orchard and having a tree-climbing contest. The boys and girls boasted about who could climb the highest tree.

For as long as Joshua could remember, he believed he was on the outside. He always believed no one would like him or listen to him. He feared hanging out with other kids. Instead, he hid within his imagination. There, he could be whoever he wanted to be. He did whatever he wanted to do.

In his imagination, he couldn't be hurt.

Unfortunately for Joshua, the other children felt his fear and his desire to be left alone. They didn't know it, but they were playing by *his* rules. They were following *his* lead. His mind was a powerful thing that dictated much more than he could conceive.

He believed they would hate him, so they did. He believed they would think he was stupid, and so they did. He believed they wouldn't want him around, so they didn't.

As Joshua read the pages of the story in his hands, he realized that this nerdy boy bitten by a radioactive spider stopped being a nerd to the world when he believed that he was invincible. It wasn't that he could just climb buildings. When he put on the special suit that hid his normal identity, he felt like a superhero and he acted like a superhero. An entire city loved him, but only because he chose to be bold. Had he told everyone that he would one day be a superhero, the world would have laughed, because he wouldn't have believed it himself. He had to just become one.

Something welled up from deep within Joshua as his classmates bragged about who was the best tree climber. The superhero on the pages stared him in the face and dared him to take a stand. Without a rational thought, Joshua jumped from his seat, faced the back of the bus and declared that he was the greatest tree climber who had ever lived, and he would climb any tree of their choosing to prove it.

The bus exploded in laughter. Many jeered at the declaration and poked fun at Joshua's weight.

Joshua rolled his comic book up and clenched it tightly against his chest. Like a shield of truth, he reminded himself that it wouldn't do any good to talk about being a superhero, he just had to become one.

The leader of the pack spoke up. "All right, Tubby Tubs McGee, we'd love to see you out climb us. As soon as we get off this bus, we're all headed to the orchard. Are you in?"

"Yes!" Joshua boldly declared.

"This should be a riot!" the leader shouted in laughter, and returned to bantering with the rest of the kids.

Joshua sat back down, confident that he would do what he said he could do.

You see, when Joshua fell from Oakie that day and all the children laughed, he realized that he felt stupid. But the thing was, they didn't make him feel stupid. That was his feeling, and he had chosen to feel it. As his mother drug him away, his stubbornness kicked in and he decided things would be different. He didn't need the other kids to see him climb that tree. He needed to *see* himself climb it. He needed to put on his own superhero costume. When he conquered this nemesis and saw what he was truly capable of accomplishing, everyone else would believe it as well.

Remembering why he had returned to his nemesis gave Joshua the fight to move forward. As the woodpecker took flight, he stood up, dusted himself off, and started again.

Oakie watched Joshua with admiration for his tenacity and heart.

You know what? That day Joshua didn't climb to the top of Oakie, no matter how much fight he put up. In fact, day after day over the next month, Joshua returned and spent the afternoons climbing away at his nemesis and still couldn't come close to mounting the highest branch.

Even though that little people hadn't immediately fulfilled his dream the way he thought he would, his presence brought a delightful joy to the orchard. His wild imagination was as contagious as the flu. Out of Joshua came a spring of life that flowed through the orchard and filled the hearts of all who played there, including Houdini and Dakota, who embraced the charming boy's beautiful madness. Oh, and might I add that Oakie became especially fond of Joshua and his games.

As the time passed, and Joshua persistently toiled toward his goal, a transformation began. The afternoons spent rigorously climbing up and down Oakie's towering body changed more than just Joshua's belief about himself. His clothes seemingly became larger and larger until his pants hung loose by a tightened rope used as a belt. His shirt now had room for not just one extra person, but maybe even two. Muscles bulged from his forearms and biceps. Now a slimmer and much stronger Joshua stood holding his head high in confidence. A new chiseled face now graced the orchard. Joshua pushed harder and longer every day until one afternoon, he mounted Oakie's highest branch.

There, atop Oakie, Joshua stood quietly admiring the view. A simple triumphant smile adorned his face. Not a word, nor a howl, left his mouth. Joshua's silent celebration of this holy moment went unnoticed by the orchard below.

Since Joshua had lost so much weight, Oakie found it increasingly difficult to feel him climbing. Naturally, it took some time before Oakie realized Joshua had climbed to the top. Though he was surprised and excited, Oakie honored the sacredness of the moment and remained silent.

Joshua stood tall, basking in the victory and power he felt.

As Joshua absorbed the sight from highest branch, Oakie remembered the victorious feeling he had felt so long ago after surviving the great flood that almost destroyed the orchard. Joshua may have started out as a little boy, but in Oakie's eyes, he was ending as a little man.

CHAPTER

20

DREAMS
OF GRANDEUR

20

Toward the end of his journey to conquer Oakie, Joshua realized he had become excited and happy about his life. Friends became abundant at school, and no one even knew about the great thing Joshua had done—they just liked him now. His imagination budded and opened like never before. Creativity captured his mind. Defeating his nemesis was the beginning of so much more.

During math class, Joshua had an ingenious idea. He began sketching plans for a secret base he would build in Oakie's branches. A mighty fortress reigning high above the orchard would be the perfect place to stage the greatest adventures the world had ever known. He would need an intricate defense system to guard against any invading hordes, super-villains, pirates, dark creatures of the night, or communists.

The first line of defense would be poop-mines. A collection of dog poop could be gathered from all the neighbors' yards and hidden under piles of leaves along the trail leading to the fortress. The foul stench would burn the nose of all those passing through and drive them in a different direction, keeping Joshua's lair secret.

Joshua had a scary, evil old grandpa. Everyone feared him. If the poop-mines didn't work, scarecrows dressed in grandpa's old clothes hanging from the trees would send them away, shaking in their boots. Beyond the scarecrows, he would need traps. Within a fifty-foot radius around Oakie, Joshua could tie his father's fishing line between the trees to act as trip wires to slow down any advancing enemies. Past the trip wires, he would dig holes all around Oakie's base and cover them with sticks and leaves. He could acquire thousands of tacks from his father's office to scatter on the ground below the fort. He would have four catapults designed to launch giant water balloons filled with toilet water stationed on each of the four corners of the secret sanctuary. With those in place, Joshua would have 360 degrees of protection. If the advancing armies made it, they would have to face buckets filled with rotten eggs hanging under the base. With holes cut in the floor he could reach his hand through and tip the buckets over and onto the invaders.

But what if they made it past all the defenses and stormed the ladder? Joshua turned the problem over in his head until he finally had an idea. The better question to ask was, *What if there wasn't a ladder for them to storm?* After completing the mighty fortress, he could build a rope ladder that he could pull up into the base after himself. He could remove the original ladder leading up Oakie altogether, and then he could control who came and went. If someone was capable of climbing up Oakie's side, he could hang a rope off the end of a far-reaching branch, swing down quickly and escape through the woods on a hover-bike hidden in the brush.

Besides defenses, Joshua needed much more to make this the ultimate base station. He needed a laboratory to start his work on cloning zombies. After a month of hard time and solitary confinement, Joshua knew his dad's precious stockpile of tools were off limits. He had to have the proper equipment for the laboratory, or it would just be another fancy zombieless room. An old man named Arnie, who lived across the street, seemed to be an inventor of sorts. He was always in his shop, shooting sparks at metal with a rod, most likely building some sort of Frankenstein monster. He could raid the workshop and borrow what he needed. The crazy old man probably wouldn't even notice.

Beyond a laboratory, he would need a vault for the vast treasure of diamonds, rubies, and Bakugon that he discovered, a room to house his secret-identity attire—like his capes, magician robes, camouflage pants, robot armor, so on and so forth. Then he would need a training room to keep in shape and practice his kung fu. Above and beyond all the sophisticated rooms, a toilet seemed to be the staple that would hold the paper together.

After school, Joshua made his rounds through the neighborhood, pulling his red Radio Flyer wagon. He made his first stop at old man Arnie's workshop. There he raided the drawers and cabinets, taking anything that seemed helpful in creating scientific experiments. After borrowing the tools he needed from old man Arnie, Joshua combed through the neighbors' lawns and gathered as much dog poop as his garbage bags could hold.

As he walked through the neighborhood, thinking about his plan, another idea came to him. The wood needed to build the fort wasn't coming from his mother's antique furniture this time around. His butt still felt the sting of his mother's swing from that mishap. Besides, the wood needed to build something of this magnitude would take something much larger than a piece of cherished antique furniture. Joshua needed a storehouse of wood, and he knew the perfect place to get it!

At the end of the block, surrounded by a fallen white picket fence, stood a towering, decrepit, abandoned manor buried beneath years of overgrown trees and grass. The shimmering white paint that once adorned the house now lay speckled on the ground from years of rain and wind chipping away at it. Behind the shattered stained-glass windows, broken long ago by neighborhood vandals, stood sheets of plywood covered in graffiti. Anchored by a solitary screw, a squeaky screen door shivered in the wind, waiting for the day when it would fall to its grave on the front porch. The vacant house stood occupied by nothing more than dark tales of a witch that once lived there. During Halloween and full moons, many dared to explore the home, but only one brave soul had ever stepped foot inside ... never to return. That's what the kids in eighth grade said, anyway. Joshua knew that dark sorcery might protect the home, but that wouldn't be enough to stop him from building his mighty base.

All the children in the neighborhood were warned by their parents to stay away from that house. They said it wasn't safe. Surely the stories of the witch had to be true. It wasn't going to be easy scavenging wood from the home without someone seeing him and trying to interfere.

Timing would be everything.

Cloaked in the shadow of night, he could safely forage through the house with minimal worry of being apprehended. Dressing up as the world's most notorious cat burglar, Jacque La Kaht, would ensure his success. Joshua's eyes bubbled with delight as he relished his ingenious scheme.

The remainder of the day was spent collecting his grandfather's old clothes, rounding up a shovel to dig holes, and getting his hands on some nails and tacks. He returned to the orchard and unloaded his wagon so he would have plenty of room to carry all the wood he was going to collect that night.

Later that evening, after the family dinner, Joshua brushed his teeth without being told and tucked himself into bed. The sooner everyone thought he was asleep, the sooner he could sneak out and comb through the eerie house at the end of the block and gather everything he needed to finish his masterpiece.

After Joshua's parents turned off the last light, he slipped out of bed and into a black turtleneck shirt and the black slacks he wore to church every Sunday. From his dresser drawer, he retrieved a black stick-on mustache and placed it firmly against his upper lip. After two tugs, Joshua felt confident his mustache wasn't going anywhere.

He rummaged through the dark for his black running shoes, but came up empty-handed. If he turned on his bedroom light, his parents might see it shining in the hallway from under his door. He simply couldn't risk it. Diving under his bed, he felt around until he grasped hold of the Converse high-tops that he had spray-painted bright red and yellow. Not the ideal shoes for a secret night mission, but they were shoes nonetheless.

While opening his window, Joshua listened carefully for any footsteps in the hallway. Before leaving, he snagged the flashlight lying on his nightstand. Leaping from the first story of the house, he dove like a ninja into a barrel roll, jumped up, and ran for the backyard.

Hidden behind the shed was his wagon with a claw hammer in it. Grabbing the wagon, Joshua moved quietly into the alley. Cautiously slinking along down the alleyway, he eagerly headed to the manor.

As he pulled up in front of the home, an annoying lump formed in his throat. Without hesitation Jacque La Kaht bravely swallowed away the nuisance.

Hidden behind clouds, the full moon gave the adventurer no help. Flipping on his flashlight, he scanned the scene. The cement sidewalk, cracked and jutting upward from the ground, was more of an obstacle course than a pathway to the porch. Carefully maneuvering over the dangerous terrain, he made his way to the first step where he parked his wagon, grabbed his hammer, and took the first of what might be his very last steps as a burglar extraordinaire.

Like a tactical SWAT team member, Joshua moved past the dangling door and slowly peered around the corner. Scanning the room with his light, he made note of the spiders clinging tightly to giant webs. Dark sorcery was one thing; man-eating spiders were a whole other danger he was all too happy to avoid.

As Joshua continued to wave his light around the entrance, the beam glided up and down over the debris cluttering the hallway. Baseball bats and fists had left holes in the walls and piles of plaster on the floor. To the right of the entrance stood a giant staircase leading to the second and third floors. Past the staircase was a large room where the rusty skeleton of a couch sat with its springs wobbling in the air. Filled with families of mice, nests carefully fashioned from the cotton of the couch were scattered about the ground.

Feeling confident there was no immediate danger, Joshua pushed on down the hallway before him. With each step, the crackle of broken lightbulbs and plaster echoed from under his feet. Moving from room to room, he scouted for wood. Luckily for him, the years seemed to have brought many intruders who had already knocked loose walls and doors ripe for the picking. Rummaging through the mess, he gathered anything he could find that would easily fit in his wagon. After stacking a teetering tower of wood atop his red Radio Flyer, Joshua made a trip to the orchard with his first load, then returned for more.

As he entered the front door a second time, the enormous staircase leading up to the second and third floors caught his attention. Many of the supplies he had gathered didn't fit well together. The steps, however, were the same length and width. If he could pluck them from the staircase, they would work perfectly for the flooring of his fort.

Joshua walked over and stood at the foot of the steps. Many of the nails in the boards had come loose. Little work would be needed to pry them up. Leaning down, he hooked the claw of his hammer and yanked away the first step. It was easy enough, but before he got carried away he decided it was in his best interest to begin at the top and work his way down.

Quickly and carefully, he climbed to the top. As he ascended to the third floor the steps shrieked out in what sounded like a symphony of pain. Both the second and third floors held unexplored rooms and, for safety's sake, it was best they stayed that way. After clearing the steps leading to the third floor, Joshua made his way back down. Like an overloaded pack mule, he carried the pile of boards in his arms stacked high above his head.

With all the extra weight in his arms, every step he landed on barked louder and louder. Finally, without warning, a weak link in the stairs gave way and Joshua's foot sank through it. His flashlight and the boards launched from his hands, sailing like shards of glass down the steps, and then scattered about the floor at the entrance of the house. Luckily he caught himself on the banister before toppling down as well.

A little shaken, Joshua stood for a moment, gathering his bearings.

His heart began to race.

A clamoring sound on the first floor was still continuing, well after the boards had come to a stop. He gripped the banister tightly. Standing paralyzed, he lowered his breathing and listened carefully. As quickly as it had begun, the noise was gone.

He wasn't alone.

After pulling himself out of the hole in the step, Joshua crept downstairs, weaving through the shrapnel along the way. As quickly as he could, he whisked his flashlight from the ground and scooped up a broken piece of wood to beat off any attackers.

Like a laser beam, he whipped the flashlight back and forth, shooting it around as he made his way to the back of the house on the first floor. Another booming crash rang out toward the end of the hall in a room he had yet to explore. Could it be the ghost of the witch that lived here so long ago? Had she come to punish him for invading her home?

Fiercely, he raised the stick above his head in preparation for battle. With his back to the wall, Joshua shimmied along as he neared the door of the room with all the commotion. Something within him screamed to run away, but running away wasn't an option for a brave adventurer. Whatever was on the other side of this door was in for the fight of its life!

Breathing heavily, Joshua counted to three under his breath as he unconsciously bit his lower lip.

One ...

Two ...

Three ...!

Without hesitation he leaped around the door and shouted a warrior's cry.

To his surprise, nothing stood waiting for him except a kitchen filled with broken cabinet doors, a toppled-over oven, a broken table, and a sink filled with moldy food.

A sense of relief overcame him as he realized something must have shaken loose and fallen off the counter or out of one the cabinets. Giggling to himself and feeling silly, he made his way over to a storage cabinet that was hanging open to search it for any remains.

Dropping his stick, he grabbed the door and pulled it open. Like a rocketing missile, a beast exploded from the cabinet and latched onto his face! Though he hadn't seen the creature with his eyes, he knew it had to be an alien like the one he saw in his dad's old films. If he didn't ditch this thing immediately it was going to plant baby aliens in his stomach. When it was ready to be born it would rip out of him like a jack-in-the-box.

Frantically running in circles, Joshua whipped back and forth trying to shake off the monster. While blindly flailing around, he smashed into the oven, toppled into the wall, and stumbled down the hallway. Making a last-ditch effort to save himself, he swung the giant mag light at his attacker. Like a fly being swatted, the alien leaped from Joshua's face to safety. Unable to dodge the flashlight, like the monster, he accidentally clocked himself in the forehead. Dazed and confused, he stumbled down the hallway through a barrage of spider webs. Caught in their webs and covered in spiders, he frantically swatted at his body, trying to lose the creepy crawlers. Unaware of his steps in all of the chaos, Joshua's foot landed on a loose board in the floor. Like a well-devised booby trap, the other end of the plank shot from the ground and smashed him in the back.

Unaware of what had hit him, Joshua spun in circles, judo-chopping and karate-kicking the air. "If it's a fight you want, it's a fight you'll get!" Not backing down from the brawl, he battled on. Like a boxer being backed into a corner, he retreated to the bottom of the staircase where the boards he had dropped lay scattered about. Tripping over them, he tumbled end over end, landing amidst the city of mice that had built their homes from the tattered couch.

The army of slumbering mice woke from their rest. In a desperate panic, the horde stampeded around the room, trampling over Joshua as they sought safety.

Frightened, Joshua leapt back to his feet and dove to the front door where he wrestled around like a turtle on its back.

Defeated, he lay holding his head and wincing in pain.

"Go ahead just do it! Plant your alien babies in me and quit toying with me. I'm not going to be some mouse a cat plays with before eating it for dinner. Just know that your babies took the life of an entrepreneurial imagineer! I'm a boy genius, not just some idiot!"

Joshua waited courageously, but nothing happened. The gavel of death didn't strike. After bracing for a moment longer, he decided it was time to look death in the face.

Without any further hesitation he pulled his hands back from his eyes, only to be met with a peace treaty.

Not quite sure what to make of Joshua, the plump raccoon extended its paw. It was holding a half-eaten sandwich, offering up his midnight snack.

"A truce, huh?" Panting, Joshua breathed a sigh of relief. "Well, I guess I can't just reject a truce." Covered in cobwebs and dust, he took the sandwich from his attacker and tore a bite from it before returning it. "Peanut butter and jelly!" he exclaimed through a mouthful of food. "I love peanut butter and jelly!"

The raccoon smiled and continued munching away at the delicacy.

Joshua struggled to his feet and stood before the raccoon. With confrontation in his eyes, Joshua began. "What's the matter with you? I'm just hanging out collecting supplies, minding my own business, not hurting anyone, and you jump out of nowhere and ambush me? What do you have to say for yourself?"

Staring back blankly, the raccoon shrugged his shoulders and continued to nibble on his sandwich.

"Yeah, I suppose you're right. Sorry for interrupting your dinner. Just so you know, you should be more careful in the future. These hands are so lethal I've been banned from fighting in the UFC. They say I'm a liability."

The raccoon sprang up from the ground and perched on a step to get a better look at Joshua.

Startled by the sudden movement, Joshua stumbled backwards, tripping over some clutter, and then caught himself on the edge of the doorframe.

Not skipping a beat, he bent down with a bruised ego and started gathering the wood from the stairs. The raccoon finished his snack, licked his fingers clean, then jumped down and scurried over to the mess to lend a helping hand. Dragging the lightest board he could find, the raccoon presented Joshua with a gift.

Joshua stopped what he was doing and grabbed the board from his new friend's hands. "You'd make a great sidekick. Have you ever thought about being a professional sidekick?"

The raccoon squeaked back at him.

"Well, believe me, you would. You already have a great disguise," Joshua said, referring to the black mask around the raccoon's eyes. "I could be your Batman and you could be my Robin. How does 'Midnight Bandit' sound to you?"

The raccoon tilted his head down to eat a piece of leftover sandwich that was caught in his fur.

"You're right, that sounds too much like an arch-enemy's name." Joshua squinted, trying to squeeze everything he could out of his brain.

"Ah ha!" He pointed his finger in the air. "You can be Smokey. Like a cloud of dark smoke, you enter the room and bring evildoers to their knees, begging for mercy!" He chuckled in pleasure at his idea.

"I dub thee Smokey!" Joshua pulled a half-eaten power bar from his pocket, broke a chunk off, and rewarded his new friend and sidekick. "As for me, you can call me Metamorphosis because of my power to become anyone or anything at any moment. My powers are limitless, and together we are unconquerable!" Joshua declared while grabbing the last of the wood he could carry. "Follow me and we will change the world." He marched out the door and back to his wagon.

Smokey sat for a moment.

"Quite a fine young chap. I wonder if he might be willing to part with any further food in exchange for the loyal service and protection of a royal knight?" Smokey said aloud in his classy English accent.

When Joshua realized his sidekick wasn't next to him, he turned around to see where he had gone. Smokey sat upright in the doorway, staring hungrily at Joshua. Joshua reached into his pocket and pulled the power bar from it. He knew how this worked; food used to be the way to his heart, too. Breaking off a piece, Joshua chucked the power bar to Smokey, then turned back and loaded the last of his wood in the wagon.

"Sir, you are a scholar and a gentleman," Smokey exclaimed before gobbling up the chunk of food.

"Smokey!" Joshua hollered as he grabbed the handle of

his Radio Flyer and headed off toward the orchard.

"The honorable services of a brave knight are clearly need-ed," Smokey declared. Leaping up, he chased after Joshua.

INSPIRED ACCEPTANCE

21

Returning to the orchard, Joshua sorted his supplies under the light of the full moon with the help of his new sidekick and honorable knight. Smokey dragged boards one by one to different piles based on size and shape. Oakie and the other trees watched as the newcomers worked up a sweat.

"What do you think they're up to with all the dead trees?" Oakie asked, watching Joshua prepare the supplies below him.

"I'd say they're planning on making you into Frankentree!" Dakota proclaimed.

Oakie became a little antsy.

"Dakota, now stop it, please," Morgan asked kindly. "Oakie, he's not going to make you into Frankentree."

Oakie calmed down a bit.

"He's going to make you into Zombietree! Rarrrr!" Morgan rolled his eyes into the back of his head and swayed his branches around like a beast reborn from the dead.

Dakota exploded in laughter.

"I guess the apple didn't fall far from his father tree." Oakie looked at Dakota and then motioned toward Morgan.

"I'm sorry, Oakie," Morgan said through tears of laughter. "But there's no need to worry—I've seen this before. He's building a fort."

"You're about to become a nest for a people!" Dakota shouted and laughed.

"What do you mean? How do you know?"

Morgan motioned to Dakota, who turned over one of his branches. Nailed to the backside of it hung a wooden board. "It's not the most comfortable and it's a lot of weight to carry," Dakota told Oakie. "But you're a huge tree and you shouldn't have any problems. Besides, he seems just crazy enough that it should be fun."

"Consider it an honor. It means you're a safe place for him to hide and play. He'll discover all of his greatest adventures in you," Morgan said tenderly.

"So what happened to your fort?" Oakie asked curiously.

Morgan chimed in for Dakota, "Oakie, I believe that as peoples grow taller and larger they slowly begin to stop using their imaginations. In time, their imaginations begin to shrink smaller and smaller. Imagination is the source of all creativity, happiness, fun, and life. Somewhere along the way, most of them stop using their imaginations altogether. A few stay childlike and imaginative—they're not hard to spot. But for the most part they grow old, fearful, and dull. Their days are short and filled with little expectation. Very little changes, but when it does, it usually upsets them. Worry sets in and they hide in their dwellings and stop adventurously exploring the world. I've only seen one full-grown people build a fort and play. That was here on Dakota."

Dakota smiled almost sadly as he listened to his father tell the story.

"Every afternoon he returned with a beautiful innocent little people that looked much like him. They had adventures until the dark of night. Sometimes they even camped out. He was too large for the fort, so he played outside of it as the little girl played with her stuffed animals. She was a princess in distress and he was a noble and powerful king. She stood high in her 'castle,' as peoples call it, and cried out to be saved from an evil dragon. Each time the large people stormed the 'castle' and slayed the dragon, saving the beautiful little princess. They returned for many seasons until one day the little people returned all alone with big tears in her eyes."

"What happened?" Oakie asked with great concern.

"I don't know, Oakie." Morgan shook his trunk sadly. "The little people spent many days curled up in a ball weeping quietly in the fort."

Dakota sat solemnly as tears trickled down his bark.

"The pain was felt by all in the orchard just as strongly as the joy that she had once expressed. It was one of the worst feelings any of us had ever known. Her innocence had captured all of our hearts. Then one day, she returned with some tools much like the people below you."

Oakie looked down to watch Joshua arrange the supplies.

"Through great anger and tears, she chipped away until every piece of that castle lay splintered on the ground. All that remains of her and the large people is that board stuck to Dakota's branch and the memories of them that fill our hearts."

Oakie thought for a moment before responding.

"That sounds terrible and painful. You would have been so much better off without them."

"No, we wouldn't be," Dakota replied. "I know I wouldn't be, anyway. They were amazing. Some of the better, if not the best, memories that I have here in this orchard are the ones with that little girl giggling and climbing around in my branches. I can still see the giant smile across that big people's face as he tossed her high in the air and caught her. Sure, I'm sad sometimes. Sure, it was painful losing them. But, having them here helped me become a big part of who I am today."

"He was boring, serious, grouchy, sarcastic, and a big pain in the knot before they came around," Morgan interjected. "Now he's just sarcastic and an occasional pain in the knot." He winked at Oakie.

"He's right, I was and I am." Dakota grinned. "But at least now I'm not serious, boring, or grouchy."

"Well not as much as your were," Morgan playfully poked.

Dakota ignored him. "Something about their carefree love and playfulness changed me forever."

Joshua climbed the steps at Oakie's base wearing an oversized yellow hard hat and carrying wood, hammer, and nails. After mounting the first branch, he stood on his tiptoes to nail the first piece of wood to the next branch.

Oakie looked at Morgan and Dakota. Everything they had said moved his heart. Looking down again, he bent his branch lower so Joshua could easily get to it.

With big powerful swings Joshua pounded the nail deep into Oakie's branch.

"So is it going to be a fort or a castle?" Oakie asked.

"It'll be whatever he decides," Morgan replied.

"I think you'll be a beautiful princess, though," Dakota jabbed.

"At least I'm not the ugly stepsister! Shazaam! Oh dang, that must sting!" Oakie shouted in triumph.

As they bantered, Houdini stood on his hind legs, fuming with anger and staring Smokey down.

While Joshua hammered away in Oakie's branches, Houdini introduced himself to the new sidekick.

"You're a thief!" Houdini shouted.

"Sir, with all due respect, if I am in fact a thief, what is it that I have stolen?" Smokey asked calmly between bites of the sub sandwich Joshua had made for him.

"I know your type!" Houdini barked. "You skulk through the shadows of the night and steal the hearts of the innocent. You feed off their kindness. You're infectious. You're a disease-carrying bag of bones!"

"Houdini, easy does it, you just met the guy," Oakie insisted.

Houdini spun around and hissed at Oakie while striking the air with his paws like a praying mantis.

Oakie backed off and decided to mind his own business for the moment.

Houdini spun back around, readying for Smokey's retort. The raccoon finished his sandwich, wiped the crumbs from his fur, then let loose an earthquake of a belch, shaking the leaves from the nearby trees and whipping Houdini's ears behind his head. Then he grabbed a leaf, stood up on his hind legs, and marched regally toward his accuser.

Houdini braced himself and pulled back a bit, unsure of Smokey's intent.

Without hesitation, Smokey slapped Houdini across the face with the leaf.

"Sir, accusations are one thing. Outright rudeness and name-calling are another. Either you apologize for your crude taunts and explain without offensive rhetoric what you are truly feeling, or you can consider this the challenge to a duel." Smokey wiped a few more crumbs from his face with the leaf. Then he stood tall with his arms at his sides, waiting for Houdini's response.

"How dare you—" Houdini began before taking another leaf to the face from Smokey.

"You walk a very thin fine line at the moment, Mr. Houdini. Choose your words wisely."

"You're only here because this people feeds you. You're stealing from him. When he doesn't have any more, you'll just leave and make him sad. He deserves better."

Smokey's eyebrow rose as he scratched his chin. "Sir, if my observations are correct, as they usually are, I would deduce that you have in fact been following this young chap for quite some time. I caught your scent near my resting quarters, again near his dwelling, and lastly along the trail to the orchard. Since my intentions have been nothing but honorable and forthright, I would say your aggression has formed because of something far beyond my simple presence. Is this an accurate assessment?"

"You're crazier than he is. I don't have a clue what you're talking about."

"Oh, but I have a rather good clue as to what you, sir, are talking about. I would say you are fond of this people. Judging by your lashing out about the food, I believe that he's fed you before. The food was a common bond that made you feel like regular old chums."

"This isn't about food!"

"Precisely. I perceive that this is about camaraderie. You followed us as we made our rounds and traveled here to the orchard. Our playfulness and good times on the journey drove you to jealousy. Now you stand before me making false accusations and using harsh, degrading language to belittle me, hurt my feelings, and drive me away in shame. Unfortunately for you, Mr. Houdini, your badgering will not break me. Quite the contrary. I am a noble knight and I do not fear a battle."

Houdini raised his paws like a well-trained boxer.

Smokey chuckled heartily. "It seems I've already won

the first round." He bowed his head and scurried off to help Joshua with the fort.

"What do you mean you already won? Hey, get back here! I said get back here!" Houdini shouted at the top of his lungs. All the trees in the vicinity looked down at Houdini and shook their heads as he threw a tantrum.

"You're a snake, a slithering snake!" Houdini shot anger like laser beams from his eyes at Oakie, Dakota, and Morgan, just to let them know he didn't need their input. Then he vanished.

High above, climbing through Oakie, Joshua searched for good strong branches to hang ropes from. While watching Captain Jack Sparrow, one of his favorite adventurers in one of his favorite movies, swing about a pirate ship and battle his enemies, Joshua had had a brilliant idea. He could use ropes to swiftly fly about his fortress, and in the event of an invasion, intruders would find it impossible to capture him.

With four fingers, Joshua whistled to Smokey and signaled for one of the ropes below. Smokey wrapped a rope around his waist and ran up Oakie's side. Joshua untied the rope from Smokey's waist and tied it around the branch, tugging hard on it to make sure it wouldn't come loose.

"You're going to become the greatest base station ever built," Joshua said, patting Oakie.

Oakie smiled warmly.

Without hesitation, Joshua leaped like a frog from the branch and swung to the other side of Oakie, screaming like a wild Indian.

As Joshua sailed through the air, Oakie couldn't help but to be filled with an enthusiastic sense of life and a desire to dream for bigger things than apples.

And why not? Joshua was a funny, imaginative, playful boy. I don't think there's anything more contagious than a little boy or girl who dreams and creates without the weight of concern.

Joshua landed on another large branch. Then he sent Smokey back for the three remaining ropes that sat in a pile below. Smokey made two more trips.

On Smokey's final trip for the last rope, Houdini reappeared for Round Two. He tied the end of the rope to his waist again, and made his way back up Oakie.

Houdini shot over, grabbed the other end of the rope, tied it around his waist, and then readied himself to run the opposite direction, away from Smokey.

"I've got this—you look tired," Houdini shouted as he took off sprinting. As the two ran separate directions, the pile of rope quickly slithered away until all the slack disappeared. Unfortunately for Houdini, he wasn't a match for Smokey, who weighed at least three times more and was easily five times stronger. The jolt whipped Houdini off his feet. He sailed backwards like a yo-yo up the tree behind Smokey. Bouncing up and down, he hung defeated in his own plan.

"Mighty Ox Warrior!" Joshua shouted. "Where have you been?" Joshua untied the rope from Smokey's waist. Then he pulled Houdini up to his face and kissed him on the forehead.

Houdini struggled in his grasp and acted annoyed at the whole ordeal. But his eyes said he felt differently.

"I haven't come across any venomous ogres or slime-slinging snails in the orchard, or any other monstrous ghouls, for that matter. It looks like you've done your job rather well." Joshua patted Houdini on the head and handed him a bite of his power bar.

Houdini hesitantly took the bar from Joshua, thinking about what Smokey had said. He felt rather sorry.

Smokey grinned and nodded with a wink at Houdini, as if to say all things were forgiven.

Houdini smirked back reluctantly. "Smokey and I can't do this without you. Now you stick around and help this team out." Joshua kissed Houdini on the head and continued to build.

Smokey lovingly padded Houdini on the shoulder as he passed on his way down to gather more rope.

Houdini followed Smokey. Banding together, the three worked through the night until it was time for Joshua to return home.

As the morning sun rose, the deformed shadow of a

failed science experiment became visible on Oakie.

"Whoa!" Dakota shouted as he woke up, startled by Oakie's appearance. "You looked much better under the moonlight."

Morgan slugged Dakota in the side with one of his branches. Morgan could see Oakie was feeling a bit insecure.

Dakota did his best to clean up his mess. "What! I'm just saying the moonlight brought out the beauty in Oakie's eyes, that's all."

"Save it," Oakie said glumly. "I know the kid smeared me with ugly."

"Hey, ya know, don't worry about being ugly. That's not even a big deal. If it helps, I didn't think you were that good-looking in the first place," Dakota said in an attempt to comfort Oakie.

Morgan shook his head.

Dakota noticed the hole he was digging for himself.

"What I mean is, looks aren't important. The real issue is all the dead trees' body parts hanging on you. Now, that's going to take some getting used to."

Oakie looked frantic as reality of his situation sank in. Morgan sighed.

"What! It's not like I haven't had to deal with it, too. It comes with the territory," Dakota defended himself to Morgan.

Before Morgan could jump all over Dakota again, Oakie chimed in, "You know what, I don't care what I look like. The people that is building this taught me that. Furthermore, I'm different than everyone else—unique, and that makes me happy."

"Whatever helps you get through it," Dakota shrugged. Morgan lovingly scolded Dakota with his eyes. Dakota decided to just shut his mouth altogether.

"Well they do have quite a bit of work still to get done on you, but in my opinion it was a great start," Morgan said.

"Thank you." Oakie stood tall and regal, embracing his new look.

CHAPTER

22

AN UNLIKELY BOND

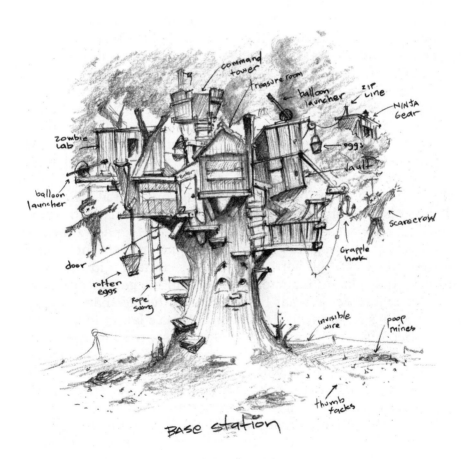

command tower

treasure room

balloon launcher

ZIP LINE

NINJA Gear

zombie lab

eggs

vault

balloon launcher

scarecrow

Grapple hook

door

rotten eggs

Rope swing

invisible wire

poop mines

thumb tacks

Base station

22

Day in and day out, the band of brothers returned and tenaciously hammered away at the Great Metamorphosis' secret lair. Oakie began packing on the pounds, looking like a well-fed father bursting at the seams after a Thanksgiving meal. Everyone from trees to animals stood eagerly awaiting the end of each day to see what Joshua would create, and for good reason. That boy was nothing short of a brilliant imagineer.

Everything was looking just as Joshua had planned it, but better. Even Dakota stood impressed. No one could have envisioned what Joshua would build. Only he could truly see the dream he had within him. The beginning of it had looked pretty rough. In fact, it was downright ugly—as Dakota so eloquently put it.

The secret lair expanded throughout Oakie. High up into his branches, Joshua had built platforms and other rooms only accessible by climbing a rope. He made zip lines spanning between the platforms for quick travel. The rooms were filled with all sorts of treasures. In fact, old man Arnie caught Joshua snooping around in his garage one day. After telling Arnie what he was doing, the old man happily donated a wagon full of tools for Joshua's laboratory.

Because of old man Arnie's kindness, the laboratory in the secret lair now had a workbench covered in tools. There was also a room filled with ninja gear, superhero cowls, pirate attire, scientist scrubs and so much more. The armory room was stacked high with rotten eggs, toilet water balloons, rotting fish carcasses, and extra poop for the mines. Joshua had built catapults with recycled rubber bicycle tubes and large sticks and securely placed them at each of the four corners. He upgraded the trap pits below by adding wet, sloppy, rotting food he had collected day after day from the trash bin behind the school cafeteria. Everything he had dreamed of in school, as he scribbled down the ideas for this secret base station, was now in front of him.

Feeling satisfied with what he had built, Joshua began the final stages of the defense system. While he fashioned the spooky-looking grandpa scarecrows, Houdini and Smokey set off to do the dirty work of setting the poop-mines.

Together, Smokey and Houdini dragged the large black garbage bag filled with the deadly mines.

"I have some fresh mines of my own I'm going to plant when we get to where we are going," Houdini declared proudly.

"I'd rather be left out of the loop on the status of your bowel movements, if you don't mind," Smokey said snobbily.

"What, it's not like you don't poop. Don't act smug."

"I'm not acting smug, I just find it rather inappropriate to discuss such things. It seems almost rude."

"So do you poop, or don't you poop? Simple question."

"Yes, of course I have bowel movements, but it doesn't mean I want to broadcast the activity to my peers. It's a rather foul thing."

Houdini continued dragging the bag alongside Smokey. Without missing a beat, he farted a booming thunder that echoed through the orchard.

"Oooooh my!" Smokey shouted. "That's disgusting! What is wrong with you?"

Houdini chuckled to himself.

"That is absolutely wretched-smelling! Why must you be so foul?"

Houdini dropped the bag and stood defiantly, not budging an inch.

"What are you doing? I can't just drag this alone."

"You need to lighten up," Houdini said sternly.

"You need to be more proper," Smokey retorted.

"My smell is foul? Talking about 'bowel movements' is inappropriate?" Houdini slammed his hand deep into the garbage bag and pulled out a fistful of animal dung. "Do you realize the irony of what you are saying?" Houdini thrust his hand toward Smokey.

Smokey recoiled from Houdini with utter contempt on his face.

"We're dragging a bag of poo behind us. Our mission is to plant this poo all along this trail," Houdini said, pushing his hand closer to Smokey's face.

"You're being dramatic, Houdini. Your problem is that you are extreme and you have a need to shock people. It stems from childhood—"

"Your problem is that you're always analyzing me and you act like you know everything. You act so prim and proper! You need to let loose and enjoy life."

"I do enjoy life—I just don't need to be crude in order to do so."

"No, you're uptight and mildly judgmental. I don't know why, and I don't care! But if we're going to be friends I need you to relax and have fun. So relax, or I will *make* you relax."

"This conversation is over. I'm not going to engage your madness any longer. Now please place the excrement back in the bag so we can continue on."

Houdini stood for a moment before a mischievous smile cracked his cheeks.

Smokey quickly became concerned that Houdini was going to try something vile again, and stepped backward.

Without warning, Houdini flung the fistful of poo smack dab into Smokey's chest.

Anger steamed from Smokey's eyes as the splattered mess dripped to the ground.

"Now breathe in and relax," Houdini prompted his victim.

"I'll relax when I see you buried six feet under!" Smokey shouted at the top of his lungs as he exploded after Houdini. Houdini dodged Smokey like a matador would gracefully dodge a bull. The two started a cat-and-mouse chase, dashing and diving around the orchard. Houdini sprinted in circles, smiling from ear to ear.

"I can do this all day long, big fella," he hollered over his shoulder.

"I demand that you stop where you are and take the

pounding you have coming to you!"

Houdini could see Smokey tiring as beads of sweat streamed from his brow. All the dumpster food and Joshua's extra portions Smokey was always eating hadn't helped his fitness in the least. Houdini doubled back to the garbage bag for more ammo.

As the two neared the bag, Smokey burst forward with all the energy he had left and leaped at Houdini.

Houdini dodged left, avoiding Smokey's pounce. Looking back, Houdini watched as Smokey dove face-first into the giant bag of poop-mines. Houdini disappeared, then reappeared over Smokey.

"Well I guess you've won, haven't you?" Smokey mumbled through the mess covering his face as he lay defeated and humiliated.

"The real winner here is potentially you. Now breathe and relax," Houdini coaxed the victim lying before him.

Smokey sat for a moment, wound up tightly inside before letting go of control. Taking a deep breath, he gathered all his frustration and then released and relaxed.

Houdini smiled joyfully. "So how is it?"

"It stinks. Literally."

"But it is oooh soooo good. Now stand up and shake it off," Houdini politely commanded Smokey.

Smokey, reeking terribly, slowly climbed to his feet and shook the mess away.

Houdini was showered by the flying shards, getting a taste of his own medicine.

The two stood silently staring at each other for a moment before breaking into hysterical laughter.

"It's not so bad after all," Smokey said, shrugging. "It's actually rather refreshing. Breathe and relax ... just breath and relax." With that, Smokey leaned down and grabbed a corner of the bag. Houdini followed his lead and grabbed the other corner. The two continued on down the trail.

Back at the secret base, Joshua had finished building and hanging the scarecrows. Now he was littering the ground with tacks. His grandiose plan was almost complete. As he worked below, the trees chatted about Oakie's new attire.

"It looks magnificent!" Morgan declared. "Only a strong, powerful tree of your size could carry the weight of such a mighty secret base. The greatest dreams he has yet to dream will be conceived in your branches."

"Yeah, it's big and all, but not as cool as the castle that used to be in my branches," Dakota chimed in.

"Sounds like you have a case of secret-base envy, little guy," Oakie playfully jabbed at Dakota.

"It's not about how big the base is—it's about how much fun you can have with it," Dakota replied.

"Well, my base is *huge*, and it's fun!"

"It certainly seems so," Morgan cut the two of them off.

Below Joshua was cleaning up the mess scattered about by all of the building he had done. The place was shaping up rather nicely.

Quietly stalking in the bushes behind him, Frederick and Caleb plotted their next torturous attack.

"You go around over there," Caleb motioned to the bushes straight across from them. "When I signal, you bolt out of the bushes and chase him my direction. I'll jump out of the bushes and drive him back toward you. After he feels the sting of your quills and is flopping around on the ground, I'll run up and leave our calling card. When we're done, sprint back to the watering hole and meet up there. Got it?" Frederick nodded in understanding.

Joshua continued cleaning as Frederick snuck around to the bushes.

At Caleb's signal, Frederick stampeded toward Joshua. Joshua saw Frederick out of the corner of his eye and turned to run.

Caleb followed suit and burst from the brush as they had planned.

To their surprise, Joshua was about to get the best of them. The bed of sharp tacks pierced their paws. Both of the attackers danced around in pain, stumbling about until they collided and fell through a pile of branches hiding the pit of rotted food. The orchard listened as the sound of defeated moaning echoed from the pit. Oakie, Dakota, and even Morgan wore smiles of satisfied justice.

Below, in the pit, Caleb and Frederick rolled around pulling tacks from each other's paws.

"I'm too beautiful to die!" Caleb shouted as Frederick sat frowning. "The world needs me! I'm nature's perfume! Someone help me."

Houdini and Smokey appeared above the pit, back from their mission.

"Oooh! You two smell horrible," Caleb gagged while laying in the rotten slop below.

"Says the skunk," Smokey jabbed, chuckling to himself.

Joshua appeared beside Houdini and Smokey, carrying a lengthy stick, looking down at his captives. Frederick and Caleb fearfully peered up, bracing for the worst. Without hesitation, Joshua raised the stick high above his head, then plunged it down toward the culprits. Caleb and Frederick winced, waiting for death ... but nothing happened.

"Come on, it's all right," Joshua said comfortingly, shaking the stick at them. "It's okay, just grab the stick."

The two sheepishly reached out and grabbed for it. "That's it, go ahead," Joshua reassured them.

Slowly they crawled up out of the pit. Joshua reached out and grabbed each of their paws. He pulled them out and set them down gently.

Everyone stared at the delinquents as they sat, sopping wet, covered from head to toe in soggy rotting food. They hung their heads timidly.

Like a caring physician, Joshua bent down and checked each of their paws for tacks. Frederick still had three stuck in his back foot and Caleb had two in his front. With all the practice he'd gotten removing Frederick's quills from his own backside, Doctor Joshua had become a pro plucker. After a few quick yelps, the patients were tack-free once more.

"The two of you need to be more careful," Joshua said kindly. "This is a well-fortified and protected base now. You can't just go running around without watching where you're going."

The two continued standing with their heads hung low in guilt.

"Here, take some of this," Joshua offered, pulling some pieces of a chewy granola bar out of his pocket.

Each took a piece and nibbled away at it.

"If you want more, there's plenty of chow in the mess hall up there." Joshua pointed to the third platform from the top of Oakie. "If you can't get to it, Smokey will help you out. Won't you, Smokey?"

Smokey shrugged. "As you wish, sir."

"Wow!" Joshua waved his hand over his face. "Stink armor! Now that is a brilliant idea!" Joshua patted Houdini and Smokey on their heads. "Let's get going, we have some more work to do." With that, Joshua grabbed the wagon handle and marched out of the Orchard.

Smokey followed.

"Enough of your funny business." Houdini shot his finger toward the two troublemakers and glared so intensely that his eyes bulged from his head. "Or else! You hear me?" Houdini's finger shook with might. In ninja-like fashion, his hand whipped through a patch of dandelions, grabbing hold of one. Without breaking his stare, he bit the head off the dandelion and spat it on the ground. "Let this be a warning."

The orchard stood tensely in silence as Houdini dealt his threatening hand of cards and slowly backed away. With that, he disappeared.

CHAPTER

23

SELF–DEFENSE

23

The fourth of July was approaching. Back at Joshua's house, a giant bag of fireworks sat waiting for the family's enjoyment. Every year, Joshua's dad purchased enough fireworks to put on a display in the neighborhood that would make the Chinese jealous. In previous years, Joshua had only been allowed to play with sparklers and boring snap-pops that made a bang when thrown on the ground. They were fun for harassing dogs and cats, but sooner or later they got boring.

Lucky for Joshua, this year was going to be different. His dad had convinced his mom that Joshua was plenty old enough to have his own firecrackers. Since the day hadn't arrived yet, the bag of goodies was packed away in the basement. Joshua had a great instinct for finding things, though. Every year, he found his Christmas gifts before his mom had a chance to wrap them. No one could hide anything from Joshua. It was the treasure hunter in him. Before rummaging around the basement, he grabbed a flashlight and a baseball bat. Then he threw on his Indiana Jones hat, a gift his dad had given him after watching the old movie together. The hat brought the explorer out in him.

With the flashlight in one hand and the bat in the other, Joshua was ready to go. Carefully, he opened the door to the basement and descended the stairs into the darkness.

Now, as every child knows, giant trolls dwell under stairs. The trolls lurk in the darkness of all basements, skulking around the shadowy crevices. Thirsty for human blood, they wait patiently for the perfect opportunity to pounce on unsuspecting children. Because Joshua's parents were always hiding goodies in the basement, our hero had become a seasoned pro at dodging trolls. He had years of experience rummaging around in his basement, and had survived without a single scratch.

The key, as Joshua had discovered, was stealth and light. Trolls were slow and allergic to light, just like vampires. If they stepped into light or light shone on them, it burned their skin. It seemed to be kryptonite common to all creatures of the dark.

Joshua led the way with his flashlight, swinging it around like a light saber, cutting through the blackness of the basement. Beams of light shining through the basement windows cast safe passageways across the ground. Joshua carefully leapt from one beam of light to the next, making his way to a closet that commonly held birthday presents.

The door to the basement slammed loudly, shaking Joshua's confidence. He stood still, breathing slowly, listening intently for danger. Had the troll outsmarted him? Was he locked in the basement? Would he have to fight for his life? A moment passed before Joshua was convinced things were all right.

Finally Joshua eased back into searching for his treasure. If the troll was growing more clever, he could be hiding near Joshua's treasure, hoping he would come looking for it. Taking that into consideration, Joshua inched slowly toward the closet door. Holding his bat high, ready to swing with one hand while holding the flashlight in his mouth, Joshua reached out his other shaking hand and ripped the door open.

An explosion of debris came cascading down atop the treasure hunter. Buried under the weight of a prickly monster that had tackled him, Joshua thrashed about violently, attempting to escape. Rolling out from under the pile of carnage, Joshua leaped into the nearest beam of protective light and caught his breath. He frantically looked around and noticed his flashlight within reach. Without hesitation he snatched the light and shined it in the direction of the attack.

Lying in a brutal mess on the ground were the collective Christmas decorations for the entire house, inside and out.

The attacker was the family's fake Christmas tree.

Joshua scanned the area with the flashlight, just to be safe, before returning to dig through the pile for his baseball bat. To his surprise, he stumbled upon the fireworks, mixed in with the Christmas decorations. He struck gold on his first dig. What luck! To celebrate, he danced in circles, waving the flashlight around like he was at a dance club.

Unfortunately, the celebration was short lived. Letting down his guard left him vulnerable to attack. From out of the shadows a monster pounced on him, screaming like a banshee.

Shrieking in return, Joshua whisked the bag of fireworks into his arms and tore up the stairs, still screaming. At the top, Joshua blew through the door like a hurricane and frantically ran to safety in the backyard, where he collapsed on the ground to catch his breath.

Behind him, a hand appeared from the door of the basement. The attacker slowly crept out.

"What a baby," Katie proclaimed, stepping around the corner, deviously chuckling aloud.

After recovering from what felt like a minor heart attack, Joshua gathered himself and sorted through his bag of plunder. Boxes upon boxes of explosives lay organized on the ground in front of him: Artillery shells, Mortar Rounds, Thundercrackers, Killer Bees, Crackling Thunders, Midnight Furies, Widow Makers, Jumping Jack Blasters—the list went on and on. Then there was Joshua's stash, a roll of five hundred firecrackers. They were all interconnected. If he wanted, he could light one fuse and all of them would take turns going off. Or, he could pull them apart and throw them individually. In his mind, it was glorious!

Like an act of Providence, an idea flashed inside of Joshua's mind. Without hesitation, he ran back into his house, ignoring the dangerous trolls that could be lurking within, and rummaged through the kitchen drawers and refrigerator. Reappearing in the backyard with an egg in one hand and a lighter and small drill bit in the other, Joshua began working out his idea.

Holding the egg carefully, so as not to break it, Joshua

took the drill bit and gently began turning it into the pointy end of the shell. Soon he had a hole big enough to hold a firecracker. Untangling one from the giant roll, Joshua slowly eased it into the hole he had drilled. Holding his creation in the air, he marveled at what he had made. It was an egg grenade!

Through the side gate to the backyard, Houdini and Smokey appeared, looking for Joshua. They had been hiding in the bushes out front, where Joshua had told them to stay quite some time ago. They finally became restless and decided to hunt down their fearless leader.

"Hey!" Houdini shouted. "What's the holdup? Our butts are cramping from all the sittin' around we're doing out there."

In one moment, the entire world slowed to a standstill as the two onlookers watched Joshua light the egg grenade and launch it high into the air. The egg climbed higher and higher, veering over their heads.

Unable to react quickly enough, the two watched their fate unfold.

An evil grin grew on Joshua's face as the grenade exploded and the slimy guts of the egg came showering down on his friendly minions.

Houdini sat in utter disgust, boiling with anger. Meanwhile, Smokey made the most of the situation and licked the yolk dripping down his forehead onto his nose.

Joshua hollered with excitement, jumping up and down and cheering for his accomplishment.

Returning to the pile of goods, Joshua made a last assessment. Egg grenades were definitely fabulous, but there was so much just sitting here. He couldn't leave it all behind. He could easily make medieval cannons out of all the explosives lying before him. With so much, his dad couldn't possibly notice if he took some of it. Picking through the supplies, Joshua gathered what he thought he needed, then tossed the weapons supply into his wagon.

Before returning to the orchard with his bounty, Joshua had to make a daring trip to the basement and put the fireworks back where he found them. Rather than risking another attack, he rummaged through the garage to find insect repellent. If it killed bugs, it had to be deadly to trolls. Taking the bottle of spray in one hand and covering his face in the other, Joshua sprayed himself from head to toe with the deadly poison. The cloud of pest repellent filled the garage, choking him and driving him into the backyard to find fresh air. Gagging and coughing, Joshua gathered his composure, pulled on a set of Flash Feet Boots, and ran at sound-breaking speeds to the basement, where he returned the bag of fireworks.

Before any troll could notice he was there, Joshua blew back up the stairs and returned to the wagon, where his disgruntled employees, who looked like a poorly made omelet, impatiently waited. Without noticing the frustrated funk his friends were in, he ignorantly grabbed the handle of the wagon and went on about his merry way as the other two reluctantly followed behind.

CHAPTER

24

A DAUNTING REALITY

24

Back in the orchard, two peoples walked around Oakie, hanging yellow caution tape and marking him with orange paint.

Morgan and Dakota looked at each other with great worry, and Oakie quickly grew concerned.

"Morgan, what are they doing?" Oakie asked.

"This is really bad. This is really, really bad," Dakota stammered.

"Dakota, please stop." Morgan urged. "Oakie ... I'm going to be very honest with you."

Oakie could feel the heaviness in Morgan's words, as if what he was going to say would not be good.

"The few times we've seen peoples do this, they left and then returned only a few days later to cut down the tree they had marked." Morgan's eyes filled with tears.

Oakie felt paralyzed.

"Why, Morgan? Why would they cut me down?" Oakie became emotional and distressed. A great sickness filled his stomach. Dakota hung his head.

"Oakie ... I don't know. I wish I could give you a reason." Morgan held back his tears as best he could while the peoples continued to mark off the area for safety purposes.

"This means I'm going to die."

The truth and pain behind Oakie's words echoed through the orchard. The mumblings of the other trees could faintly be heard as the word spread from one tree to another. Trees began to whimper and cry as mourning spread through their hearts.

"I don't want to die. Why would they do this, Morgan? Why? Why would they cut me down and kill me?"

Helpless to comfort Oakie, Morgan cried.

And for good reason. I promise you this: The moments when a father feels powerless to comfort and protect the ones he so deeply loves are filled with the greatest pain he will ever experience, rivaled only by death. It is in these moments when a father's only weapon is faith.

As Oakie struggled to understand, a hefty, choking weight bore down on Morgan's heart.

"I haven't done anything wrong. I haven't been bad. I haven't hurt anyone. Why would they kill me, Morgan?" Oakie pleaded for an answer, hoping the truth would change.

"Maybe you've just become too big for the orchard. Or maybe the orchard has become too small for you. Your roots are growing everywhere. Maybe the soil can't support all of us anymore. I don't know—there could be so many answers." Even the hopeful Morgan lost the wind from his sails.

"I don't want to die. I haven't made apples! I've just barely enjoyed Joshua and the fort he's built in my branches. I want to see Verstand again. I want to hear about Otis's wild adventure to Vulture Desert. I want to laugh at more of Dakota's jokes."

Dakota ached with wrenching pain as he imagined not getting to play with Oakie. Life would feel so boring and mundane without him.

"I REFUSE TO DIE!" Out of nowhere Oakie shouted at the top of his lungs as he thought of the dire storm he had so bravely survived.

The power of his words shook the orchard. The grief that had so quickly flooded everyone's heart was driven away.

"Do you hear me? I REFUSE TO DIE."

Hope captivated his audience.

Fear fled.

Morgan's tears dried up as the power of Oakie's statement resonated through his own branches.

"Then that's it. You shall live," Morgan declared, unwavering from the faith and hope that he had rediscovered through Oakie's bold declaration. "Something will happen. Something magnificent that none of us could foresee. You will be protected. You will live on. The dreams and desires that you have long carried will come to pass. I'm with you, Oakie."

Even Dakota knew that somehow, in Oakie's resolve to live, things would change.

Below, the peoples finished marking out the ground. Suddenly, one them stepped onto Joshua's trap and fell down into the pit filled with rotten food. The trees looked at each other with hope and excitement. Grumbling and complaining, the people climbed out of the pit and stood in frustration, cleaning away the mess.

"What are you doing to my secret base?" Joshua's familiar voice demanded as he stampeded through the trees, dragging his wagon full of weapon supplies. Stopping, Joshua looked back and barked at Houdini and Smokey. "The two of you stay here and guard the weapons. If things go bad for me, and I have to retreat, hide them until I return."

The two nodded in agreement.

Joshua saluted his soldiers. Then he dropped the wagon handle and rushed toward the two men, puffing his chest out and clenching his fists like the Incredible Hulk.

"Take it easy, kid," one of the men said, trying to calm Joshua. "We're here to clean up the orchard and this tree has to be removed."

"What do you mean by 'remove'?" Joshua demanded with fire in his eyes.

"We're cutting it down. It doesn't belong here."

"Yes, it does. Now get out of here and leave it alone!" Joshua bent down, scooped up a handful of rocks, and began throwing them at the two men.

The men dodged back and forth, trying to avoid the rocks, until both of them fell into another pit.

The trees cheered Joshua on.

Boiling with anger, the two men fumbled around until they could get their bearings. As they struggled to get out, Joshua climbed up into his fort, pulled up the rope ladder and prepared for battle.

"Listen, you little punk!" shouted one of the men. "You get out of that tree right now! You're in so much trouble. You just wait until we find out who your parents are!"

"Yeah! They're going to paddle your butt with a big stick after we tell them what you did," The other man chimed in.

"A general doesn't back down in the face of threats. A general fearlessly marches forward!" Joshua shouted.

The men were through playing around. Both of them stormed toward the tree.

Joshua tipped over a bucket full of rotted food onto their heads.

The orchard cheered wildly.

Oakie couldn't believe what he was seeing.

Morgan and Dakota roared with laughter.

The act only infuriated the men more. While they looked for a way to climb the tree, Joshua ran to the armory, grabbed a crate of rotten eggs, and returned to show them who was boss. Below, the men floundered as one attempted to climb the other's shoulders.

Looking down, Joshua took careful aim, then screamed at the top of his lungs, "You guys thirsty for more?" Without remorse, he began to unleash a fury of foul egg guts, hailing down egg after egg toward his victims below. The men fell over onto the ground.

Joshua had to decide whether to stay in the fort, in hopes that the punishment he was dealing out would drive them away, or Plan B—run!

Below, the men angrily barked up a storm, shouting the harsh things they would do to Joshua if they caught him. They looked tenacious enough to stay.

To Joshua, Plan B seemed to be the safest bet. Running to a rope hanging behind him, he leaped fearlessly and grabbed hold of it. Swinging like Spiderman through the trees, he let go and dove into a large pile of leaves that he had raked together for an emergency just like this.

The two men climbed to their feet and began sprinting his direction, like sharks after a wounded seal.

Joshua laughed to himself as he bobbed and weaved through the trees, carefully leaping over every trip wire he had tied.

His pursuers caught the trip wire and tumbled end over end.

Seeing an opportunity for a good time, Frederick leapt from the bushes and braced for impact.

The two men yelped as they slammed butt-first into Frederick's quills. Coming to a painful stop, they lay defeated. And as usual, Caleb pounced on his powerless victims and broke their spirits with a satisfying spray to the face.

For the first time ever, Morgan, Dakota, Oakie, and the rest of the orchard unanimously celebrated Caleb's stench and cheered him on.

Though seemingly defeated, Joshua knew the two would return for retaliation and finish what they had started. He headed home, knowing all too well this wasn't over. Tomorrow he would have to return and prepare for war.

Houdini and Smokey followed orders, dragging the wagon into the bushes and concealing it until Joshua came back.

After taking some time to regroup, the two men hobbled out of the orchard with broken egos and a hunger for vengeance.

As night fell, the orchard celebrated the triumph, chattering on and on about Joshua's bravery.

That night the moon sat hidden behind a cluster of clouds. Beyond them, stars decorated the sky. They glimmered as though they were living and breathing. They seemed like they were somehow watching over Oakie, working with him, and cheering him on. Oakie suddenly had an unexplainable value for them he had never felt before.

Without Joshua, most would say Oakie was defenseless against the forces that were determined to take his life. But our favorite tree was on his way to discovering that he wasn't just a bystander in the battle. No, sir. Sometimes when you got nothin' left to fight with, you discover your most powerful weapon—belief.

As the orchard slowly faded into sleep, Oakie let the silence of the night blanket his heart and bring him comfort. A peace inside of Oakie told him there was something much bigger than Joshua on his side.

If this was his last night, though, he wanted to drink in life and enjoy every last moment of it. Reflecting on his past, every painful moment faded away as he thought about everything good that had happened in his life. Only the things that made him happy remained. Everything else seemed so trite. It didn't matter anymore. This moment might be all he had left, so he had to enjoy it to its fullest. Hopeful, yet realistic, Oakie drifted off to sleep, letting the next day come to bring whatever it might.

As the morning light broke through the horizon, Oakie slowly woke from a deep slumber while the rest of the orchard slept on. Across from him, the eyes of a proud father stared quietly, patiently waiting for Oakie to wake up. For hours Morgan had watched his precious son Oakie sleep. There was such awe in Morgan's heart. What a gift Oakie had been. Though Oakie had not come from Morgan's seed, he was as much his son as Dakota was. The night had brought Morgan an insightful dream, one he had to share with Oakie alone.

"Good morning, son." Morgan smiled.

The word "son" caught Oakie off guard. That was the first time Morgan had ever addressed him as "son." Almost sheepishly, Oakie replied, "Good morning ... Dad."

"Last night I had a very interesting dream. I thought I might share it with you before the others woke—if that would be all right?"

"Heck yeah!" Oakie whispered in excitement, realizing he wanted to share this moment alone with his *dad*.

"All right then, listen carefully and I'll do my best to describe it."

Oakie nodded his head in agreement.

"I saw a magnificent field filled with apple trees. The field of trees grew just as any field of trees would. Theirs was a beautiful yet ordinary existence. Then I watched as a cloud came, carrying with it a rainbow. From the cloud a single golden seed dropped from the sky and planted itself in the ground below. The same cloud that dropped the seed also watered it. Soon the seed stood as a giant golden tree in the center of the field."

Oakie could see the golden tree vividly in his mind. The picture was magnificent.

"The tree glimmered and shined, reflecting the light of the sun. Soon the golden tree could grow no more because the field was filled with all it could hold. The earth began to cry, and soon it shook for reasons no one knew. As the earth shook, the field shifted. Where there was once flat land now there grew giant mountains. A hot, fiery liquid spilled from the earth, consuming all the trees, except the golden one that could not be touched. Left all alone in the deep valley stood the solitary golden tree. The shadows from the mountains that surrounded this tree blocked the light that had once illuminated it and caused the tree to shine. Then the golden tree slowly began to crack and crumble to pieces."

Oakie's eyes saddened as he felt the pain of the golden tree.

"Broken beyond repair, the golden tree withered away until one day, the cloud carrying the rainbow returned. The colors of the rainbow burst through the shadows of darkness and mended the golden tree."

Oakie's eyes filled with hope.

"After the passing of many nights, the earth shook again—only this time, the mountains came down and the ground beneath the tree rose up. Now the tree stood alone on top of a great mountain, illuminated once again by the beautiful light of the sun. Before long, vines began to grow and wrap themselves around the golden tree until the gold could no longer be seen. The sun returned day after day, hoping to see the brilliance that once shined from the tree, but it could see nothing."

Oakie's heart ached. He wanted the tree to shine again so badly.

"Eventually the sun grew sad. In time, the sadness of the sun became anger. The anger was so great that the sun became hotter and hotter until the vines could no longer take it and could do nothing more than wither away."

Oakie felt relief as he imagined the vines dying and falling to pieces.

"The golden tree now shined brighter than ever, but the sun had yet to cool. Gold began to melt from the leaves of the tree and drop to the earth. Dripping slowly down the side of the mountain, covering the earth like a waterfall, the gold found its way into the crevices of the land.

"Yet again the earth shook and the mountain holding

the golden tree shrunk down until all that was left was a flat field. Soon the cloud carrying the rainbow returned for its last time and showered the field with purple rain. The earth swallowed every last drop, and from it burst forth mighty golden trees for as far as the eye could see."

The moment seemed almost holy as Oakie imagined the field of golden trees shimmering, almost blinding the sun that blanketed them.

"What does it mean, Morgan?"

"I'm not completely sure," Morgan said, reflecting for a moment on the dream, "but I do believe that no matter what happens, *all things will be made beautiful in the end.*"

"I like that." Oakie smiled as he repeated the words Morgan had said in his mind. All things will be made beautiful in the end. There was such comfort in that.

"Hold this truth close to your heart, despite what might happen," Morgan said. "Let it lead you when things seem too dark to see anything in front of you."

Oakie didn't completely understand what that meant for his future, but he knew Morgan's words always held wisdom he could trust. The two continued to talk and share their thoughts about life while enjoying the quiet, intimate time they had alone. Soon the rest of the orchard awoke to begin the day.

CHAPTER

25

THIS MEANS WAR

————— 25 —————

Trucking down the beaten path, Joshua charged toward Oakie, eager to start preparing for war. That morning he had dressed appropriately for the occasion. Digging through his father's hunting gear, he clothed himself in his father's oversized green camouflage pants and shirt. His feet sported a pair of his mother's hiking boots, which seemed to fit rather well with the help of crumpled newspaper stuffed into the toes. A red beret he'd found at a swap meet adorned his head. As he marched forward, Houdini and Smokey followed behind, playing a game of tag with each other.

Houdini, as always, appeared and disappeared at will, confusing his playmate and getting the best of him.

"You may have the upper hand in this child's game of tag!" Smokey declared, "But in a gentleman's duel, I would have your floppy ears and the head they're attached to."

Houdini snuck behind and gave Smokey's tail a tug, playfully letting him know who would get the better of whom.

Joshua stopped abruptly, then spun around and faced his soldiers. "Attention!" he commanded.

Smokey and Houdini stopped their games and stood like statues while they listened to their commander's orders.

"This is not a game! Today we prepare for the coming war that lies ahead. The battle before us will be of epic proportions. It is our strategy and preparation that will either yield us victory or deliver us into the hands of defeat. Though I vow to do all I can to protect those that serve this cause, I cannot promise everyone will survive."

Smokey and Houdini looked at one another with concern. Since there were only two of them, the chances of survival seemed bleak.

"I thank you all for your courage, bravery, and unwavering dedication to the cause. May God be with us as we fight valiantly against those that would come to steal that which we have given our lives to build." Joshua saluted his soldiers and then continued, "Our main objective today is to mount the cannons that we confiscated during our raid on an enemy's secret bunker. The cannons will be mounted throughout the base in a three hundred and sixty-degree manner, leaving us one hundred percent protected.

"Now as for the two of you, though you are brave, you are not physically prepared for what lies ahead. Because of this, I have taken the liberty to commission our leading genetic scientists to create a super-soldier drug that will transform each of you into an individual army of one. The scientists said it couldn't be done, but I urged them with great faith that it could and would be done. And so it is, after grueling, painstaking research, I hold before you in my hand the Super Soldier Cocktail. Though it has not been tested and is not FDA-approved, I administer it to you today with complete confidence that it will far surpass all expectations. As I am required by law to share with you, the side effects are as follows: Nausea, vomiting, explosive diarrhea, loss of sight, headaches, back cramps, numbness in fingertips and toes, stomachaches, and last but not least, violent fits of smelly gas."

Houdini and Smokey stared at Joshua in confusion.

"Do you agree to the terms and conditions of the use of this drug?"

The two continued to stare.

"Good, I would expect no less from the men of honor that stand before me." Joshua placed his hands in his pockets and pulled from each of them a handful of the Super Soldier Cocktail. Leaning down, he opened his hands to reveal a mixture of crushed granola bar and smashed-up chewable vitamins.

"I never understand his ramblings, but eventually he always speaks my language," Houdini said referring to the food in Joshua's hand.

"I certainly can't turn my nose up at a nice treat,"

Smokey mumbled before gobbling the snack.

Joshua backed away and watched as the two mutated into genetic freaks capable of tearing a semitruck in two. "YES! We have accomplished what no scientist dared to believe possible!" Joshua shouted at the top of his lungs.

Houdini leaned over to Smokey as Joshua celebrated. "Do you feel gassy?"

"I didn't think of it until you said something, but yes, I do feel a bit gassy."

Houdini and Smokey's stomachs grumbled. Joshua returned his attention to the soldiers before him.

"Your first orders are to retrieve the surplus weaponry that you concealed yesterday. In the meantime, I'll return to the base station and drill holes in the remaining rotten eggs we have stored in preparation for the egg grenades I must build."

The animals sat for a moment, waiting for something more to eat. Joshua gently nudged and shooed them away.

While his soldiers went to gather the supplies, Joshua returned to Oakie. As the brave general stepped into sight, everyone began to cheer for him.

Oakie's eyes became a bit misty.

"Are you crying?" Dakota asked, a hint of teasing in his voice.

"No." Oakie choked back the mounting wall of tears.

"You are crying!" Dakota chuckled.

"No ... whatever. Yes, I'm crying. Geez, can't a tree have some emotions without being badgered?" Oakie said playfully.

Dakota became a bit misty-eyed himself before laughing it off. The truth was, the entire orchard felt a great deal of emotion in that moment. The bold general before them that was once so weak in stature now stood with strength and determination. The little boy had grown into a little man, and that little man was the only thing standing between Oakie and death. He was fighting for an innocent life that couldn't fight for itself, and that moved the hearts of all within the orchard.

Joshua climbed to the base and drilled holes in the remaining rotten eggs. As he finished, Smokey and Houdini appeared, dragging the red wagon full of fireworks. Joshua grabbed a large bucket attached to a rope and lowered it down to his soldiers, waiting below. After they filled it, he pulled it back up and unloaded it. The two continued to help until all the explosives had made it into the fort.

Morgan and Dakota watched with curiosity as Joshua jumped from one platform to the other, carefully aiming fireworks toward the ground as he nailed them to the branches. Soon Roman candles, mortar rounds, Booming Bettys, and fireworks of all sorts laced Oakie's branches. The red, white, and blue that made up the fireworks' packaging left Oakie looking like an American Flag. He was a finely decorated Fourth of July display, and no one could argue against that.

Climbing down, Joshua backed away from his well-armed base station and took a moment to admire his work. Nodding his head in approval, he climbed back up and went to work in the armory. He filled all the rotten eggs with their firecracker detonators. After finishing dozens of egg grenades, he gathered the leftover fuse that had tied the giant string of firecrackers together. With a roll of electrical tape and the firecracker fuse, he connected every firework nailed to Oakie's body. When the time was right, it would only take one match to end the war. Finally, hungry and tired, Joshua dragged himself to the mess hall and grabbed the sandwiches his mother had made for him from the food cooler. He ate slowly while he imagined running around and throwing grenades at his enemies. In his mind, he watched as they fled, jumping up and down in pain as the tacks pierced their feet. He could hear them screaming the word, "Retreat!" at the top of their lungs. He laughed as they fell into the pits and begged for help. He rejoiced as they stumbled through the orchard and fell over the trip wire that he had strung everywhere. Victory was within reach and the battle hadn't even begun!

After cleaning up his dinner mess, Joshua broke out the face paint his dad used for hunting. Looking into a cracked mirror that hung from a wall, he carefully painted his face in hues of green and brown until he was a camouflaged warrior. Ready for battle, all he needed now was for the enemy to return. Since it was Friday, he had convinced his mother to let him sleep over at a friend's house for the entire weekend so he wouldn't miss anything at the orchard. But Oakie was really his home for the weekend, and since night was falling, it was time to prepare for bed before all the light disappeared. Joshua pulled out the sleeping bag and flashlight that he stored in the fort for nights like this.

After laying out the sleeping bag, he rummaged through a crate to find his protective sleep stabilizer. The sleep stabilizer was an invention he had created a few years back. For quite some time, an evil Dutch Gnome had been living under his bed and terrorizing him while he slept. His grandfather had told him that he'd better sleep with one eye open. After dozens of sleepless nights trying to keep one eye open, a picture in his imagination inspired him. He saw a spring-loaded contraption that could be used to hold one eye open. With the help of the spring from a dismantled mousetrap, some popsicle sticks, and a roll of string, he fashioned himself a protective sleep stabilizer. Now he could have the protection of sleeping with one eye open, but still get his much-needed warrior rest.

Under the cluttered mess of creative experiments, Joshua found his sleeping apparatus and jammed it into his eye.

Behind him, Smokey had silently climbed into the fort. As Joshua turned around, the monstrous sight of his bulging left eye and the fresh paint on his face scared Smokey, sending him running in a panic.

"Houdini! The kid is mutating into some sort of freakish monster. He turned different colors and his brain is exploding right out of his eye socket. Houdini! You disappearing lunatic, where are you? We have to do something!" Smokey frantically barreled around the room, trying to decide what to do.

Joshua stood wondering if Smokey somehow got that rabies thing his dad always said wild animals had. If he did, that would mean Joshua would have to "put him down," whatever that was.

Smokey climbed the branches until he was safely above Joshua. Like a seasoned skydiver, he dove from the branch and latched onto the top of Joshua's head.

Joshua spun in circles, trying to lose his attacker.

Like a bull rider, Smokey gripped Joshua's cheek tightly with one hand and slapped the side of his face with the other.

"You stupid rabbit, if you can hear me, just forget it!" Smokey screamed at the top of his lungs. "Save yourself!"

Joshua dove for the cooler, tore a peanut butter sandwich from it, and shoved it in Smokey's face.

The instant peanut butter touched Smokey's lips, panic fled and euphoria filled him. He went limp, high on his love for food, then fell to the ground and cradled the beloved peanut butter sandwich in his arms. "False alarm," Smokey mumbled as he devoured the sandwich in ecstasy.

Below all the havoc in the fort, Morgan, Dakota and Oakie chuckled as they reflected on all of Joshua's antics. Like any imaginative boy full of life, Joshua's presence fed the hearts of those closest to him with entertainment and joy. There were no dull moments when he was around, and because of him, the orchard couldn't help but feel a greater sense of purpose. Such is the gift of any little boy or girl.

After cleaning up the mess Smokey made in the fort, Joshua grabbed a lighter he had taken from Old Man Arnie's garage. Gripping it tightly in his hand, he lay down to sleep, prepared for the war that lay ahead.

CHAPTER

26

THE GREAT TRIBULATION

26

Rrrrrrrrr! Rrrrrrrrrr! Rrrr! Rrrr! Rrrr!
The wail of a rabid chainsaw, starving for the flesh of a tree, tore through the orchard, shaking the world from its peaceful slumber.

Rrrr! Rrrr! Rrrrrrrrr!

Joshua shot from his sleeping bag, dazed and groggy with confusion.

Startled, Smokey leapt up from where he lay and bolted through the branches, lunging from Oakie to Dakota, then to Morgan.

Terror filled Oakie's eyes as the vicious attacker dressed in orange barreled toward him, wielding a smoking chainsaw.

Rrrrrrrrr! Rrrr! Rrrr! Rrrr!

The sound pierced Oakie's heart as he braced for death and gave both his father and his best friend a look that said goodbye ...

As the thunderous growl of the chainsaw rained down upon him, a shimmering ray of hope appeared upon a branch in the form of a little people. The general stood valiantly clothed in courage. He held an egg grenade in one hand and a lighter in the other. Sparking the lighter, he touched the fuse to the flame and sent the grenade whistling at the man below.

The egg shattered into thousands of pieces and painted the man with sticky, stinky goop. Gagging from the putrid smell, the attacker dropped his chainsaw and curled over. As he violently ripped grass from the ground to clean his face, four other men wielding chains and axes, dressed in orange, broke through the trees and charged toward Oakie.

Swift as a ninja, Joshua sprang from his post back to the

armory where the stash of grenades sat waiting to be thrown. Without mercy, he blindly chucked one grenade after another over his enemies' heads. The foul slop hailed down from the heavens upon the gang of death-dealers advancing below.

No one could escape the chaos. The goop splattered the trees and the innocent animals fleeing for their lives.

Try as he would, Houdini couldn't dodge the vile egg grenades. While peeking out from the hollow stump where he hid, an egg burst above him and covered his face. Joshua cackled at the top of his lungs as he watched the men slipping about on the slimy goo until they crumbled to their knees.

With great persistence the men forged on, determined to conquer the boy and his tree. As helpless bystanders, Oakie and the rest of the orchard anxiously watched the war rage.

One of the men dropped his ax and raced toward Oakie, only to find himself crashing into the bottom of a pit. The other three dropped what they carried and rushed toward the base. One stopped to help his fallen companion in the pit, while the other two dashed past the traps and started their climb up Oakie.

Rrrrrrrrrr! Rrrrrrrrrr! Rrrrrrrrrr!

The man with the smoking chainsaw stood once again and barreled toward his victim with angry vengeance burning in his eyes.

From above, General Joshua dumped one bucket of rotten food after another on the invaders as they climbed toward him.

His persistence only fueled their fire.

Turning his attention to the chainsaw-yielding maniac below, Joshua realized if he didn't stop him immediately, Oakie would be firewood. The time to act was *now*! Joshua turned to light the end of the fuse that would set off the barrage of fireworks. But before he could get two steps from where he stood, an invader latched onto his ankle. Joshua fell down, his head bouncing off the ground. Stars filled his eyes as he lay dazed from the hit.

The intruder in orange tugged fervently on his leg, dragging Joshua toward him.

Getting his bearings, Joshua struggled, kicking at the attacker with his free leg. It was no use; the man wouldn't let loose.

Rrrrrrr! Rrrr! Rrrr! Rrrr!

The chainsaw screamed angrily below. The future grew bleak as Joshua thrashed about violently to free himself.

From above, a dashing knight appeared in the leaves of Oakie's branches. The shining light of this hero broke through the shadow of Oakie's darkest hour. Time slowed to a standstill.

For a brief moment, the world simply stopped as a giant rotten watermelon rocketed out of Smokey's hands and plummeted toward the man gripping Joshua's leg. With pinpoint accuracy, the bomb hit its target and sent the man sailing through the air.

Joshua was free!

Shaking his head, Joshua knocked the stars from his eyes and sprang to his feet. From his pocket he pulled his lighter and gave it a flick. The tiny flame burned brilliantly as it danced in the wind. Before anything else could go wrong, Joshua thrust the lighter like a sword at the fuse and set the finale in motion. All his effort and hard work would climax in this one moment.

Like a flash of lightning, the fuse blazed from one cannon to the next. The fireworks erupted one after another in a beautifully orchestrated symphony. Greens, reds, blues, yellows—sparkles, crackles, bangs, pops, pows, whistles, one after another after another—the fireworks exploded and sent shards of fiery debris all about the orchard.

The men below ducked and dashed, jumped and dove, flipped and flopped. Their escape was nearly impossible as one fireball after another pummeled the ground below the fortress. The roar of the chainsaw died as the giant man in orange gave up his weapon and fled for his life. The remaining four ran in terror, chasing after their leader.

Joshua danced around the fort, leaping about and shouting a victorious war cry that almost drowned the sound of the fireworks still exploding throughout the orchard.

The trees cheered and laughed in celebration as the men

tucked their tails and ran.

Oakie breathed a sigh of relief. Joshua had done it. He was safe. He would live on, and not a day would pass that he wouldn't remember the valiant efforts of his dear friends.

As Joshua bounced around, a flicker caught his eye and stopped him abruptly. The heat of a rainless summer had sucked every drop of moisture from the foliage below. All around Oakie, the embers of the fireworks began to burn brightly as the dry leaves and brush turned into fuel for their fire. A giant blaze erupted in the orchard. Like a python, the flame twisted and turned, slithering its way through and around every apple tree.

Sheer terror gripped the orchard as the fire chased the trees down and tore away at their bark. The fiery python coiled its tails around the trunk of every tree and made its way to their branches. One by one the trees screamed as their leaves erupted in flames.

The hidden creatures of the orchard bolted from their sanctuaries, flooding the paths free of fire. Smokey lay below Oakie, coughing heavily as he choked on the ashes that filled the air.

Houdini saw his friend battling for his life. A snarling vicious flame flared up and stretched its arms wide as it dove toward Houdini. He darted past the fire's reach and sprinted to his friend's side. Grabbing a dirty, shredded cloth lying on the ground, Houdini covered Smokey's face.

"Give me your hand! Follow me, and don't let go!" Houdini shouted, and began dragging his friend through the obstacle course of flames in front of them.

A crippling pain gripped Joshua's stomach as the fire painted the orchard in hues of red, orange, and yellow. What had he done? How did this go so wrong? He had to do something! Anything! Joshua ran to the armory and tore through the mess of supplies until he found a shovel. Like a swashbuckling pirate, he leapt from Oakie's branches with the shovel in one hand, grabbing a rope with the other. Swinging down to the ground, he sliced away at the fire, pounding the flames with all of his might.

But as quickly as one flame went out, another started.

Sweat and tears covered Joshua's face as the fire fought back. Working his way around Oakie, he stopped the fire from devouring his refuge, but the rest of the orchard was being swallowed alive.

Oakie stared into his father's eyes as the flaming monster reached out and grabbed hold of his dear dad.

Morgan didn't flinch.

Peace that Oakie couldn't understand rested on his father. The fire scaled Morgan with a ravenous hunger.

In terror, Dakota watched as the fire lunged from Morgan's branches to his own. Dakota shrieked in pain, joining the others as they cried aloud for their lives. Oakie could hardly breathe as he frantically looked around the orchard, seeing his family burn alive.

"Oakie," Morgan said softly, under the screams around them.

Oakie's eyes shot back and forth, his heart filled with remorse and regret. This was his fault entirely, he thought, as he sat powerless to stop any of it.

"Oakie, please look at me," Morgan said softly once again.

Oakie continued to stare as Dakota wept in pain. Self-hatred filled his heart as he watched his beloved brother being eaten alive.

"Oakie!" Morgan shouted. Oakie finally turned to him. "Keep your eyes fixed on mine. Don't look away. Even when I am no more, remember to keep your eyes fixed on mine. If you look away, you will only see pain and suffering. If you look away, you will quickly forget all the goodness. When I'm gone, close your eyes and remember us as we were.

"Morgan ..." Oakie muttered as a tear fell from his face. It was followed by others until a river of tears cascaded down Oakie's bark to his roots, where the heat of the fire swallowed them.

"Just watch my eyes, son and don't lose hope. It is the anchor of life when nothing remains," Morgan said calmly as the fire engulfed him.

As Oakie stared into his father's eyes, the chaos seemed to disappear and everything went silent. It was as if he was alone with only his father standing before him. Oakie felt like he had transformed back into a tiny sapling and was looking up from a place of innocence as Morgan showered him with care and affection. It felt as though life was simple and the worries few. Here in this place, he knew everything would be okay.

"Oakie, you are truly a precious tree. I am so thankful that you found your way into my orchard. I have longed to have sons like you since Dakota was born. I've dreamed of having sons who would sit before me and allow me to enjoy their company. Thank you for being here with me. Thank you for sharing yourself with me. It has been an honor and a joy to know you."

"Morgan?"

"Yes, son?"

"Is everything going to be all right?" Oakie asked with a childlike curiosity.

"Yes, Oakie, in time all things that are wrong will be made right."

"I'm scared."

"I understand. Life can be scary, and sometimes very tough. But I will be with you forever in your heart."

Oakie's eyes dropped at Morgan's words.

"Oakie."

Oakie looked into his father's eyes. "Yes."

"I love you." The power of those three words was driven deep into Oakie's heart. Then the pain of the present crisis returned, along with the screams and the cries that were muffled by the sound of the crackling fire.

Morgan's face disappeared as the blaze wrapped itself around him. All that remained were fingers of fire dancing through the dark smoke that consumed the orchard. Oakie looked down, and there below him, Joshua fought fervently against the blaze and the exhaustion that was slowly overcoming him. The cause was hopeless, but he pushed forward, battling the guilt that rested on his shoulders. Oakie feared for Joshua's life as he finally collapsed, unable to breathe from all the smoke that filled his lungs.

As Oakie watched Joshua lying beneath him, unconscious and helpless, something rose from deep within.

He closed his eyes and silently cried out, "Please save my friend. Please help him. Please don't let him die."

At the pleading of his heart, a tree tumbled over, startling Oakie. Two men dressed in yellow, carrying axes, broke through the flames and discovered Joshua lying on the ground.

"Did they say if anyone else was with him?" one fireman shouted to the other as he placed his mask over Joshua's face.

"They didn't know! I'll check his fort just to be sure!" the other fireman replied.

While the first fireman gave Joshua CPR, the other stormed up Oakie. Without regard for Joshua's hard work, the man tore through the fort, knocking down planks, smashing walls with his ax, and clearing Oakie's branches of the base station. He frantically searched for any other children. Satisfied that no others were left, he jumped down and hustled back to his partner.

"Please be okay, please be okay," Oakie begged as the fireman worked on his dear friend.

Suddenly, with a violent cough, Joshua returned from the dead.

The fireman scooped him up in his arms and wrapped himself around the fragile little child. Leading the way with his ax, the other fireman chopped away at fallen debris to cut a path for their escape. As Joshua was carried to safety, his eyes opened just enough to catch a glimpse of his secret fort that was now in shambles.

Oakie watched with gratitude as his friend was carried away through the flames. Now all alone, Oakie sat blinded by the fire encompassing him. The pleas of his family were no more. The fire was left to pick away at their remains.

It should have been me. Again and again, Oakie thought to himself like a broken record, *It should have been me.*

As the day turned to night, the fire burned on. Oakie's crying turned into weeping. His weeping turned to sobbing, his sobbing became wailing. Before the night was through, his wailing finally fell silent. No matter how many tears Oakie shed, they weren't enough to extinguish the flames.

Sadly I tell you that many flames will burn through life,

delivering to us devastating moments and circumstances that are far outside the bounds of our control. Sometimes we are left having to stare into the face of tragedy as it takes from us our dearest treasures … those we love.

Though I do agree with what Morgan said—"Don't lose hope, it is the anchor of life when nothing remains"—I would have to add that it's not just the anchor, it's also the shovel that digs you out of the deepest hole when you've fallen into your lowest low. Though I am fully aware that much larger trees have been destroyed by much less, I am confident that in time Oakie will find his silver lining, even if he must face the darkest hour before the dawn.

CHAPTER

27

THE VALLEY OF DEATH

27

The next morning, a fog of ashes floated through what used to be the orchard. A graveyard that resembled a gray winter was all that remained. No chirping, no growling, no cawing, no playing, no fighting, no grumbling, no celebrating ... nothing. There was nothing more.

Amidst the nothingness stood the last source of life—Oakie. But he didn't feel very alive. As if he had died with his family, Oakie stared blankly at an ember as it slowly drifted to the ground in front of him and then was extinguished. Like a sad clown whose face was painted by the ashes of the blaze, tears that had long dried left a trail running from his eyes to his roots deep in the ground.

His friends ... his family ... all gone.

Only the cries, screams, and horror remained. Over and over, the movie played out in his mind. So helpless. So powerless. So incapable of stopping any of it. The fire spread so fast. One moment they were all smiling, laughing, celebrating their victory, the next ... they were shrieking in panic with no way to run, no way to escape, and all Oakie could do was *watch*.

A cool breeze swept through the cemetery that now surrounded Oakie, gently peeling away the veil of haze that hid the painful tragedy. Morgan had often described the beauty that he could see before the other trees in the orchard had grown. Oakie daydreamed regularly about it, but he never actually believed that he would one day get to see it for himself.

To his disappointment, this was nothing like Morgan's description. The hills, once a home to so much life, lay barren, covered in black soot. Nothing splendid. Nothing magical. Nothing inspiring. Death had wiped its hand across the fields and hills, leaving behind only a mess of pain and heartache. Complete desolation. Although Oakie still stood untouched by the flame, he felt as though he was no more. The flames that took his family also took his heart. What now?

And so he stood silent and still. The sun set. The moon rose. Day after day, Oakie stood silent. Slowly the wind gathered debris and began to sweep it away. Under the ash lay the bones that had not fully burned. Trunks of trees too large to be fully consumed remained as a chilling reminder of those that once shared this place with Oakie. No motion. No life. Oakie simply shed his leaves. First a few, then the rest, until a giant mound of leaves lay below and Oakie was naked and bare.

Cresting over the distant hill, a black shadow filled the sky. As the shadow grew closer, it seemed to become alive, like a swarm of locusts. As the swarm approached, it became clear that it wasn't a swarm at all. It was a murder of crows—the most reviled of all birds. Crows wait for those that have died and feast on their carcasses. They thrive on death. Trees pulsing with life will have nothing to do with crows. They whip their branches wildly at the mere sight of these wicked birds, refusing to be a resting place for them.

Yet, as the murder made its way toward Oakie, he did nothing. Although it was the first sign of life in quite some time, Oakie continued to stare blankly into the distance. Stiffened, he stood motionless as the murder descended on him. His branches were soon filled with crows, replacing all the leaves that had been lost. From a distance it was quite a dark and frightening sight to see.

The murder cawed loudly, surveying the land. After a long journey, the crows had grown very hungry and tired. Oakie made a wonderful place for them to settle and rest.

Scanning the field below, a crow caught sight of something that looked rather tasty. Without hesitation, he leaped from the branch and swooped down to the pile that had caught his attention. Scavenging through the debris, he discovered a treasure—the carcass of a deer. One by one the rest of the murder noticed what he had found and made their way to the field. Tearing through the clutter, they discovered a feast that had been prepared for them. A wildly dark celebration began as they dug up the victims of the fire. Still hardened, Oakie watched quietly as each crow found a tasty treat to carry back to his branches.

While the murder dug through the graveyard of Oakie's family, one crow remained. Mysterious and regal in nature, she quietly stood with her head held high while the others fought over their pillagings. Perched in the crevice of Oakie's trunk where his branches split off, she waited as the crows returned with their banquet and presented her with a portion of what they had found. There at her feet, the sacrifices began to pile high with no acknowledgement of the offerings.

Days passed and the murder continued to gorge themselves on the banquet that surrounded them. The bounty seemed neverending. The crows grew large and plump. Some grew so large that they even struggled to fly back to the branches where their brothers and sisters rested and digested. The weight of the murder was so heavy that even the strongest of Oakie's branches couldn't help but bow under it.

The crows chattered.

"We've for sure found ourselves a home here," said one as he shoved another piece of meat in his mouth, which was already too full.

"Reminds me of the stories my grandfather used to tell about the fields they found after the war. It was a perfect paradise," one chimed in.

"There's so much, it's like it never ends," added a crow lying on his back.

"There's almost too much," responded another.

"Don't be silly, there's no such thing as too much," one pointed out as he tipped back and threw a piece of meat in the air, attempting to catch it in his mouth. Losing his balance, he toppled over and fell from the branch. Plump as a pig, he struggled with all his might to fly, but his wings were no good. Spiraling out of control, he plummeted to the earth, where he landed on his head. The murder erupted in laughter as they watched their fallen friend flop around, dazed and confused. Some laughed so hard they spit all the food right out of their mouths. The fallen crow collected his bearings and broke into hysterics along with his friends.

Emotionless, the crow in Oakie's crevice sat quietly amid the stacks of food piled high around her and observed the childish play of the murder. Her eyes were full of irritation and distaste as they pierced the party's fun and games. Carefully watching her demeanor, a crow in the middle of the murder commanded the attention of the group.

"Silence!"

The group continued laughing.

Glancing over, the crow took notice of the continued foul demeanor of the mysterious crow in the crevice.

"I said SILENCE!" the crow barked louder.

The murder began to quiet, but a few continued.

"ENOUGH!" Finally all submitted to the order. "You're right to be excited. It's been a long time since there's been such abundance. We should celebrate. We should be excited. We should laugh, and grow fat, but let's not do so without honoring the one to whom we owe all of it. Let's keep in mind our queen, who with her keen sight led us to this 'paradise,' as one of you so eloquently put it."

The murder exploded with a cheer. At the top of their lungs they began, "Long live Queen Morte! Long live Queen Morte!" The chant continued, over and over again.

There in her crevice, Queen Morte perched in elegant darkness. Not a smile, not a bow—she simply stood and received their adoration.

Her subjects sporadically leapt forth and added gifts to the tower of food before her. Though she had not eaten even one bite of what had already been brought, they continued to honor her with their sacrifices.

Without warning, she abruptly extended her wings.

A shiver of silence echoed throughout the murder. Like statues they stood waiting to receive words from their queen.

"My beloved, your gifts of admiration and adoration are received and always welcomed. Although expected, they do not go overlooked."

A few crows began to cheer.

The queen's eyes silenced them quickly. "I will attempt

to continue without interruptions. We were created for a time such as this. Where others have drowned in tragedy, we bathe in it. We drink from it."

The murder stood hypnotized by every word.

"Their pain and suffering is ours to glory in. It's only right that we feast on their destruction and fill our bellies. All will perish and when they do, *we* will feed. Even the flesh of the mightiest kings will one day touch our lips. Where others fight and toil to survive, we thrive. When all have gone to their graves, who still stands?"

"We do!" cried the murder.

"Feed until you can eat no more. Dispose of all that is a remembrance of that which once lived. When we have left our mark and nothing remains, then we will move on. Hear me! Listen closely. We will find those that have fallen to misfortune. The earth is ripe with them. I will lead. Where I go, so you shall thrive!"

The murder burst into a war cry. Their hearts rallied behind their queen. Each and every crow was prepared to follow Morte and plunder the earth of all those that had fallen.

"Do you miss them?" Queen Morte addressed Oakie for the first time. "Do you dream of them? Do you long for them?"

Oakie sat motionless.

"It must be so lonely here all by yourself. Lucky for you we came."

Oakie peered up to look at the queen where she sat on her throne in the crevice.

"My subjects will scour the ground and wash it clean of their blood. In the meantime, we will keep you company, and when we leave, you can die in peace with only the memory of your loss to haunt you."

Oakie's branches bent even more under the weight of the murder, so much that they began to touch the ground. Some had become so brittle and burdened by the crows that they simply snapped.

"What is your name, my dear?"

Oakie remained silent, locked tight like a jail cell. "Come now, you must have a name. What kind of queen would I be if I didn't thank you for your hospitality by at least learning your name?"

Oakie didn't budge.

"Suit yourself. Die alone, nameless and unknown, but don't say this queen didn't do her best to bring you comfort."

Oakie sat quietly for a moment longer, and then spoke softly, in pain.

"Oakie."

The queen peered off into the distance momentarily before responding. "Oakie ... sweet like a child. Sounds almost helpless and slightly boring—surely not the name of someone who is great. It's very odd that you, out of all the great trees that were once here, would survive this tragic ordeal. Tell me, Oakie, do you regret being the only survivor?"

Morte's question violently twisted the dagger that still pierced Oakie's heart from the passing of his family. As he stood heavy with guilt, shamed and condemned by the role he had played in the loss of those he loved, a marching wave of invaders stormed the field of rotting corpses.

Queen Morte squinted tightly trying to make out what was causing the disruption. Seeming pleasantly surprised, she changed the subject.

"Well Oakie, it looks as though we have some visitors. I do so love termites. Occasionally we cross each other's paths, and I have to say I am always quite delighted. Some of them are very enlightened and can be enjoyable conversationalists, unlike yourself."

The termites invaded the field. Digging into the dead trees, they burrowed deep down and began devouring the remains from the inside out.

Three rather large termites made their way toward Oakie. As they approached his roots, the queen addressed them. "Hello darlings. I am Queen Morte. Welcome to my feasting grounds."

"A pleasure to meet you, Your Royal Highness. My name is Colpa. I am the High Queen of these termites and I share my throne with my lovely two sisters."

The others bowed their heads before Morte.

"My name is Vergogna," said one.

"And I am Condanna," chimed in the other.

"Three very beautiful queens ... it's a pleasure to meet you," replied Queen Morte.

"The pleasure is all ours," the three said in unison.

"I'm sure it is." Queen Morte paused for a moment. "Is there any way I can be of assistance to you?"

Colpa took the lead and began sharing the needs of the colony.

"We've been traveling for quite some time. The colony is in need of food and shelter. The sun is burning us alive. We must find a place to hide from the sunlight or surely we shall all die. Providence has led us here."

"Seemingly so," Morte replied.

"Our soldiers and workers feast in the field to regain strength. As for us, we are searching for the perfect place to build our nest. Do you have any suggestions?" Colpa asked.

Queen Morte's eyes twinkled in delight. "Look at me! Where are my manners? Please allow me to introduce you to Oakie. He's very quiet. Not a conversationalist at all, but perhaps he simply needs the right company ..."

The three replied in unison. "It's an honor to meet you, Oakie."

Oakie sat quietly.

"Oakie, please don't make a fool of me. Greet our guests and quit being rude."

"Hello," Oakie responded hesitantly.

"He's very cute," said Vergogna.

"Cute is a way to put it, I suppose." Morte carried little affection for Oakie. However, she did see great value in his ability to accommodate her guests. "I have a suggestion," she continued in her regal manner. "May I share it with you?"

"Please, Your Majesty, share with us your insight." Colpa sat confidently before Morte, perceiving her affection for the sisters and their colony.

"My dear Oakie seems to have been very lonely before we graced him with our presence. Although I'm sure we've been good company to our host, there will come a time when we must move on. Surely he'll be sad. As a great queen, I can't imagine leaving such a precious soul all alone just to slowly rot away. It just wouldn't be honoring to him."

The three sisters looked at one another, trying to understand Morte's words.

"Here is what I suggest. I propose that you build your nest deep down in the most hidden places within Oakie."

The sisters began to glow with excitement at the idea.

"It serves you both very well. After the troubles and terror this poor tree has seen, your comfort is more than welcome, I'm sure."

The three sisters nodded in unison, sympathizing with Oakie's loss.

"And as for you, well, you will find protection behind his thick hardened wood. Nothing will harm you, especially not the taxing light of day that burdens you so."

"May I interject, Your Majesty?" Condanna asked respectfully.

"By all means, please share with us your thoughts."

"Clearly your friend is carrying great sorrow."

Oakie turned his eyes down to his roots, realizing how true Condanna's words were.

"I think it would be selfish of us to look elsewhere for a place to call home. The troubles of our colony are so small in comparison to that of this tree."

The other two sisters nodded in agreement.

"This is truly someone in need, and my heart breaks at the thought of Oakie being left here alone. It's my humble opinion that we stay here, if for nothing less than his benefit. Would you agree, Colpa?"

Colpa glanced back and forth between Morte and Oakie's lifeless face. "Yes, wholeheartedly. This tree needs us. If we don't join him, who will?"

The queens shrugged their shoulders and shook their heads as if to say, "No one."

"Who will be here for him? Who will watch over him? Who will love him and tend to his needs? I refuse to turn my back on a creature in such need."

"Then it is settled?" Morte asked.

"It is for us," Colpa replied. She looked at her sisters and prodded them for an answer.

They both nodded their heads in agreement.

"Yes!" they declared in unison and excitement.

"Well, Oakie," Colpa began. "As queens governed by honor and integrity, it would go against all we stand for to simply impose our desire to care for you. Just because our presence would benefit you does not mean you want it. It is our heart to protect you."

The weight of the word *protect* struck Oakie.

"Care for you ..."

Someone to care for him again? Could they really care for him like Morgan or Dakota?

"Comfort you, and love you."

Comfort and love? Everything felt so cold inside. The idea of comfort and love seemed scary.

"But we do need a proper invitation. We simply won't go anywhere that we are *not* welcome."

Morte added her own two cents to the high queen's invitation. "Although their offer is very noble and selfless, please do keep in mind that they are in need of food and shelter, and without you they will die like your family."

The entire group waited patiently for Oakie's response.

A moment passed before he took a deep breath and began, "What if I let you in to make your nest and you die?"

Vergogna had something to say about that.

"How could we die?" she asked. "We'll burrow into the deepest places of you to build our nest. You'll protect us as much as we'll protect you. After all the destruction that happened here, you are still alive and well. Nothing could destroy you, so we'll always be safe."

Oakie paused to let the thought sink in.

"What if I get tired of you and don't want you around anymore? What if you make yourself at home and get all settled in and I want you to leave?" Oakie had so many fears. He just couldn't be sure he could let someone get close so quickly. Condanna chimed in.

"Oakie, first and foremost, you'll never tire of us or desire for us to leave. I know you can't see that right now, but in time you'll understand the absurdity of the question. But, to settle your heart, I promise you that we would wholeheartedly and graciously move on if you asked. You have my word as royalty. If that doesn't count for something, I don't know what more I can give you."

Oakie surveyed the empty field. For a moment he could see the orchard as it was before the fire. He remembered the days just as he broke through the ground and discovered his new self. He reflected on all the wisdom and love Morgan had shared with him. He could hear Dakota playfully throwing wisecracks his direction. He replayed the soothing lullaby of the insects' chatter that lulled him to sleep every night. Flashes of peoples running wildly and playing tug-of-war with the branches as they picked apples shot through Oakie's mind. It seemed as if just yesterday Joshua had been struggling to climb him for the first time.

Joshua.

Oakie loved the boy so dearly, yet oddly enough, hated him equally as much. If it hadn't been for Joshua, everything would have been fine. Everyone would still be alive. If it hadn't been for Joshua, Oakie wouldn't be alone. Oakie's anger blazed toward Joshua until he came to his senses.

Joshua didn't know better. He was so lovable and caring. He would never purposely hurt anyone. Joshua wasn't the problem—Oakie was. If Oakie had never been born, he would never have been buried in the orchard. He would never have grown so large. Joshua would never have been able to build his fort. The fire would never have started. If Oakie had never been there, everyone would still be alive.

Oakie was to blame.

He had killed his own family, not Joshua.

"Oakie."

Morte startled Oakie from his thoughts.

"Don't just sit there. You're being rude. Do you want to spend the rest of your life alone and lonely?"

"No."

"Well then, receive their wonderful offer, because you won't find a better one. After what happened here, I'm amazed by their courage and bravery. No one else would dare come near you."

It hurt to hear, but Morte was right. Being close to him

was risky and dangerous. He couldn't protect the orchard, but he could protect these termites. He could give them all a home and help them out. He could do for them what he couldn't do for his family.

He could save them.

With the most enthusiasm Oakie had felt in a long time he welcomed his new friends. "Yes, of course!"

The queens cheered together.

Morte smiled for the first time since she had landed in his branches.

"We'll give the command and begin burrowing immediately!" Colpa declared. "For all the trouble you have caused, you have begun redeeming yourself very nicely."

Oakie felt good about getting to help, but something about Colpa's words stung.

28

FOOLS' PARADISE

28

The three queens summoned their workers. Instantly, a tidal wave of termites erupted from the debris where they had been busy gathering and eating. The colony drove forward and surrounded Oakie. Pushing in as closely as possible, the vast sea awaited instruction.

Having ascended midway up Oakie, the three queens peered down on their loyal subjects.

Colpa began the task of inspiring the colony. "Today dawns a new day! No longer will we toil in the fields under the oppression of light. No longer will we go to bed with our bellies empty and hurting. Providence has been faithful and granted us a gift. I stand here before you today with my feet planted on our future. The name of that future is Oakie. Now let's honor Oakie with the affection of our applause."

The colony went wild with yelling and clapping.

Flapping her wings, Morte joined the celebration. The rest of the crows followed suit.

Even under the heavy weight of the murder, Oakie felt more alive than he had since his loss. Anything was better than the ache of the nothingness he had been feeling. A smile slowly crept across his face.

Colpa raised her hand and in an instance there was silence.

"Truly we thank you," Vergogna interjected. "You will make a wonderful host for all of us, and all of the generations to come."

Colpa began again. "I commission the workers of this colony to begin burrowing immediately. Dig to the core of this tree, where the light will never shine. Prepare our quarters so we may be refreshed and begin to replenish this colony with brothers and sisters. Gorge yourself on the fruit of your labor as you do so. Eat heartily. This tree is abundant with food."

The colony went wild with ecstasy.

Colpa raised her hand again to settle the crowd. "Oakie, you are ours and we are yours. Today we make a covenant with you. Today we are one."

"Don't just stand there! You've got your orders. Now get moving," Condanna demanded.

The termites flooded Oakie's trunk. Tearing away the bark, they broke through the tough outer shell with ease. Thousands of them chewed away at Oakie. Devouring everything they could as quickly as they could, they made their way into him. They scratched, tore, and ripped at Oakie's insides.

Fresh, lively trees were much too tough and chewy. Termites rarely had the strength or tenacity to burrow into them. Luckily for the colony, Oakie's recent loss in the fire made things much easier. It was almost as easy as digging into one of the charred trunks lying in the field.

Oakie began to shake. The pain was nearly unbearable.

Morte quickly became irritated with the commotion Oakie was causing. "Oakie! Stop your shaking."

"It hurts so bad. It's horrible!"

"Quit whining and don't be a child. Ignore the pain. A strong tree looks past the pain."

Oakie squirmed some more, wincing as the colony tore his insides to pieces.

"Do you think this is easy for them? Imagine the pain they're going through. Having to build a whole new nest has to be so difficult for those workers. Although they're insignificant in the grand scheme of things, you have to realize that you're not the only one sacrificing. Do you hear them complaining?"

"No. But, I wasn't complaining. I didn't even say a word."

"Your shaking around said more than enough. Besides, you're disturbing my rest. When you have my level of responsibility, then you can complain."

"I'm not complaining, so leave me alone."

"Hold your tongue and mind your manners. Quit being selfish and self-centered."

Oakie glared with fiery anger.

Morte raised her head smugly. "Clearly I'm wasting my breath. I don't care how you feel—just quit disturbing my rest."

With every passing moment, Morte's company felt less and less satisfying. Besides her rude, entitled behavior, Oakie began noticing how badly his branches ached under the weight of the morbidly obese crows.

As the colony continued to hollow out a nest, the three sisters took time to become better acquainted with Oakie. "The peasants will be busy for a little while before our home is prepared and ready for us to settle in. Please indulge us with the story of what happened here," Colpa asked.

Hesitantly, Oakie shared the tale.

When he finished, Colpa asked to hear it again.

And so Oakie shared it once more.

Colpa seemed intrigued and so caring. Nothing else mattered. She cared only to hear Oakie's story again and again. Each time it seemed so fresh, as though Oakie was telling it for the first time. Although it was extremely painful for him to relive, Colpa's care for his story somehow felt comforting.

As Oakie continued to repeat the tale over and over again, Vergogna grew frustrated and overwhelmed. "I can't believe what happened. If I caused the demise of this colony, I don't know what I would do. I certainly could not show my face ever again. I would dig a hole into the center of the earth and hope to never be found."

Oakie dropped his eyes in shame.

She continued, "I simply could not feel good about myself."

Condanna broke in. "I would certainly hope that Providence would give me the proper punishment that I deserved. I couldn't imagine getting away with such an atrocity. I would do everything in my power to pay back such a weighty debt.

"Easy now, girls," Colpa began. "Oakie's been through a lot."

Oakie smiled at Colpa's validation and protection.

"We'll have plenty of time to help Oakie grieve, but let's

take it in strides."

The girls respected Colpa's wishes.

"Now Oakie, as you were sharing your story, I had quite the bright idea. Would you like me to share it with you?"

"Yes, please."

"Good. What would you say about sharing your story with the entire colony? I know how bad you feel and how heavy a burden it is that you carry, so I thought it might be a bit therapeutic to confess all the horrible things that happened to the orchard because of you. If you will give yourself the opportunity to bleed it all out, I think it might be helpful."

Oakie looked hesitant.

"You seemed comforted each time you shared your story with us, so I thought it might help. I'm just keeping your best interest in mind. That's all."

"I think so." Oakie nodded. "I think you're right. I should share it. I know I felt much more than I've felt in quite some time when I shared with the three of you."

"Wonderful!" Condanna shouted.

"Even Condanna is excited. You don't know her well, but she rarely becomes excited. This will be wonderful for both you and the colony," Colpa reassured him.

"When should I share the story?"

Vergogna jumped in. "I believe he should share when they're halfway through the completion of the nest."

"And why's that?" asked Colpa.

"The story of Oakie's loss will strengthen them, and give them a sense of purpose. It will help the colony understand the cause better. They'll be able to see how much greater than them this project is. This is truly about helping out Oakie. How could they listen to his story and not feel the need to burrow faster and deeper? A better understanding of Oakie will help them to get acquainted with him. Their compassion for him will drive their hearts to be closer. The only way for the colony to really love Oakie well is to become one with him, and his story is the way to do this."

"Vergogna, you're brilliant. I have completely overlooked the kindness and compassion of the colony. His story will certainly fuel them to do things they couldn't without it," Colpa said.

Oakie had no idea his story could inspire so many. He could help the colony help him. What an amazing thought!

It was settled, and so the days passed. Oakie waited impatiently for the opportunity to tell everyone about the horrible things that had happened because of him. As the termites continued to dig away, he had to learn how to block out the pain. The digging was excruciating at first, but the sisters gave Oakie their best counsel, which helped greatly. With every day that passed, they chiseled out more and Oakie was able to feel less.

The day finally came for Oakie to share his story. It was magnificent. The sisters had him repeat it again and again to the colony.

With every telling, the colony seemed to actually grow bigger, much like Oakie grew during the terrible storm. They were large and hungry and ready to burrow again. And so they did. The colony dug with a strength and tenacity it had never known. The termites dug ravenously, without relenting. They looked almost crazy, with green sticky saliva dripping from their teeth. With each bite, the saliva soaked deep into Oakie's wood.

Strangely, it seemed as though there was some sort of healing in it. Everything went numb. There was no more pain! Whatever was happening *had* to be good. The pain was going away, and Oakie wasn't alone. Even the taxing ache from the weight of the murder seemed to lessen until it was almost unnoticeable. What an amazing gift these termites had become.

Because Oakie was so grand in size he was the perfect place to build the most ambitious and dignified nest ever imagined. As the workers journeyed into his depths, the three sisters shared with each other their most elaborate and creative ideas. After agreeing on the best ones, they sent the plans with a word to the workers to build without regard for time or energy. They were determined that this nest would be talked about for ages to come. They were determined to create history.

And so it was. After much toiling, great dedication, and loss of workers' lives, the nest was finished. History was made. It was a day for celebration. It was a day for rejoicing. It was a day of victory. A great portion of Oakie had been hollowed out to create the most luxurious, majestic, regal nest a termite had ever seen. It was better than even the queens had dreamed. Their new kingdom seemed vast and neverending. This city could withstand a thousand termite lifetimes. Their home would be a sign to all who would visit that Providence was with them.

As the colony celebrated, Colpa took a moment to visit with Oakie. "Oakie, do you hear that? Do you hear their shouts of joy? Do you hear their laughter? This is about you."

Oakie smiled.

"This is all about you. This is because of you. You gave us a home when we had none. Without you we would cease to exist. We would have been burnt alive by the sun. Without you, the light would have destroyed us. Do you understand that?"

Oakie's smile grew.

"Thank you, Oakie. Thank you for protecting us. Even if you couldn't do it for your family, you've done it for us. I believe that in Providence's eyes, you have atoned for your failure."

"You're welcome, Colpa. But I owe you thanks. If it wasn't for you I'd be alone. You saw me when I had nothing and you gave me something. You gave me care, affection and attention. You gave me friendship and a new family. There's a new life thriving inside of me and it's you. All of you have made everything so much better. Thank you, Colpa. It is an honor to know you."

"Well I do suppose you're right about that. You are rather blessed."

The two sat, briefly soaking in the moment.

Colpa broke the silence. "It's time that I took off. I have a whole colony that awaits my presence and I must attend to them."

"Goodnight, Colpa."

"Goodnight, Oakie."

As Oakie watched Colpa return to the celebration inside, he reflected on Morgan. Sure Colpa wasn't Morgan, but at least she was someone who cared about him—and surely that was worth something.

CHAPTER

29

UNWELCOMED GUESTS

29

"Oakie!" Morte barked.

"What?" Oakie snapped. Something about Morte irritated Oakie. It had since the beginning. Even at her most pleasant, she was far from warm and welcoming. He wasn't quite sure what she was doing there. The murder was a rowdy bunch. Their humor was very sarcastic and their jokes about each other were rather mean. Every day, there seemed to be less reason to have them around.

"You're being a bit feisty. Maybe you should mind your manners."

"Sorry." Oakie reeled in his irritation.

"Anyways, I had a compliment for you, but I'm a bit hesitant to give it now."

Oakie softened. "I'm really sorry."

"All right, then. I will take you at your word. What I was going to say is that since the colony has moved in, you've been much more bearable to be around."

Oakie frowned.

"In fact, you're much less of a bore."

"That's not a compliment."

"Sure it is. It's just not the way you want it packaged."

"You know what? I don't think I like having you around."

"Yes, you do."

"No, I don't. You're arrogant, snotty, and you talk down to me like I'm less than you. I don't feel good even when you're giving me compliments."

The murder started turning its attention toward Oakie and Morte. No one had ever addressed her in such a manner.

"Well, I can see I'm wasting my time trying to encourage you."

Oakie began to get louder. "That's not encouragement. Furthermore, all my branches have either snapped or are breaking. All of you have gotten so fat you can barely fly. In fact, some of you can't!"

A crow sitting on the ground by Oakie's roots hung his head in shame.

"I don't appreciate your tone."

"I don't appreciate *you!*"

"That's uncalled-for, and I won't be talked to that way. Might I remind you that if it weren't for me, you wouldn't have your precious termites to keep you company. If it weren't for me, you'd be nothing. If it weren't for me, you'd be all alone, just staring at the charred remains of your family."

"You're horrible and I hate you. There's nothing good about you!" Oakie shouted.

"You will not behave like this anymore. When you can be civilized, we'll talk."

"No, I'll talk and you'll listen. I don't want you or your plump little piggies around me anymore." Oakie had the murder's full attention now.

"If you didn't want us around, you would have asked us to leave a long time ago. The fact of the matter is, you need us. You need us to keep you in check. We're here to clean up your mess, and you should be appreciative."

"You listen here—"

"But instead you're smug and abrasive. You talk to me with lack of appreciation and honor."

"I hate you and I want you to leave! Now leave!" Oakie screamed at the top of his lungs."

A handful of crows lost their balance and plummeted to the ground.

"Don't you dare scream at me, you foolish, insignificant tree!" Morte shouted back.

The entire murder became extremely uncomfortable and fearful. They had never seen Morte like this; there was no telling what she might do.

"Leave me! Get out of here!" Oakie began to shake his branches, but they had become so brittle and weak that rather than shaking the crows off, they simply broke and fell to the ground.

"Stop this now! I demand that you stop!"

"You can't tell me what to do!"

Crows lay scattered, rolling across the ground. Most had become so large they could barely stand.

Off in the horizon, a billowing white cloud rapidly approached.

"I *can* tell you what to do, and I will!"

"Well, I don't have to listen, and I *won't*!"

"I will make you pay for this. You will not be forgiven. You had your chance you weak, insignificant—"

"Shut up! Just shut up. I have had enough!" Oakie shouted furiously.

The cloud grew larger as it approached. In fact, as it drew nearer, it became clear that it wasn't a cloud at all.

The crows began cawing loudly. Terror overcame the murder. Morte and Oakie stopped fighting and fell silent.

A parliament of white eagle-owls, staggering in number, stormed their direction.

Morte's eyes widened. Like a band of brothers in war, the parliament flew fearlessly, as a mighty force.

"It can't be!" Morte's mouth fell wide open.

"What is it?"

"Verstand ... Today you will die," Morte scowled.

Oakie stood in shock as Morte took flight from the crevice where she had sat for so long. Bolting as fast as she could, she jetted away from the parliament.

Behind her, the murder fell from Oakie and began running as fast as their legs would carry them.

As the parliament descended on the murder, Verstand broke away to chase fiercely after Morte.

The crows that could still fly leapt from the branches in which they sat, hoping to escape. One by one, members of the parliament swooped down below Oakie and plucked the plump crows from the ground as if they were rotten fruit hanging from a tree. They took them away to feed on them. The crows that still had the luxury of flight didn't have the luxury of speed. They had fed so long on the dead that they couldn't escape their own fate.

As the parliament continued its assault on the murder, Verstand gained on Morte. Although the sacrifices presented to Morte from the murder were great, she had eaten little, preferring the taste of her own power as they worshipped her splendor and greatness. Because of this, she remained thin and light. There was nothing weighing her down. She was faster now than she had been in her youth. Jetting through a field, she could see a swamp at the edge. It would be the perfect place to make her stand—all she had to do was out-fly Verstand.

"Give up, Morte. The parliament is making dinner out of your murder. Before this is over, I will make dinner out of you as well."

"Verstand, when I carry your head back to the parliament, they will fear me. They will bow before me. They will worship and adore me. They will lavish me with the proper respect and honor one deserves for defeating a queen such as yourself."

"Even if a tragic miracle such as that were possible, not one of them would stop until they either destroyed you or saw their own demise."

"Even the greatest of kings will grovel and beg for mercy when facing the sharp side of a sword."

"Then you've not met a truly great king."

They were quickly approaching the swamp. Only a moment more, Morte thought, and Verstand would be hers. "Tell me this, Verstand—do you have any regrets?"

"Only one."

"And what is that?"

"That I haven't killed you before now."

"What a large regret you will take to your grave. But even larger will be knowing you didn't kill me at all."

"When I die, it will be regret-free."

"When you die, it shall be as a fool."

Morte exploded through the trees that stood like a gateway to the damp, dark swamp. Without hesitation Verstand followed, tracking closely behind. Though Morte had not visited this swamp before, it was rather easy to navigate. Swamps were a home away from home—she found their dark, damp aura rather inviting.

It wasn't easy to keep up with Morte as she wove her way through branches and thick foliage, but Verstand enjoyed a good challenge. Diving toward the marshy water below, Morte skimmed across the top of the pond. Seeing an excellent opportunity, she tapped the back of the swamp's natural booby trap. A crocodile burst out of the water. Verstand whipped straight up in the air, just ahead of the mouthful of razor-like teeth. The croc's mouth came snapping down, but grabbed nothing more than a feather from Verstand's backside.

Morte smiled sinisterly. Dodging behind a tree, she positioned herself like a cat waiting to pounce on an unsuspecting mouse.

Verstand scanned the area as she climbed above the swamp to regain her composure. Then, like a bomb dropped from a fighter jet, she aimed herself downwards, wings tucked tight to her body, rocketing toward the earth. As she broke back into the swamp, she could see the croc settling back into the water as she returned to her path. In front of her was a trail of crow feathers that Morte had purposely left behind.

While Verstand swooped through a cluster of vines, Morte made her move and leaped from behind a tree onto Verstand's back. Grasping tightly with her claws, Morte began to peck viciously at Verstand's neck. Verstand lost composure and barreled, out of control, toward a tree.

"It ends now, you pompous do-gooder!" Morte shouted.

Verstand retorted, "I haven't battled your tyranny my entire life to die here and now."

Extending her wings, Verstand spun her back toward the tree, cushioning the blow with Morte's body. The two fell to the ground.

Verstand leaped to her feet.

Morte lunged for Verstand's throat.

Ravenously, the two tore at each other while rolling around on the ground.

Morte snapped at Verstand's ear, clipping it off.

Verstand caught sight of something just quickly enough to turn the tide in her favor. She threw Morte backwards, then stood tall and proud with her wings spread wide, waiting as Morte quickly regained balance and shot back. Timing was everything. As Morte got close, Verstand tucked in her wings, rolled backwards and grabbed Morte with her talons. Using the crow's momentum against her, she threw her backward.

Morte landed abruptly. Disoriented, she shook it off, stood up, and addressed Verstand.

"Though your efforts were valiant, they were trite in comparison to what I'm about to do to you. You have no hope of winning this. Submit and taste my wrath."

"Submit and taste *his* wrath." Verstand pointed at the crocodile: Morte was sitting in its mouth.

"Caaaaaaaaw!!!!" Morte's shriek echoed throughout the swamp, scaring the creatures hidden within the deepest parts.

All that remained of her were a few feathers that slowly floated to the ground, and a very satisfied crocodile who smiled widely as he returned to his resting place.

While Verstand was hunting down Morte, the parliament waged war on the murder. One by one, the crows fell to the power of the owls' talons. Putting all their trust in Morte without thought or question and overly indulging on the dead that surrounded them had left the murder powerless to withstand the parliament. The owls celebrated as they feasted on their fallen foes.

And might I add that they celebrated with good reason. You see, generation upon generation of eagle-owls had fought long and hard to free the earth from the oppression of the crows. Some would argue that the crows did the earth a favor, washing the world clean of its dead. As noble as that sounded, the truth had been wrapped up tightly in lies: The crows carried great diseases, plagues that would wipe out not only animals, but also entire villages and sometimes even cities of peoples. The crows created more death than sometimes even they could clean up. They were more harmful than they were helpful.

The story behind the feud, as I understand it, is that before the war between the crows and eagle-owls that began so long ago, a noble eagle-owl queen named Verita pleaded with a dark crow king named Inganno. She begged him to take an honest look at the destruction his kingdom was bringing upon the earth.

The king was very selfish and ambitious. His dream was to become the most powerful king any kingdom had ever known. He told the world that the endeavor he and his noble followers were embarking upon was a gift that would better everyone, so many believed in and came to embrace his dream. They praised and honored his murder for all it did. With open arms, kings received Inganno into their forests and gave him and his murder free rein to do as they saw fit.

At first, the kingdoms celebrated the murder as heroes, but soon their anthem changed. The murder brought disease and wiped entire kingdoms out with death. They feasted and became fat. When the food was no more and all they had stored was gone, they moved on, leaving once vast and thriving kingdoms barren and lifeless.

Inganno was drunk with power. Verita reasoned that if the king would not put an end to his madness there would be no kingdoms left to feast upon. All would be dead with the exception of the murder itself. With only Inganno's kingdom left, soon even they would cease to exist as starvation stole their lives.

Inganno refused to listen. His lust for power was greater than the harsh reality of Verita's foresight. He banished the queen from his presence and organized a plan to kill her.

But Verita was no fool. As a queen of wisdom, she had already planned an attack on Ingonna in the event that he would not listen. And so it was, before the king could assassinate the queen, Verita launched her attack and the war began. Verita and her parliament slayed Ingonna, as well as a great portion of his murder. Unfortunately, Ingonna II, the king's son, escaped death and planned retaliation. Generation after generation continued to battle. Uncountable lives were lost, including that of kings and queens.

Though the price had been immense, the mighty eagle-owls continued to stand for the greater good of the earth.

Upon returning from her battle with Morte, Verstand—the great-great-great descendent of Verita—met with Oakie.

Perched in the crevice where Morte once sat, she shared this story with Oakie in great depth and detail. As he listened, sadness overcame his heart when he realized how greatly Morte had deceived him. Morte was no different from her ancestor, King Inganno. They were the same.

Oakie shared his loss with Verstand and told her all that had happened. Verstand listened intently. Together, they grieved the passing of the orchard.

"Oakie, precious Oakie. I am so sorry. I can't imagine witnessing all that you saw. I want you to know it wasn't your fault," Verstand said softly.

"But if I wasn't here-"

"But nothing. Joshua started that fire, not you."

"But if he didn't have a place to build his fort-"

"If he didn't have a place to build his fort, the orchard would have missed out on the beautiful gift that Joshua was. You said it yourself, Oakie. He was full of wonderful creativity. He brought your heart joy. Every day, you longed for him to come play. His imaginative adventures made everyone laugh. He entertained all of you. He was the highlight of your day, as well as the others. No one grew tired of him. The whole orchard seemed disappointed when a peoples came that wasn't him. Right?"

"Yeah, I guess."

"What do you mean, 'Yeah, I guess'? You said everyone was livelier. You said everyone perked up when they heard someone coming. They were anticipating his arrival at all times. Something about Joshua changed the orchard for the better. Something about him made the normal so abnormal. Right?"

"Sure."

"He may have made a grave mistake in starting that fire. It may have cost you the lives of your family, but who he was to you and all the others brought life so abundantly that it was all worth it. To live a life of security without joy, peace, and love is not living a life at all. That orchard *truly* lived while Joshua was here. If they were alive now and had a choice to live again with Joshua, knowing the possibility that they might also die by the mistake of his hands, I believe they would risk it. I believe what he brought was much greater than what was lost. Their day of passing would have eventually come. What better way to die than feeling fully alive?"

Tears streamed down Oakie's face. "He was like the princess, the king *and* the castle," Oakie muttered the revelation to himself. "I just miss them so much."

"I know, sweetie. It was a beautiful orchard. But, as long as I have been around I have learned something. There will be loss—but if you believe in hope despite the loss, beauty will spring forth from the ashes. That ground below me is more fertile than it has ever been. The lives of your family were not lost in vain. Their bodies have replenished the earth. Given time, something will be planted in their places. Whatever is planted will grow wildly. Just as Morgan was the first of many, so too will you be the first of many. A day will come when you reflect on my words here today and you will smile as you see the grand picture before you."

There was power in her words. They dug down to the core of Oakie's being. He could feel something changing inside him. The numbness in his remaining branches began to lift. He could feel the pain again. Oddly enough, as quickly as the pain became noticeable, it began to alleviate. Cracks in the branches began to weld themselves together again. Branches that had broken were slowly growing back. New stems began sprouting outward and forming leaves.

"Everything is changing for you, Oakie. You're going to be greater than you ever imagined. This isn't the time for you to die. This is the time for you to thrive. I love you and I believe in you. I want to stay longer, but I must depart. The parliament has fed and rested long enough. There are many more murders that seek to bring death and destruction, and it is our job to put a stop to them."

"Thank you for everything, Verstand. I couldn't ask for a better friend."

"You're very welcome, Oakie. Remember, there is no better way to die than by being fully alive."

With that, Verstand smiled and leapt from the crevice where she sat. Swooping high in the air, the parliament took notice and followed suit. A breathtaking blanket of white lifted from the ground all at once, filling the sky and casting its shadow on the ground as a reminder to the earth that it was protected from above.

THE RETURN OF
AN UNLIKELY HERO

30

Verstand's tenderness, kindness, understanding, and love brought an immediate transformation. However, with that also came an angry uprising. From the depths of Oakie's belly, the three queens stormed to the surface. With rage in their eyes, they marched out in great distress.

"What is the meaning of this?" shouted Colpa.

"What is the meaning of what?" replied a very confused Oakie.

"What do you mean, 'what'? Our magnificent nest that we toiled so painstakingly to build is closing up."

"Yes, it suddenly started shaking and shrinking," Condanna barked. "The walls started closing in all around us. A great portion of our workers' quarters was lost, along with the workers. Who's to blame for this?"

"Whatever the cause there will be a price to pay for this!" shouted Vergogna.

"Quiet yourselves and let me talk," ordered Colpa. "Now you listen here, Oakie. I don't know what you are doing, but whatever it is, it had better stop immediately. I will not stand for this! Do you hear me?"

Oakie was less than pleased with the queens' behavior. He had no idea what was happening, but their manner of addressing him was not okay. "Hold on, all of you. I don't know what you're talking about, but I'm sure there's an explanation."

"I'm sure there is ... now, where is Queen Morte? I don't care to waste my time talking with you. I want to talk with her." Colpa dismissed Oakie altogether.

"She's dead, and so is her lousy murder."

The queens gasped with disbelief.

"Bite your tongue! I don't need to listen to your filthy lies. Now, where is the mighty queen?" Colpa reprimanded Oakie.

"I told you, she's dead."

"Lie to me again and you will pay dearly," Colpa threatened.

"It's no lie. Verstand and her parliament freed me from the weight of their oppression. I will never again have to listen to her or the mindless chatter of her foul murder."

"Verstand!" the three blurted in unison.

"So the stories of that wicked owl are true. I loathe her for what she's done to our dear friend." Colpa shook her head.

"She's not wicked. She saved me from that horrible crow you called a queen."

"This is all because of that worthless owl. What did she say to you? What destructive things did she plant in your mind?" Vergogna sneered.

"She didn't plant anything destructive in my mind. She told me the truth about Morte and the crows."

"You listen here. You forget everything she told you, you wretched insignificant tree!" Condanna demanded.

"I don't like you. I don't like any of you. I want you to leave me alone. In fact I want you to leave me altogether. You're no different than Morte."

"Oh, *we're* not going anywhere, you ungrateful peasant!" Colpa's anger grew stronger. "Might I remind you that you are the reason for the death of this orchard. You need us. We *don't* need you."

"Their deaths were not my fault."

"You disgust me. You've actually fooled yourself into believing that this orchard's blood is not on your branches. You can't just wash your sins away so easily. You're a murderer, and don't forget it!" Vergogna was determined to break Oakie's spirit.

Oakie wouldn't have it. "Oh, no I'm not. Joshua started that fire, not me. Besides, it was an accident," Oakie said in rebuttal.

"If we weren't here, I would suggest that you burn yourself down, so that no one would ever be hurt by you again." Condanna was sharp with her words.

"I don't need any of you. You need me. In fact, without

me you'll burn alive in the light. All of you will die, and you know it."

"I've had enough of this." Colpa stamped her foot. "We're heading back to our nest immediately to give the orders to begin burrowing. By this time tomorrow the nest will have doubled in size. Our workers will not relent. By the time we are finished, you will be nothing more than a giant shell for us to thrive in. Hopefully you'll be dead altogether by the end of the week so we don't have to waste our time talking with you ever again."

"You will not! I told you I want you to leave. You told me that if I no longer wanted you around that you would-"

"We will do nothing of the sort. You are our home and that is final. Your days are finished, you whiney little tree. There's not a thing you can do about it." Colpa took her stand.

"Oh, yes I can. I told you to leave. Now, pack up your entire colony and be gone!"

"Ladies, I'm done wasting my breath on this childish fool. It's time to return and rebuild." Colpa turned from Oakie and began to march toward the nest. Vergogna and Condanna followed quickly behind.

"You will leave. All of you will leave. I told you I don't want you here anymore!"

The three queens ignored Oakie's orders and went back inside to start the digging.

"Get out of me!" Oakie shouted at the top of his lungs. Almost immediately, an excruciating pain overcame him. His insides were being torn to pieces. The pain was greater than ever before. Every bite and every tear was intensified. There was no going numb—not this time. Oakie could feel the battle within and he couldn't escape the pain. The termites would not leave easily. Luckily for Oakie, Providence was truly on his side.

In the distance, something that sounded like rolling thunder approached. An ocean of red washed over the landscape like a tidal wave. Soon, a chant filled the air as the wave drew nearer.

"All for one and one for all.
If we stand together none will fall.

We stand for the weak and make them strong.
If we stand for each other we will live long.
All that matters is all we see.
All that matters is you and me."

Cheers and laughter followed the chant before it began again. Whatever was coming seemed vast and neverending.

Oakie squinted his eyes tightly, trying to make out the faces behind the voices. Ants ... millions of ants spread out all across the landscape! This didn't make any sense. The only ants Oakie had ever seen marched in one perfectly straight line. What was happening? As the sea of ants neared, a long-forgotten face surfed ahead of the wave.

Running toward Oakie, waving his hands in the air, The Duke shouted loudly. "Bro! Bro, over here!"

"The Duke," Oakie whispered to himself in relief.

"Bro," The Duke stopped at Oakie's base. Huffing and puffing, he continued, "Bro, where's the orchard? I swear there was an orchard here, bro. There was a little green dude somewhere near here too. If they're all on vaycay, this is gonna be a major disso."

"Disso?" Oakie didn't quite understand.

The Duke rolled his eyes. "Disappointment, boss. Where's the little greenie?"

Oakie chuckled. "*I'm* the little greenie."

"Seriously, bro? The Duke has seen the little greenie dude, and you are not him."

Behind The Duke, the wave settled and began to build forts to camp in for the night.

"Well I was him. I mean, I still am him, but not little and not green anymore."

The Duke paused reluctantly for a moment. "*Viva la* what, bro?" The Duke waited for an answer.

"What?"

"I said *viva la* what, bro? If you are the little greenie dude, then you should know, '*viva la* what'? Answer me, dude, or this convo is D.U.N."

"*Viva la* ... *revolución?*"

"Little Greenie! Dude!" The Duke grasped his head between his hands and shook it wildly. "The Duke's brain is bleeding from overload. What happened? Did you eat the whole orchard or something?"

"No, no, not at all." Oakie chuckled heartily.

"Are you in The Duke's mind? This is a trip. You're in my dreams, aren't you?"

"This isn't a dream, Duke."

The Duke picked up a rock. "The Duke's gonna hit himself in the head. When The Duke wakes up, if you're still here, it means this isn't a dream and the Duke wasn't sleeping."

Before Oakie could say anything to stop him, The Duke slammed the rock into the side of his head. Spinning around in circles, he teetered to the left, then to the right, and then fell flat on his face.

After seeing The Duke smash himself in the head, an ant came marching Oakie's direction.

"He thought he was dreaming," Oakie said.

With little surprise on his face, the ant responded, "I know. He does this. All the great inspirers have their quirks. I call it being eccentric. This is just *one* of his quirks. I'm Lieutenant Dan, by the way."

" 'Eccentric' is a good word for it. I'm Oakie."

"Are you the reason for the *revolución*?"

"What *revolución*?"

"The one you see before you. The Duke said a great and most wise little greenie dude—his words not mine—sparked the candle that lit a blaze in his soul. That blaze freed us all from vast, neverending lines of marching mindlessly nowhere."

"Well, I hate to brag."

"Then don't. Are you or aren't you him?"

"Yes, I am."

Lieutenant Dan knelt and bowed his head before Oakie. "It's an honor to meet you, sir. I, and millions of others, owe you our deepest gratitude. Your wisdom and inspiration purchased freedom for our generation, and many generations to come. We owe you our lives."

Oakie's heart burned with life and passion. He never could have imagined that such a simple, random moment so long ago would alter the course of history for so many.

The words of Lieutenant Dan echoed throughout Oakie with the same power that Verstand's had. The thought that his life seemed to have little significance seemed foolish when he gazed at the mighty army camping before him.

Transformation started once again. Immediately, leaves began to bud and branches strengthened. His insides tightened. It would only be a matter of time before the termite queens returned for Round Two.

"Lieutenant Dan."

The Lieutenant raised his head.

"Do you think Duke is dead?"

The Lieutenant laughed. "No disrespect, sir, but you must be joking me. The Duke has a head harder than a rock! I'm surprised it wasn't the rock that passed out. He's done this plenty of times before. The only effects he's going to suffer, besides a mild concussion and a headache, are more of his blackouts."

"Blackouts?"

"Yeah, he'll be talking and, mid-sentence, boom!" Lieutenant Dan stared blankly for a moment, then continued, "He isn't 'there' any longer. He passes it off like it's war trauma, but I know better. You take enough hits to the head, and you're bound to knock something loose. His episodes can last days at a time, so that's why I stick by his side. I have a strong back, so I carry him until he wakes up."

"Speaking of waking up, I think he's moving."

The Duke began to struggle to his knees.

Lieutenant Dan rushed over to help him up. The world was still spinning, so it took The Duke a moment to adjust. Wincing from the pain, he stared at Oakie for a moment.

"You!" The Duke addressed Oakie. "Bro, The Duke had a dream that he was dreaming that you were a dream. He hit himself in the head to wake up from the dream, but when The Duke woke up, you were still here. Now either you're not a dream, dude, or The Duke needs to hit himself in the head again and wake up."

"The Duke doesn't need to do that, sir." Lieutenant Dan grabbed The Duke's hand as he was about to hit himself in the head again, stopping him just in time. "As your lieutenant and dear friend, I can most assuredly promise you that this is in fact the 'little greenie dude' that you referred to. And in no way is this a dream, sir."

"Little greenie dude ..." The Duke sat in awe. "You're not little or greenie anymore. You're like BIG and brown. You're big brownie dude now. Riiight on!" The Duke slapped Lieutenant Dan on the shoulder, causing Dan to lose his balance. "Do you see this, bro?"

"Oakie's fine," Oakie said to correct him. He didn't care much for "little greenie dude" and he cared even less for "big brownie dude."

"Right on." The Duke nodded his head. "I'm glad your friend is doing well. How are you, bro?"

Lieutenant Dan rolled his eyes, shrugged his shoulders and smiled.

"I'm getting better. It's great to see you, Duke!"

The Duke turned and looked at the army behind him. "We did it. You and me—we did it. Our vision's complete. The *revolución*. Not *one* line. No more mindless chants. No more *the man*. It's just me, you, and a few million ants livin' life, bro."

"What about Commander Brick?" Oakie inquired.

Just then an ant came sailing through the air, swinging on spider webbing. He hung from Oakie's branch and pounded his chest like a monkey. "*Viva la revolución!*" the ant yelled at the top of his lungs. Letting go, he did a triple back flip and landed in a pile of ants that was waiting with open arms to catch him.

"His back flips are getting better every day."

The three had a good laugh. "So bro, what happened to the orchard?"

Oakie shared his story in great detail.

The ants were very moved by the loss. "Sir, my condolences to you and your family," Lieutenant Dan said with sympathy.

"The Duke is sad for you too, big brownie dude."

"Thank you both. Things really are getting much better, especially now that the crows are gone. Now, if I can only get rid of Colpa, Vergogna, Condanna, and their colony, I would be really good."

The Duke and Lieutenant Dan looked at one another as if to question if they had heard Oakie correctly. "Are you referring to THE three termite queens Colpa, Vergogna, and Condanna, sir?" Lieutenant Dan asked.

"Yes, do you know them? They're not very friendly at all. They seemed so at-"

"Bro," The Duke cut Oakie off. "You mean the three wicked stepsisters? The treacherous termite terrors?"

"Yeah, I guess." Oakie seemed puzzled.

"Dude, bro, our mission since we rallied together and got liberation has been to hunt them down."

"Why?"

"*Why?*" The Duke clenched his head tightly between his hands and began to shake it.

Lieutenant Dan kicked a nearby rock away as a precaution. Oakie braced himself.

"Because, bro, they're for sure pure evil. Before the *revolución* and before the mindless marching, there was only ... them. They're crafty and manipulative. They're sly and cunning. They're sweet on the outside and strictly sour on the inside. They started out telling us they were our friends. We broke breadcrumbs with them. The Ant Nation welcomed them with open arms. We believed they would be the answer to our problems. They came with a message of change. And change they brought, bro. They invaded the mighty ant kingdom Antropolis, a kingdom that had thrived for ages. They made slaves out of ants. They made slaves out of all us. They made all of antkind do the work not even the lowest of termites would do. They worked us without food; they punished us harshly when we had no strength to do the grueling tasks they demanded of us. They slaughtered many—all in the name of greatness. They went so far as to use our kind as footstools just to humiliate us and break our spirits."

Oakie's eyes grew wide with horror. As The Duke spoke his heart sank.

"They oppressed our people nearly to the point of extinction."

"I didn't know. I'm so sorry."

"An ant by the name of Esperanza, who had been born into slavery, rose up with a message in her heart."

The very mention of Esperanza caused Lieutenant Dan to lift his head in respect and honor.

"Esperanza thought in a rebellious way that contradicted everything the queens stood for and believed in. Secretly, she began to spread her message and awakened the hearts of her people. At first, it was long and hard. The Ant Nation had been so brainwashed by the termites," The Duke swirled his hands around his head, "that unwashing them was the biggest mountain to conquer. With time and patience, she rallied enough ants together to devise a most gnarly plan to overthrow the queens' rule. It wouldn't be easy, not just because they were weak with hunger, but the fear the queens had beaten into them was deep."

Oakie listened intently, hanging on every word.

Even Lieutenant Dan, who knew the story by heart, waited in anticipation to hear the outcome.

"She finally convinced her compadres that fear was the only thing standing between them and victory. One night, all ninja-like, while the colony slept, Esperanza and a small group of her freedom bandits snuck through the shadows, rolling, dodging, climbing, and crawling past fierce security. Locked away deep in the heart of Antropolis was *Amore*. Amore was an ancient fire given to our kind by Providence. Hand-delivered by lighting long ago, the Ant Nation fed the fire day and night in order to keep it thriving, protecting it at all times so that it would never go out. Amore was the most powerful *discovery* the Ant Nation had ever *discovered*. With it, we could protect ourselves from the dark, treacherous, carnivorous, ant-eating ghoul that sought to feast on our flesh."

The Duke startled Lieutenant Dan, snapping at him with his large teeth. Then he proceeded to storm around in circles with his hands lifted high and pretended to attack Lieutenant Dan just as the ghoul would have.

Lieutenant Dan backed away, slightly annoyed.

"The ant-eating ghoul is actually real?" Baffled, Oakie looked at Lieutenant Dan.

"Yes, sir. It is very real, sir. In fact it's too real in my opinion, sir."

"You doubted The Duke?" The Duke looked a little hurt. "Tsk, tsk, bro. Tsk, tsk."

"Well what happened?" Oakie urged, dying to know the outcome.

"Keep your leaves on, bro. I'm getting there. While the bandits distracted the guards that kept watch over the sacred fire, Esperanza slipped in and seized Amore. Dashing as quickly as possible through the maze of guards, Esperanza raced to the royal nest where the termite queens took refuge. Esperanza set the nest ablaze. Amore rapidly consumed everything it touched and drove the queens and all who lived there out. As the termites fled in confusion and fear, the freedom bandits slayed their oppressors."

Jumping into the air, The Duke came pouncing down on Lieutenant Dan with his arm stretched out as though it was a mighty sword.

Lieutenant Dan dueled back and forth with The Duke. Racing to the top of a rock, The Duke leapt through the air and conked Dan on the head, sending him to the ground and ending the play battle.

Lieutenant Dan stumbled to his feet as The Duke continued.

"Lurking in the shadows, Esperanza stood silently watching for the queens. Soon the nest had all but crumbled to ash. A victorious cry rose from the field as the ants watched the termites run away, shaking in their booties. Esperanza stood mesmerized by the sight. A voice whispered from behind her, 'You may have your colony's freedom, but today I have your life.' And with that, Queen Colpa drove a spear through the heart of Esperanza. That day Esperanza lost her life, but in it, an entire colony gained theirs."

Lieutenant Dan hung his head in mourning.

Oakie got a little teary-eyed.

The three paused for a moment of silence.

"Though she's dead, she's not gone. She lives on in all the hearts of this Ant Nation. Next to you, she was my greatest inspiration."

Oakie smiled, feeling a little inadequate to be compared to this heroine.

"She reminded me that we were made for so much more, and though we may have momentarily lost ourselves since her passing, I think we're back on track."

"That's an unbelievable story, Duke."

"Well believe it, compadre, cause it's for real. And that's why we're on this mission."

"Revenge?"

"No, big brownie dude, far from it."

Becoming a little irritated with "big brownie dude" Oakie corrected The Duke, "Oakie."

The Duke looked around trying to figure out where this "Oakie" was that the big brownie dude was talking to. Not seeing anyone, The Duke shrugged it off and continued, "I figured if the queens did it once, they'd do it all over again to someone else, bro. If we don't hunt them down and destroy them, they could do a lot more damage to the innocent and weak. Given enough time it could be the Ant Nation all over again. This *revolución* isn't just for us—it was meant for everyone!"

"Pardon me, Duke, if you don't mind my interjecting," Lieutenant Dan chimed in.

"Interject away, Senor Dan."

"Oakie," Dan began as The Duke looked around yet again, completely baffled about this "Oakie" fellow. "Sir, back to the beginning of all this. You made mention of the three queens and their colony, but I haven't seen one termite yet. Have they left?"

"No ..." Oakie was a bit hesitant to answer, remembering how Esperanza dealt with the queens in the story.

"Where exactly is their nest, might I ask?"

"You might."

Dan and The Duke waited for a response. When they got none, The Duke jumped in.

"Okay, so where's their nest then, bro?"

"Inside of me."

The ants sat in shock.

CHAPTER

31

THE POWER OF AMORE

31

"BRO! What do you mean they're *inside* of you?" The Duke paced in circles, looking for a rock. Lieutenant Dan kicked every rock he could see out of sight while The Duke continued pacing.

"Well they're inside of me. It's a long story—"

"We don't have time for a long story! We gotta figure out a plan, bro." The Duke began hitting himself on his forehead with his open palm. "Think ... think ... think!"

"Sir, please be careful not to knock yourself out," Lieutenant Dan pleaded.

"Now's not the time to worry about me. If we don't-" Lieutenant Dan's worry came true as The Duke blacked out.

"He didn't just-" Oakie began.

"Oh he did, and at the worst possible time," Lieutenant Dan replied.

"AHHH, OOOOH!" Oakie groaned.

"Sir, are you all right?"

"No, I'm not. The queens are rebuilding their nest inside of me. A lot of it got destroyed. The pain is horrifying. It's getting worse and worse.

"Aaaah! They stopped for a while. I figured they were finished, but they must—ooooh, aaah!—have just been on a break." Oakie's eyes screamed with pain. "You have to do something, Lieutenant Dan! I don't know how much more I can handle. Ooooh!"

Lieutenant Dan thought quickly. Oakie moaned quietly, trying not to distract him.

"I've got an idea, sir. Not a whole idea, but it's a place to start. I'm going to go round up a team of our most elite warriors. We'll try to brainstorm together. If nothing else, they'll be assembled and ready when The Duke comes to, and maybe he'll have an idea."

"That's better than nothing," Oakie said between tremendous jolts of pain.

Lieutenant Dan saluted Oakie and took off, running to assemble the team.

In the meantime, Oakie remained strong and battled through the trouble at hand. Below, The Duke remained frozen in time.

As the termites tore away at his insides, Oakie wondered if he would have been better off never letting them in at all. What if he had rejected Colpa's offer? It seemed so comforting at the time. Verstand had eventually showed up, and so did The Duke and his army. Maybe he never needed the termites in the first place ... Maybe they didn't actually help him at all. Maybe Oakie was worse off now than he had been before. The queens really *were* sly and cunning. They had fooled him *so* well. They had made themselves seem *so* sweet, *so* kind, *so* caring. They never *actually* wanted to help Oakie. All they wanted was to find a home for their own selfish purposes.

"—act quickly, we might not get the jump on them. Lieutenant Dan, assemble a team of our most awesome warriors. In the meantime, I've got an idea to share with my compadre here." The Duke had come out of his coma and was spinning around looking for Lieutenant Dan.

Despite the pain, Oakie couldn't help but laugh. Out of nowhere, the great Duke had returned.

"That dude is one eerie dude. Like *abracadabra*, he disappears right before your very eyes. He's a mystical ninja assassin and I'm stoked he's on our team."

The pain was becoming unbearable, but Oakie knew he had to push through.

"What's your idea?"

"The Duke had a vision, bro. In the vision The Duke and some of his own freedom bandits stormed through that termite nest, each of us carrying a piece of the sacred fire Amore. Like well-trained pyro-technicians, we napalmed the nest like Esperanza, and burned our way to victory."

The Duke smiled from antenna to antenna, overwhelmed with pride at how ingenious his vision was.

Oakie took a moment to gain composure. "There's only one small problem, Duke."

"Small is easy. The Duke can handle small."

"I AM THE NEST! Are you out of your mind! You'll burn me alive."

"Bro, that's the brilliance of it." The Duke stood unshaken by Oakie's incredibly strong reservations.

"That's extremely brilliant Duke," Oakie continued sarcastically, wincing in pain.

The Duke smiled.

"Kill the termites and kill me. Maybe while you're at it, you should light a cute cuddly bunny on fire, just for fun."

The Duke frowned.

"Bro, that would not be fun at all. I have no idea what's going on in your head, b-"

"I have no idea what's going on in your head, Duke, but let me tell you this—you're crazy!"

"Dude, chill out and hold onto your cookie crumbs for a minute before you drop them all over the place."

Oakie glared at The Duke.

"First off, The Duke's not sure what happened between the moment you thought his idea was brilliant and the moment you decided to harm a defenseless bunny, but he does know something's gone amok."

"How am I supposed to react to you *killing* me?"

"The Duke would never kill you, bro. Why would you think The Duke would kill you?" The Duke was hurt.

"Setting me on fire would burn me. Burning me would kill me. What don't I understand here?"

The Duke started laughing.

"What's so funny? This isn't funny!"

"Sure it is. Dude, Amore won't kill you. It's a sacred fire. Sacred fire doesn't kill stuff—it protects stuff, that's what makes it so sacred. It only burns things that are dead. It won't burn the living."

"Will it burn the termites?"

"Yeah."

"Will it burn an ant-eating ghoul?"

"Oh, for sure."

"Will it burn a cute furry bunny?"

"What's with you and harming bunnies? That's just messed up, bro."

"If it only burns dead things, then why won't it burn me?"

"Look, it's all mystical and sacred-like. The Duke doesn't get the logistics of it. All The Duke knows is that it won't burn living plants and trees. If it's dead, it'll burn it up. If it's not dead, it won't."

"Is this the only way?"

"Yes."

"Are you sure? Are you one hundred percent positive it won't burn me alive?" Oakie had watched his entire family go up in flames, and now The Duke wanted to use some wild sacred fire to burn the termites out of the deepest places inside of him.

"The Duke crosses his heart and swears on Esperanza's grave that you'll be okay. The Duke would never do anything to hurt you! You're The Duke's hero."

Oakie wasn't convinced, but The Duke seemed confident. "All right. Let's do it. I'm putting my trust in you, Duke," Oakie said hesitantly.

"You won't regret this, big brownie dude," The Duke shouted with excitement, and ran off to get Lieutenant Dan.

Oakie shook his head and wondered how he got himself into such a mess.

As evening approached and the moon climbed into the sky, Oakie had time to consider the situation. He was having second thoughts. He said he trusted The Duke, but with every passing thought, that trust was dwindling. He was faced with a large decision that few would ever be brave enough to make. On one hand, he could let The Duke try his crazy idea. Letting Amore consume him was risking a quick, painful death. On the other hand, he could back out and keep on living with evil termites until they slowly killed him from within.

I always say it's best to just rip off the band-aid. The pain doesn't get to linger that way. But what do I know? I don't have to make the decision, I'm just telling the story.

GREATER LOVE HAS NO ONE THAN THIS

32

As the moon went to bed and the sun awoke, The Duke and Lieutenant Dan returned to Oakie, along with a group of their strongest and most fearless freedom bandits. Among them was Commander Brick.

"Commander Brick?" Oakie was shocked.

"Well, if it isn't the sassy civilian. Lucky for you I'm not carrying a stick." Commander Brick laughed and saluted Oakie. Behind him, four of the bandits stood carrying a beautifully crafted box held by poles. Inside the box danced a vibrant, colorful flame that looked as though it was crafted from a rainbow. Colors of all hues lived within it.

Instantly, Oakie remembered the dream about Verstand he'd had as an acorn buried in the ground, so long ago. The flame looked exactly as the caterpillar had in his dream. There was nothing scary about the fire at all.

Everything about it instantly settled Oakie's fear and worry. Peace overcame him. The ants stood in awe as a miracle took place before their eyes: There was an explosion of life. All of Oakie's branches strengthened and began lifting. Leaves that had already begun appearing during Verstand's visit grew full size. Leaves that hadn't been there appeared everywhere.

"Dude, that was not part of the plan." The Duke was stunned.

"I'm ... I'm ... p-pretty sure I'm okay with it," Oakie stammered in wonder. "So ... wha— ... what's the plan, Duke?" Oakie asked, almost speechless.

While The Duke stood in a daze, watching Oakie grow new branches, Lieutenant Dan chimed in, "Sir, if you don't mind, I'll share the plan with you. I think The Duke is a bit preoccupied, along with the rest of the bandits."

"Go ahead ..." Oakie slowly pulled out of his own trance to give his attention to Lieutenant Dan.

"Well sir, each of us has a special torch forged by the early elders of Antropolis. They made the torches so they could carry the flame without it burning out. Last night, we sent a group of scouts to survey the nest. There are only two main entrances to it. Beyond those, there's a maze of tunnels that they successfully mapped out. The tunnels all lead to the center of the nest, where the colony lives. The nest is fantastic in size. In the middle of the living quarters stands a giant tower. At the top of the tower, the three queens reside. The security is rather limited, as there is no known threat to the colony."

"Except for you." Oakie smiled.

"Yes sir, except for us." Lieutenant Dan smiled back. "Most of the warriors are working alongside the workers, trying to expand the nest. They seemed rather tired and aggravated. It was almost like taking one step forward and two steps back. The walls keep closing in around them. I guess you're growing on the inside?" Lieutenant Dan shrugged, not really understanding what was happening. "Needless to say, our scouts had no trouble getting in because everyone was so busy. We have a battalion positioned at the rear entrance. Our platoon—" Dan motioned at those standing before Oakie, "—will be going through the front. We're each going to take a tunnel and light a fire behind us. Once we're in, no one can get out that way. The only other exit will be the rear one, forcing the termites into the hands of our well-positioned warriors."

"Brilliant!"

"That's my idea, compadre," The Duke said proudly, pulling himself out of his rapture.

"Of course it is," Oakie assured The Duke.

Lieutenant Dan continued, "When we reach the center of the nest, if things work out as planned, the queens should still be in their tower. With nowhere to escape, we'll set the base of the tower on fire, trap the queens, and leave them to their proper demise. Once that fire has been set, we'll head to the tunnels that are currently being built, set them ablaze, and navigate our way to the rear exit. Amore will do most of the work for us. We just have to release her to do what she does best."

"What about me? Will I be okay?"

"As far as I know you'll be fine, sir. You may have a large hole left where the nest existed, but other than that, you should come out unharmed."

"Other than that you *will* come out unharmed, civilian. It is a soldier's duty to protect the lives of the innocent," Commander Brick reassured Oakie.

You can take the brick out of the commander, but you can't take the commander out of the Brick. Oakie was thankful for Commander Brick's presence. "So are you waiting until tonight to strike?" Oakie asked Lieutenant Dan.

"We actually talked at length about when to set the plan in motion, sir. We concluded that the appropriate time was during the day. If any of the termites should escape our forces waiting at the rear entrance, the rest of the army will be positioned down here, circling the area. The termites will be much easier to see, giving us an even greater advantage. If by some miracle any of them get past our vast army, we're counting on the sun to finish what we started. The termites won't survive long in this heat. Light is their natural enemy."

"So, big brownie dude, what do you think?" The Duke asked, nodding at the greatness of his plan.

"Oakie," Oakie corrected The Duke.

The Duke looked around. "Bro, where *is* this Oakie you keep talking to?"

"Right in front of you." Oakie shook his branches toward himself.

The Duke looked around again. "Dude, what are you talking about?"

"My NAME is Oakie."

"What? Big brownie dude, why didn't you tell The Duke that a long time ago?"

Lieutenant Dan shook his head.

"Lieutenant Dan, big brownie dude's name is Oakie." The Duke slapped Lieutenant Dan on the shoulder.

"Sir, do you approve of our strategy?" Lieutenant Dan asked Oakie.

All Oakie's hesitance from the night before disappeared. The choice was clear. "I love it!" Oakie was filled with excitement. As weird and quirky as The Duke was, no one could deny his brilliance.

"*Viva la revolución!*" The Duke shouted, pumping his fist in the air.

"*Viva la revolución!*" Oakie shouted back.

Lieutenant Dan grabbed a torch and buried it deep in Amore. Pulling it out, he raised the flame high in the air, signaling the army to get into position. Each of the bandits plunged their torches into the sacred fire and stood waiting for their leader.

The Duke walked over to the chest. Lifting his head to the heavens, he dipped his torch in. Amore gripped it tightly. Valiantly he raised his torch high in the air and waited for the full attention of the freedom bandits. "Today we stand as Esperanza once stood. Today we stand for a better tomorrow. Today we stand for justice. Today we stand for peace. Today we stand for hope. Today we stand for freedom!"

The bandits cheered.

"All for one and one for all!"
The freedom bandits joined in,
"If we stand together none will fall.
We stand for the weak and make them strong.
If we stand for each other we will live long.
All that matters is all we see.
All that matters is you and me!"

The bandits rallied behind The Duke as he led the way up Oakie's side to the nest's entrance. Pausing for a moment before entering, The Duke looked Oakie in the eyes. "Oakie … I like that name. I'm proud to die for that name. This is for you, Oakie." With that, The Duke disappeared along with the rest of the bandits.

Inside the path was dark and eerie. The termites had made quite a mess. The Duke turned back and signaled the bandits to light the fire. Amore began to blaze wildly, illuminating the entrance, immediately consuming the dead wood.

"We've got to hurry," Lieutenant Dan ordered. "Each of you know the plan. Pair off and we'll meet up at the center of the nest. May Providence be with you!"

The Duke and Lieutenant Dan took the shortest tunnel that led directly to the nest. It was their belief that leaders not only led with their words, but also with their lives.

As the ants made their way through the tunnels, Oakie could feel his insides being engulfed by the warmth of Amore.

When The Duke and Lieutenant Dan approached the end of their tunnel, they saw two guards clothed in armor and posted for security. Since there was no immediate danger to the nest, the guards were wrapped up in playful chatter, paying no attention to the tunnel. Leaping out, The Duke and Dan seized the guards and dragged them off into the shadows, then emerged clothed in the guards' armor.

"Whoaaa …" The Duke gazed up in amazement. The nest was carved in the shape of a dome. Homes that had been burrowed right out of the walls were stacked on top of each other almost as high as the dome itself. Pillars lined each walkway, which went from every tunnel entrance into the nest, and all the way to the center of the dome where the palace stood. Reigning high above them were the quarters where the queens lived. Their palace rivaled any they had ever seen. The tower had been carved out in such a way that deadly spikes, beginning at the base, wrapped around it all the way to the top. At least a dozen guards surrounded the tower, protecting the entrance to the queens' lair.

"Sir, the spies didn't mention anything about the guards," Lieutenant Dan whispered.

The Duke smiled mischievously. "I know, bro. What a sugary little cookie for us this is. We're gonna have some sweet, sweet fun. Give me your torch, bro."

Lieutenant Dan looked reluctant.

"Dude, hurry up! We don't have all day."

Lieutenant Dan surrendered his torch.

The Duke ran to some nearby rocks and hid both their torches behind them. "Just stay quiet and let me do the talking."

"Whatever you say, sir."

"Hey!" The Duke shouted. "Hey, over here." The Duke waved his arms wildly.

"I hope you know what you're doing."

The Duke continued waving, ignoring Dan's lack of faith.

"I said, OVER HERE!"

One guard finally noticed them and came running. "What is it? Is everything all right?"

"No bro, quite the opposite. Get the royal guards. There are intruders down this tunnel. I don't know how many. We took off immediately to get help when we saw them."

"You deal with it soldier—we have strict orders not to leave our post."

"If you don't leave your post and the queens get upset because intruders make it into the nest, then we're all gonna have our heads on sticks. Do you want your head on a stick, bro? Do ya?" The Duke made like his head was on a stick, hanging his tongue out as if he were dead.

"You're right. If you two buffoons don't do your job, we're all in for it."

The guard returned to his post and rallied the other troops together as quickly as possible.

"Thank you, Commander Brick, for all those heads on sticks. I guess The Duke learned something from you after all." The Duke chuckled to himself.

"Sir, what are we going to do next?"

"Watch and learn from your sensei, young grasshopper."

The guards jogged in their direction. As they approached, The Duke waved them through the tunnel. "Hurry up! Move it. They're down the tunnel. You've got to stop them before they get here."

The guards blew past Duke and Dan on a mission to hunt down the invaders. As soon as the last soldier passed by, The Duke rushed over and grabbed the torches. Tossing one to Lieutenant Dan, The Duke whipped around the corner of the tunnel and started his side on fire. Lieutenant Dan followed suit.

"Termite kabobs, bro. Tasty termite kabobs."

The two smirked as Amore flooded the tunnel.

"Ingenious, sir."

"You're welcome."

Out of the remaining tunnels burst the other bandits with their torches.

"All right soldiers, The Duke and I are headed for the palace. The rest of you make your way to the entrance of the other tunnels where all the workers are. Light 'em up and head to the rendezvous point!"

The bandits scattered to fulfill their mission while the Duke and Lieutenant Dan made their way to the palace. Smoke from the tunnels that were already burning began to billow into the nest. The smell rose to the top of the tower.

Condanna was the first to catch the frightening smell, and rushed to the window of the queens' chambers. Below, thousands of termites exploded out of their homes and began racing for an exit. Pandemonium broke loose.

The bandits unleashed Amore down all of the tunnels, with the exception of the one leading to the exit, and trapped all the workers inside, sending them to their doom.

"Colpa! Vergogna! Come quickly." The two queens frantically ran to the window where Condanna stood in horror.

"No! What is happening? NO! NO! NO!" Colpa screamed.

"Our home! Our precious home!" Vergogna shrieked.

"Forget the nest! What about us?" Condanna snapped. "We've got to get out of here."

"It can't be!" As the fire blazed brightly Colpa immediately recognized it.

"Amore ..." Colpa stood shocked. "The Ant Nation is here. They want their revenge on me. Well they won't have it!" she screamed in terror.

Standing below, The Duke corrected Colpa, "It's not revenge, you wicked witch. It's freedom! And you're not going anywhere." The Duke signaled Lieutenant Dan, and in one glorious act, Amore scaled the palace, hopping and jumping over the deadly spikes that protected it. The fire climbed the walls and trapped many of the inhabitants in their homes. Those that escaped Amore made their way through the exit tunnel to meet their demise at the hands of the ants.

The Freedom Bandits ran with the herd of termites that were already headed for the exit. When they arrived at the palace, they rejoined The Duke and Lieutenant Dan.

"Surf's up, compadres! You know the rules. I was the first one in and I'm the last one out. So make it fast, 'cause the last thing I plan on seeing is a sandy beach with gnarly waves crashing on the shore."

Leaping and dashing over the backs of the termites that were stampeding through the tunnel, the bandits broke forth into the open and rejoined the brothers stationed outside of the exit, where they had already laid waste to piles of their enemies.

Lieutenant Dan looked around and noticed something terribly wrong. "Sir, we're one man short."

"Did you take a second count?" The Duke asked with great concern.

"Sir, I didn't need to—it's Commander Brick. He's not here."

A ferocious chill ran down The Duke's back. Commander Brick had been the biggest opposition to the *revolución*. It had taken a great amount of time, convincing, and patience on The Duke's behalf, but eventually the Commander came to his senses. Since he had joined the Freedom Bandits, a lot had changed. Sure, he wasn't the softest or the kindest, but he was changing. Commander Brick was the first to volunteer for the mission to the termite nest. Before, he had been willing to shove Oakie's head onto a stick. Now he was willing to die for Oakie and The Freedom Bandits' cause. Commander Brick wasn't The Duke's best friend, but he wasn't just a soldier either. He was part of family now—a family that didn't just serve their leader, but was served *by* its leader. That's what made the *revolución* what it was.

As weird as The Duke seemed, he was their father and he would die for every last one of them, no matter who they were.

Without hesitation, The Duke mounted back up on the wave of stampeding termites. "You're in charge if I don't survive," The Duke shouted to Lieutenant Dan as he sailed back down the tunnel. Surfing against the wave was much harder than surfing with it.

Chaos ensued as the termites trampled each other, fleeing for their lives. Smoke filled the tunnel, making it extremely difficult to breath.

The Duke bounded through the smoke, hurtling over and diving under the termites, trying his best not to get trampled. The herd of termites lessened as he approached the end of the tunnel. Soon only random stragglers were all that were left. The Duke dodged them easily.

Breaking into the main nest, The Duke witnessed the most magical sight he had ever seen: Amore had seized the walls and was swallowing the palace. She had been released in all of her power and splendor. The colors were so vivid and bright; the flame was the purest sparkling white The Duke had ever seen. The fire burned so brightly that no smoke was visible. In the presence of the flame, there was no room for darkness. It wasn't until the smoke escaped to the tunnel that its blackness could be seen.

As the fire blazed on, the nest began to shrink. A miracle unfolded as Amore consumed dead wood. The living wood behind it, below it, and above it expanded and filled the room.

The Duke would have stayed there forever if he could. There was nothing that compared to what he was witnessing.

Whipping around, The Duke continued his search. Running down the fiery path to the palace, falling debris bombarded the way. It was as if a meteor shower had exploded within Oakie. Circling the palace, he hunted frantically for Commander Brick. Hopelessness set in as he realized the Commander was nowhere to be found. From above The Duke, a vicious voice rang out.

"My sisters were two of the greatest queens this nation has ever known, you wretched, foul ant! Today I'll have your soul as reparation for their lives!" Vergogna flew angrily above The Duke. She hadn't shed her wings yet like Colpa and Condanna had. It was the only reason she had survived the fire in the palace. Pointing her spear at The Duke's heart, Vergogna lunged toward him, firing her spear.

The Duke closed his eyes, raised his hands and braced for death. In a flash, it was over. Not even the slightest drop of pain. Death didn't seem all that horrible. The Duke stood for a moment taking it all in before venturing a peek at his surroundings.

Suddenly he realized he wasn't dead at all. Relief momentarily overwhelmed him—until he looked down. There, lying at his feet, was none other than Commander Brick. Jumping at the last moment, Commander Brick had taken the spear through his chest and saved The Duke.

Vergogna hovered furiously as the martyr lay dying at her target's feet.

"Commander Brick, dude ... why? What were you thinking, bro?" The Duke fell to his knees and grabbed the hero before him.

The Commander lifted his head and gazed at The Duke. "Because, sir, I learned from the best. This ant nation needs you. They didn't need me. You needed me and now they have you." The commander began choking and coughing. "Promise me something, Duke."

"Anything, bro, you name it."

"Don't ever compromise who you are. The day you stepped out of that line forever changed the course of our history. Esperanza may have inspired you and a whole generation, but she's gone. Now is your time. You've been called to be this Ant Nation's inspiration. Don't take that lightly. I'm proud of you, my boy." With that, Commander Brick saluted The Duke and passed away.

As The Duke held tightly to the lifeless body of the heroic soldier, fiery debris hailed down around him. The nest was rapidly burning up and closing in. Vergogna's hunger for revenge was second only to her thirst for survival. Hastily glancing about she spotted the only exit left., which was rapidly closing on the other side of the nest.

In a flash, Vergogna abandoned her foe and flew frantically for safety, dodging fireballs as she headed for the exit.

Pulling the spear from Commander Brick's chest, The Duke sprinted after her. Slamming the spear into the ground, he vaulted over the fallen pillars and aimed himself for one that lay on its side, angled like a ramp. As The Duke neared the end of the ramp, he slammed the spear down once again and threw himself through the air, landing on Vergogna's back.

Vergogna bucked ferociously.

The Duke grabbed hold of Vergogna's wings and began to steer the two of them to the entrance. Fireball upon fireball pummeled Vergogna. The shower of flames was too much. They couldn't be avoided. The Duke jerked Vergogna's left wing hard to the right and spun her upside down, using her belly to protect himself from the fireballs.

The tunnel was fully engulfed in flames. As the dead wood burned away, the tunnel closed faster and faster. Like a giant drill spinning in circles, the two spiraled through it toward the light. As the tunnel shrank, The Duke knew he had to do something if he was going to escape with his life. Letting go of Vergogna's wings, he jumped to her head just as the tunnel became too small for her to fit through. Her body abruptly plugged the hole and thrust The Duke forward, launching him toward the exit. Rolling across the ground, he jumped up and ran with the spear in his hand as the shriek of the dying queen echoed past him. The Duke could taste the finish line, but the tunnel was closing fast.

Still running, he threw the spear with all his might. It stuck into the ground, stopping the tunnel from closing up just long enough for The Duke to launch himself into the group of bandits that were waiting for him outside. Looking back, he watched as the spear snapped in two and the tunnel snapped shut forever.

CHAPTER
33

BEAUTY FROM ASHES

33

Lieutenant Dan and the rest of The Freedom Bandits cheered wildly as they raised The Duke high above their shoulders and carried him down to the sea of ants waiting below.

Oakie's face sparkled with life. Everything was so fresh. Hope and peace flooded his mind. He stood proudly, with an air of newfound confidence. Amore had done more than just rid Oakie of the evil sisters and their family—Amore had consumed his heart and his mind. The evidence shone through his eyes.

Below, the ants cheered and celebrated their fearless leader and their victory. The Duke gave them time to enjoy themselves before signaling for their attention. After a moment the chants settled and the commotion died down.

The Duke looked at the *revolución* before him. He remembered the day Oakie had addressed Commander Brick so boldly, yet so innocently. He remembered the profoundness of Oakie's words. He could still feel their impact as they washed the dross from his heart and liberated his mind. He remembered the courage it took to step out of that line and let the army fade off into the grass, leaving him behind in the unknown.

Before, he had stood alone with nothing more than a dream in his heart and the words of a sapling that echoed in his mind. Now, after many dangerous adventures and duels with death, he stood where it had all begun, returning with the revolutionary army that he had so long ago envisioned. Words that had inspired a dream had woven themselves into tangible reality before his very eyes.

The Duke gazed up at Oakie's brilliance that shone from his face. Turning back toward the army, he shed a tear as the heroic act of the Great Commander Brick played out again in his mind. Without a mighty warrior by his side, this leader wouldn't have lived to see his dream become a reality.

"Please take a knee," The Duke asked.

One after another, the family standing before The Duke knelt.

"Today, as we celebrate, we must remember now and forever what granted us the victory."

The crowd waited in silence.

"Long ago, a great yet simple sapling had an idea. That idea inspired a dream in the heart of one lone ant. That ant shared his dream with you, and you shared it with each other. A *revolución* way freaking bigger than a single ant was birthed, and all of you selflessly jumped on board. In our humility and meekness, Providence granted us Amore. Against the craziest odds—like ever—we carried Amore with faith and courage into the darkest and creepiest chambers of our enemies' camp. We carried Amore where it couldn't go on its own, and it did what we couldn't do alone. The most killer victory we have ever locked down was through belief, action, and unity. Let's thank Providence and celebrate each other for the sacrifice we all have made."

The crowd began to cheer. Before it could get out of control, The Duke motioned for them to calm again.

"Bros and Bro-ettes, let The Duke finish with this ... Today we lost a mighty warrior and most awesome friend. Commander Brick took a heinous blow from a most villainous queen on behalf of The Duke. The bravest of the brave, for sure. He gave up his life without hesitation. Let's honor him with a moment of silence. Commander Brick did the greatest thing an ant can do—he died for his friend."

The ants in the crowd bowed their heads.

Oakie looked down with great respect for his friend. The Duke had become a leader worth following.

After a lengthy moment, Oakie ended the silence.

"I stood here alone, quietly waiting for death to take me," he said. "The weight of my grief left me blind to what the termites were doing. I foolishly found them comforting. Their lies were as convincing as I was hopeless. I would have rotted away to nothing had you and Verstand not fought for me. Most of you didn't know me, but you stood for me. You faced loss and certain death. You followed what you believed was right. You came for me when I had nothing. You helped me when I couldn't help myself. Words cannot describe the gratitude I feel." Tears welled in Oakie's eyes and streamed down his bark.

The eyes of the vast crowd of soldiers filled with tears as well. The Duke watched Oakie with respect.

"Thank you, Duke. Thank you, Commander Brick. Thank you to *all* of you."

"No, thank *you*, Oakie dude." The Duke bowed his head in honor.

Oakie smiled. "Now let's celebrate!" he shouted, playfully breaking the moment.

The crowd jumped up, cheering.

As the moon rose, the Freedom Bandits carried Amore out to the center of the camp to illuminate the night sky. Drummers began a tribal beat. Ant families gathered around and danced with their shadows, just as little children would.

Hearty laughter filled the air, reminding Oakie of the days spent bantering with Dakota.

The Duke broke from the party and journeyed up Oakie to meet with him face-to-face.

"Oakie, dude," The Duke said happily.

"Duke," Oakie greeted his friend.

"We're leaving tomorrow morning."

Oakie saddened at The Duke's words.

"Bro, the *revolución* must march on. It thrives on adventure and Amore burns brightest when we follow our hearts. If Amore dies down, it means we're not following our hearts. We can never afford to have Amore die out. Without Amore, the *revolución* will cease to exist. I can't squelch it by making us settle down. Amore is the only thing that will keep us safe, so the *revolución* must move where its heart takes it. The Duke's job as a leader is to carry Amore wherever it burns brightest. We've never gone wrong as long as we've followed its leading."

Oakie stared at his friend in awe. The Duke reminded him of Morgan. He carried such wisdom, honor, and integrity. What a gift it was to know such a dynamic, humble, selfless leader. Oakie looked into The Duke's eyes with great approval. "So, where do you plan on going, then?"

"Wherever Amore burns brightest." The Duke grinned. "Bro, honestly I'm not quite sure. We almost always have to take a step and just start moving. If we start moving and the flame dies down, we adjust the direction we're going."

"Is that ever scary?"

"Like, only when I start to worry about what this giant sea of ants is going to eat or where we're all going to camp."

"Do you always find food and a place to sleep?"

"Bro, since we began carrying Amore, there's always been colossal bounty to eat and the most comfortable places to sleep. Before ... not so much. We always ate and slept, but dude, let me tell you, it ain't fun eatin' dung when you ain't a dung beetle."

Oakie chuckled through a look of disgust as he thought of The Duke having to eat dung. "Well then, my dear Duke, it sounds like Amore has everything taken care of."

The Duke smiled. "And then some," he added.

"Duke. One last question, if you don't mind?" Oakie asked.

"For sure, Oakie dude."

"Since Amore burned through me, my insides feel hot. It's not painful, but it feels like she's still blazing inside. In fact, it feels like it's getting hotter and hotter. Do you think it will go away?"

"I'm for sure not a scholar, bro, but from what I know, she only stops burning when something stops living. I think you're stuck with her."

Oakie didn't really understand it, but it felt comforting nonetheless. As long as he was alive, Amore would be with him. Ironically, fire took his family, yet the fire burning inside him brought peace, joy, and hope.

Oakie and The Duke sat silently for a moment, with nothing more to say. Like old friends, they embraced the silence with ease. The sound of the celebration floated up and interrupted their brief interlude. The Duke looked toward the tribe of dancers rejoicing below.

"Well, a mighty leader can't just leave his faithful followers alone during a crucial time like this," Oakie said, smiling playfully at The Duke.

"No, he can't, Oakie dude." The Duke returned the smile before heading back down to the celebration. "*Viva la revolución!*" The Duke shouted and pumped his fist in the air.

"Cacaw, cacaw!" Oakie shouted back.

The Duke paused mid-step, shook his head and laughed to himself before continuing on.

As The Duke faded into the sea of dancers below, Oakie turned his eyes toward the sky. There in the cloudless heavens above, stars sparkled, the sky glimmering like diamonds. As Oakie gazed with awe at the beauty above, a shower of light began. One star after another ripped through the sky and soared down to earth. It had been a very long time since the heavens had rained stars. It was as if the stars danced above to celebrate the army that danced below.

Oakie closed his eyes and took a deep breath. The moment filled every part of him with life, from the very bottom of his roots to the very tips of his branches.

Opening his eyes, he was met with a miracle he had never seen before. A wave of green light began to erupt from the blackness as the shower of stars faded away. As the light grew stronger, a magnificent red erupted from the green. Pulsating and growing, the colors began to whirl through the sky. The light waved back and forth as though the hand of a skilled painter was clutching his brush and confidently moving it over a blank canvas. As the colors grew and moved about, they took on a life of their own.

Oakie was mesmerized.

Weaving through the sky, the elegant creature of light began to dance to the beat of the drummers below. It was like Providence had come as a friend to share in the victory celebration. And yet … the light felt as though it was hand-tailored for Oakie—a private party of sorts. Oakie felt an immense sense of freedom. The magic and wonder of the moment felt almost like a rebirth. After all the pain, sorrow, and suffering, the power of Amore left Oakie feeling born again.

As the night wore on, Oakie slowly faded off to sleep under the assurance and care he felt from the light above.

The next morning, he woke to the greeting of the dawning sun. After a good yawn and a stretch of his branches, he looked down to say good morning and goodbye to his friends. Surprisingly, he was greeted by the remains of packed-up campsites and the words *Viva La Revolución* etched in the ground.

"*Viva La Revolución,*" Oakie said in a bittersweet whisper.

The warmth of the morning sun washed over Oakie as he stood alone with only his thoughts. His world had never been so quiet. He couldn't hear a bug on the ground or a bird in the air. The silence would have driven him mad with loneliness in the past, but after all that had happened, he was relieved.

Squinting at the sun, Oakie began to share his thoughts.

"I've faced death more than once in my life. I've lost all that I love and cared about. I hold nothing but memories. But do you know what?" Oakie asked the sun. "I feel more alive today than ever before. I feel more hope, more peace, more joy—and I have no reason for it. I have nothing to show for my life. I am here all alone, with the exception of you and this fire called Amore that burns deep inside of me."

The sun listened intently as it slowly ascended.

"I feel more powerful now than when I stood surrounded and protected by the orchard. I am no longer a sapling easily trampled by the foot of peoples. The rain came, but it did not wash me away. The fire blazed, but it did not burn me."

Strength and power grew with every word as Oakie's very voice deepened into that of a mature tree. "The crows came to break me and the termites came to devour me from the inside out, but I would not be broken. I would not let them have my life. The world around me may have been stolen, but I am in charge of *me*. When the rain pours and fires blaze, I CHOOSE!" shouted Oakie.

"When all that I love is lost, I CHOOSE!" Oakie shouted again. "I choose what to believe. I choose what to feel. This can never be taken from me."

As Oakie's declarations echoed through the sky, his eyes glowed with a strength born of years of experience.

"The field before me is not a graveyard. Before it was an orchard, it was an empty field where only one great tree named Morgan stood alone. In time, it became so much more. In time, it became a family. In time, it was filled with peoples. In time, I stood here. And now I stand here alone. But in time, this field will be filled again. Some way, somehow, it will be filled with something grand. Something great will grow. I don't know what and I don't know how, but I do know it will be magnificent. It will be more magnificent than anything ever before!"

The sun was moved by these words of hope as they shook the heavens. Clouds suddenly began to form from thin air.

"Beauty will rise from these ashes!" Oakie thundered.

The clouds broke and long-overdue droplets of rain showered the earth. Like treasured diamonds falling into the hands of orphans, the ground grabbed every last drop, soaking them in to quench its deep thirst.

Oakie closed his eyes and breathed deeply as the water covered his bark and washed over his face. As droplets landed on branches, the skin of the branches began to crack. The dry, hardened, skin shell split open and from it, tiny green stems broke forth. A green coat covered Oakie's arms.

Below, tiny green hairs of grass began to spring up across the field. Small rodents that had long been buried in the safety of their dens dug their way out of the ground. Tiny worms came up for a fresh breath of air. The earth awakened from its grief.

As the world around Oakie began to pulsate with life, his eyes slowly opened. Through the soft trickle of water showering the field, a beautiful rainbow grew and stretched across the sky. And there, out on a hill in the drizzling rain, appeared the silhouette of a small figure beneath the rainbow. Slowly the figure drew toward Oakie. As the image neared, the face of a lost, but not forgotten, friend came into focus.

Clothes soaked, hair wet like a mop, Joshua's teeth chattered. The delightful young boy Oakie so loved and missed stood before him. His hands were hidden in his pockets, attempting to avoid the chill he felt. With remorse in his eyes, he surveyed the field. Nothing was as he had remembered it. Dragging his feet, Joshua walked around, imagining the orchard as it had once been. He recognized the remains of a tragic battle poking through the ground. As the rain washed away the soot, shards of colored plastic that had not been burned in the fire slowly revealed themselves. The Fourth of July debris littered the field—a painful reminder of Joshua's foolish decision.

Turning around, Joshua once again faced his nemesis and good friend. The two stared quietly at one another for quite some time. Joshua looked over the remains that hung about Oakie's branches. Pieces of a platform here, broken walls there, and the stairs that started it all nailed to Oakie's side. Joshua's eyes slowly followed the stairs down to the ground, where he scanned over the broken remains of his glorious base station that hadn't burned.

Oakie watched with sadness in his heart as Joshua knelt to the ground and sifted through the clutter.

There in the debris, Joshua found his protective sleep stabilizer—just one of his many inventions. Cradling the contraption in his hands, he began to cry. One tear after another slid down his face.

"I'm a failure." Joshua whispered into his hands. "I'm a failure of an explorer, inventor, hero, leader, protector. I'm a failure."

The rush of tears outran the rain falling on his face.

"I'm a failure. I'm a failure. I'm a failure!" Joshua shouted as rage grew within. Jumping to his feet, he spun around and threw his invention as far as he could. He ran through the debris, kicking pieces of wood and plastic. Bending down between kicks, he grabbed the remains of his fort and hurled them into the field.

Oakie stood peacefully, understanding all too well what his dear friend was feeling.

Stopping abruptly, Joshua uncovered a rusted hammer below the wreckage. He stood for moment and stared.

This hammer started it all. Without it, he could have never built the stairs to climb his nemesis. Without it, he could never have built the fort that he so foolishly defended with fireworks. Lunging at the hammer, Joshua tore it from the ground. With hatred in his eyes, he stormed toward Oakie, clenching the hammer in his hand. Darting up the steps, he leapt from branch to branch and thrashed around, knocking away the remaining platforms and walls.

Oakie winced as pieces of wood went sailing past his face to the ground.

Panting heavily, Joshua stopped in front of the broken mirror he had used to paint his face with camouflage. Like a stand-off between two gunslingers, he stood face-to-face with his reflection, looking with accusation at his enemy.

The reflection glared back with violent dissatisfaction.

"I hate you!" Joshua shouted before smashing the mirror to smithereens with the rusty hammer.

Oakie's heart broke as Joshua jumped around, crying, violently smashing away at the remains, clearing Oakie's branches of the final pieces of the fort.

With nothing left to hammer, Joshua descended the stairs. As he did so, he took the claw of the hammer and tore each stair from Oakie's side.

Oakie's heart dropped. Never again would he get to enjoy the company of his good friend jumping around in his branches. The inspiring and imaginative child was heading toward the exit door of Oakie's life. Though he felt the weight of another loss, looking into the rainbow reminded him that even though life would never be the same, the future held its own treasure waiting to be found.

Finally Joshua stood on the ground, hammer raised high in the air, glaring at the final step. With all his anger and strength, he brought the hammer crashing down on the plank, sending it whizzing across the ground. Attempting to breathe, he gasped for air. All the frustration and anger he had carried since the fire could no longer be boxed up and stored in the deepest pits of his stomach. Seeing Oakie and the barren field for the first time broke it all open. As Joshua caught his breath, the hate and anger began to subside. There, hidden below all of it, was the thing for which he had no words.

Sadness and pain welled up, sending the happiest and most joyful boy Oakie had ever seen buckling to the ground in tears. Leaning against Oakie, Joshua hung his head between his knees and wept.

The base station was more than just a place for Joshua to play. It was a picture of all he had fought so hard for and his decision to never give up. It was proof that he could do anything he wanted if he just believed. It was his place to be whomever or whatever he wanted without judgment. It was his sanctuary of peace. And now, it was no more.

There, Joshua cried under the light of the rainbow and the drizzle of the rain alone with his nemesis-turned-friend. "I'm sorry," Joshua mumbled through his tears.

As he mourned his loss, two small figures appeared on the hill where he had walked only a short time before. They marched toward Oakie and Joshua.

"Long time no see. I'm surprised the two of you haven't killed each other," Oakie said playfully to his friends Houdini and Smokey.

"He tried, but he can't. I'm too fast!" Houdini shot back. Smokey shook his head.

"I won't waste my precious energy engaging him."

"You just did. Ha, I win again!" Houdini reveled in his wit.

"He told us to stay put until he came back, but Big Ears here never does what he's told." Smokey pointed to his partner. Houdini slicked his ears back with his paw as if to pet them in appreciation and to scorn Smokey for making fun of them.

"It's probably better you came," Oakie said, gesturing toward Joshua.

Houdini elbowed Smokey in the side, taunting him.

"The truth is, he's going to need you both. He won't be like this forever, but he will need you to stick close so he knows he's not alone."

The two nodded as if to say it hadn't been easy, but they wouldn't leave him alone. Then, like only true friends would, Houdini and Smokey each took a side and cuddled up next to their best friend.

Joshua lifted his head from his knees and wiped the tears from his puffy cheeks. "I thought I told you guys to stay put," he said kindly.

Smokey raised a soggy piece of a peanut butter sandwich in the air and presented it to Joshua as a truce.

Joshua pulled the sandwich from Smokey's hand, brushed away a bit of dirt, and shoved the entire bite in his mouth. "Goes down better with milk," he said, trying to chew the mouthful of sticky peanut butter.

Swallowing the treat, he stood and looked around. The field below Oakie was covered in junk.

"This won't do," he declared. "We can't leave our hallowed ground in such disarray!" Pointing at his trusted sidekicks, he barked, "You two follow me!" Then he began a diligent march through the rain and mud back to his house.

"That's the ambitious kid I remember," Houdini said, and winked in Oakie's direction before following Smokey, who was already in hot pursuit.

"Remember to stick close," Oakie reminded them as they chased after Joshua.

"Already on top of it," Smokey replied, leaping onto Joshua's back and wrapping his arms around his forehead.

Turning around, Smokey gave Oakie a mischievous laugh and a thumbs-up as the trio crested the hill and disappeared.

CHAPTER

34

IN TIME ALL THINGS WILL BE MADE RIGHT

—————— 34 ——————

Each day at the same time, Joshua returned to the field. Dragging his wagon, accompanied by his companions, he made the journey determined to clean up the past. Lacking the glimmer his eyes once carried, he toiled in the field, dragging dirt-covered wooden planks and chunks of plastic back to his wagon, loading it full. Trip after trip, he piled the garbage high on the wagon, and when it could hold no more, he sadly hauled away the remains of his base station.

Each load stirred up memories of playing or the grand adventure it took to build his magical kingdom. Some days the memories were too much and they left him with tears in his eyes; others pushed him to fits of anger.

No matter what his mood, Houdini and Smokey stuck close by. Some days they quietly helped clean and other days they hassled each other in fun.

Joshua was never safe from their rowdy rumble or playful antics, and Oakie only encouraged their behavior.

With every trip Joshua's mood lightened. With each load of garbage removed from the field, he smiled a bit more. Houdini and Smokey's unwavering dedication and unrelenting games chipped away at his sadness and turmoil.

Soon Joshua was taking breaks from cleaning to play games with his friends. Using a plank like a baseball bat, he knocked rocks into the field while Houdini and Smokey took turns chasing them down and bringing them back. When that had all but worn the two out, Joshua tossed them in the wagon and dragged them wildly around the field. Like a hockey player battling on ice, he whipped figure eights as fast as he could, slowing down only to keep the wagon from spilling over.

Houdini and Smokey held on for dear life, struggling to keep their lunch down as the wagon thundered over the rocky terrain. When the ride finished, Joshua cackled with joy at the top of his lungs as the two stumbled about trying to get their bearings.

Oakie watched with delight as his friend slowly found the spark of life again. Before long, the downtrodden boy who had visited Oakie in the rain had all but disappeared. And soon, with dedication and determination, the field was clean of all the debris.

Returning alone one day, with no wagon, Smokey, or Houdini, Joshua approached Oakie and stood quietly before him. Oakie watched curiously as his friend reached into a pocket and pulled out a red Swiss Army knife. After a moment of struggle, he opened the largest blade and found the perfect place on Oakie's trunk to begin carving. Driving the knife deep into the bark, he cut and chipped until he had formed a sufficient "J."

Oakie chuckled as the digging of the knife tickled him. Soon the name "Joshua," etched deep into the bark, decorated Oakie's trunk. Marked for life, he now bore the name of his best friend.

After taking a second to be sure the name had been carved sufficiently, Joshua closed the blade and returned it to his pocket. He looked at the marking for a moment before reaching out to place a hand over his name. As he pushed softly against Oakie's bark, something electric happened.

A wild burning began to blaze from deep within. Amore was alive and well! As Joshua held his hand firmly against Oakie, Amore shot from the pit of Oakie's trunk and injected herself into the branches above. Suddenly, leaves broke forth from the green stems. Her power was mesmerizing and transforming.

Joshua closed his eyes, keeping his hand in place. "Dear God, please protect my friend. Keep him healthy and strong. Give him more friends to hang out with so he doesn't feel alone like I used to. Amen."

As Joshua finished his simple yet powerful prayer, the words stoked Amore's fire and shot yet another electric blaze throughout Oakie's branches. His leaves began to rumble. His branches felt as though they were ready to explode. Suddenly, something burst from a cluster of leaves like a kernel of popcorn.

It was an acorn!

Oakie marveled at the acorn. It seemed as though it had been an entire lifetime since he had seen one.

Squinting his eyes tightly, Joshua pushed all of his weight against Oakie, as if to shove something through the name, past the bark, and into the center of the tree. Soon the other leaves began to shake, and a miraculous sight erupted throughout Oakie's branches. First the one, then a dozen, and then hundreds of acorns exploded from Oakie's leaves!

The acorns began as little green jewels and quickly bloomed into giant brown nuggets. Oakie's branches began to hang under the weight of them. Somehow, their appearance had been ignited by the faithful prayer and love transfusion Oakie received from this simple little boy he called "friend."

Joshua opened his eyes to take another look at Oakie. It seemed as though it would be his last. "Thank you, Nemesis. You're my best friend and I'll never forget you." Then he dropped his hand from Oakie's trunk and marched out of the field.

With a heart full of memories, and the fresh markings of a best friend etched deep into his bark, Oakie sat and marveled at the transformation left by a little boy filled with love. Hundreds upon hundreds of acorns decorated his branches, and not a single apple amongst them. After all the time spent thinking and dreaming about making apples, Oakie had been thrown a curve ball he couldn't have imagined. What did it all mean? If only Morgan was around to see this! What would he say? Oakie didn't know what to feel. Was it good? Was it bad? Whatever it was, one thing was for sure—it was one big giant surprise!

As Oakie sat hypnotized by the acorns, a giant bird sailed toward him, engulfed by the sun's light. As the bird approached, two unrecognizable riders became visible. What sounded like a war cry from one of the passengers startled

Oakie. He watched hesitantly as the bird drew closer until it was upon him, circling above. Oakie hadn't seen a bird since Morte and her murder had left. With apprehension, he kept his eyes on the enormous bird and its riders.

Suddenly, without rhyme or reason, the bird dive-bombed out of the sky toward Oakie.

"Weeeeehooo!" shouted the rider, holding the reins of the bridle in the bird's mouth. Diving, diving, diving, down, down, down. The bird plummeted toward the ground. Oakie braced for impact. Then, like a parachute, the bird came to a gentle landing in front of him.

Sitting atop the bird, under a mask of yellow-and-blue face paint, was a wild and familiar friend from the past.

"You crazy squirrel! Where have you been, Otis?"

Otis looked Oakie up and down for a moment, studying his friend as though he was looking through a microscope.

"Otis, you meathead, what are you doing and why are you covered from top to bottom in paint?"

The moment the word "meathead" flew out Oakie's mouth, Otis knew he had found his friend. "It can't be! Cheveyo! I told you this was it. My knower always knows," Otis shouted in excitement.

From behind him, a horned lizard popped out. Covered from head to toe in yellow and blue markings, wearing the feather of a desert hawk strapped to his head, Cheveyo leapt from his seat behind Otis and landed before Oakie.

Otis sprang from his seat and landed next to his friend.

Cheveyo stood quietly with his arms crossed as Otis did a celebratory tribal dance mixed with some flying ninja kicks and slicing judo chops. "The great Numees Salali strikes again!" Otis shouted while continuing his victory dance.

"What is Numees Salali?" Oakie asked.

Lost in his dance, Otis paid no attention to the question and continued.

"Sister Squirrel," Cheveyo chimed in.

Otis stopped in his tracks.

"No it doesn't! It means Wise Warrior," Otis shot back.

Ignoring Otis, Cheveyo continued with a very solemn look on his face, "New to the desert tribe, Otis was eager to make a good impression. Unfortunately, not understanding the tribe's ways, Otis completed a task that was strictly reserved for women of the tribe. He was very proud of his achievement. He told all the great warriors of his accomplishment, boasting that he was the best."

Otis stared at the ground, remembering the incident.

"When he shared his story with the chief spiritual elder Nahimana, Nahimana laughed and called him Numees Salali or 'sister squirrel.' "

"Wait a minute! I remember him distinctly saying 'Wise Warrior'!" Otis retorted.

Cheveyo continued talking to Oakie. "Not understanding our language, Otis asked, 'Does that mean 'Great Warrior?' In his sarcastically funny sense of humor, Nahimana answered back, 'Wise Warrior.' "

Otis stood silent for a moment. "You mean to tell me I've been introducing myself to all the fine ladies as Sister Squirrel?"

"This is correct," Cheveyo said, not cracking a smile.

Oakie burst out in a deep belly laugh.

Otis's mind flooded with memories of meeting lady lizards. Every time they laughed at him, covered their faces, and ran away. No wonder he couldn't get a date. "Stop laughing! This isn't funny," Otis demanded.

Oakie couldn't stop thinking of Otis referring to himself as "Sister Squirrel." He tried to stop for his friend's sake, but only laughed harder.

"Why didn't you tell me about this? You're supposed to be one of my best friends!" Otis pointed at Cheveyo.

"Because it is funny."

"Wait a minute!" Otis's face grew even more shocked. "After I passed The Great Tribulation and they initiated me as a tribal warrior, they carried me around chanting ..."

"Yes, 'Sister Squirrel.' That day was very triumphant and many jokes were made at your expense, my friend."

Otis's anger built until it couldn't be contained. Leaping up and down, stomping on the ground, he shouted, "I'm a wise warrior! I'm a wise warrior!"

Otis's childish fit provoked Oakie to more laughter. All the laughing shook his branches so hard that a cluster of acorns broke loose and rained down on Otis.

One after another, the acorns bounced off of Otis's head and scattered about the ground. Dazed by the acorn beatings, Otis stumbled around, rubbing his noggin.

Even Cheveyo couldn't keep a straight face anymore as he joined in Oakie's laughter.

Frustrated and angry, Otis grabbed an acorn and spun around to throw it at Cheveyo. Before releasing it, a revelation of epic proportions hit him. Stopping dead in his tracks, Otis stared, almost frozen, not believing his eyes. Caught in blissful rapture, Otis held the acorn between his hands and raised the golden trophy high in the air. Wonder painted his face. "She's more beautiful than a cactus princess," he said in awe.

Oakie and Cheveyo stopped laughing and turned their attention to Otis and his acorn.

"Where did she come from?" Otis stammered.

Noticing Otis's reaction, Oakie began to feel even more excited about what he had created.

"Not the apple you thought I would make, but in my opinion it might be just as good." Oakie grinned from branch to branch.

"Better," Otis said, lost in the wonder of the acorn.

"There's plenty more where that came from." Oakie shook his branches and dropped a few more acorns down to Otis.

Cheveyo dodged back and forth to avoid the falling nuts. Otis watched a dozen or so acorns scatter about the ground. His eyes trailed back up Oakie. Glimmering in the sunlight was the greatest storehouse of treasure Otis had ever seen. The sight left him breathless. His heart began racing faster than a horse in the Kentucky Derby. Looking up, he grew lightheaded and fell over onto his back.

"Are those for real?" Otis stammered.

Oakie shook another branch and dropped another dozen or so.

"Do crazy squirrels ride vultures?"

An ancient carnal instinct rose from the deepest depths of Otis's stomach. Like a programmed robot designed for one single task, Otis sprung to his feet. Acting without a will of his own, he frantically ran in circles gathering up the acorns and stacking them in a pile as high as they could go. Just as he had done long ago with Oakie, Otis raced around and ravenously dug holes in the ground. Using his paws and teeth, he burrowed down as fast as he could. Then he retrieved the acorns and shoved his treasures in the holes before covering them up.

At the speed of lightning, he raced around until there was nothing left to bury. Exhausted, out of his mind, and with a mouth chock-full of dirt, he turned toward Oakie again. With his wild eye twitching, he huffed and puffed, trying to catch his breath.

"You have a little something in your teeth." Oakie motioned with a branch.

Otis licked his teeth and blew a big muddy spitball out of his mouth.

"A lot has changed since we last chatted, old friend."

Still stunned, Otis nodded in agreement.

"Is this the coveted treasure you refer to as acorn?" Cheveyo inquired, holding an acorn Otis had missed.

"Like I said, it's *not* an apple," Oakie interjected with a large grin.

"What does this acorn do?" Cheveyo asked, very interested.

"It gets gathered up and buried by me," Otis said, pointing to himself.

"Then, after what feels like eternity, it becomes me," Oakie said triumphantly.

"How did this happen?" Otis asked, perplexed by what he was seeing.

"Do you want to hear the story or bury the rest of them?" Oakie replied.

Otis began shaking like he was ready to explode. Bursting into the air, he bounced about. Grabbing Cheveyo's hands, he dragged him into a celebratory dance. "Ooooh baby! We've struck it rich!" he shouted as he twirled Cheveyo in circles. "We found what we've been lookin' for and with it, never-ending treasure!" Otis released Cheveyo and sent him flying. "Let's get to gatherin' and buryin'." He rubbed his paws back and forth, warming them up for the party.

"All right, if you say so," Oakie warned before revving up and shaking all of his branches as hard as he could. "Take cover!" he shouted as the acorns began to break loose and plummet to the earth.

Cheveyo and Otis sprang back and forth, dodging the acorns as they showered down around them. It became a game of cat and mouse as the two leaped about, evading the missiles.

Oakie's heart leapt with joy. It was a delight to see Otis playing and having so much fun. After everything that had happened, he never would have imagined someone would enjoy acorns more than the peoples had enjoyed the apples in the orchard. It was wonderful knowing what he had created was so loved by someone else. But beyond that, after all this time, it was a greater pleasure getting to be close to someone he called *family*.

As the last of the acorns fell, Otis stood for a moment, staring at the plunder. The acorns blanketed the field below Oakie. The sight was overwhelming. The longer Otis looked at the piles of acorns, the more it began to look like work, not fun. If Otis wasn't careful, the best thing that ever happened to him could become his worst nightmare.

"This is all wrong!" Otis exclaimed.

"What's all wrong?" Oakie asked.

"This!" Otis waved his hands at the field. "I can't bury all of these alone!"

"Do not fear. You are not alone. I will gladly assist you, my friend," Cheveyo chimed in.

"I'm not scared of them. It's not like they're going to bite me. I'm scared of dying from exhaustion trying to bury all of this!" Otis began to march back and forth, trying to engineer a plan. "There has to be a way to do this," he mumbled to himself.

Cheveyo and Oakie watched as their friend went into deep thought.

Suddenly, as though lightning struck, Otis spun in circles and pumped his fist in the air. "Nothing is too complicated for this adventurer extraordinaire!" he shouted as he raced over to Cheveyo. Grabbing the face of his horned friend, he jerked Cheveyo in nose to nose. "You listen up."

Cheveyo was startled.

"I want you to dig, and I mean *dig*. Dig like your life depends on it. You dig everywhere you can. You use your tail, your claws, and your mouth. You start digging and you don't stop until I return—not for water, not for food, not even to go to the bathroom."

"What if I must go terribly bad?"

"Do whatever you have to, just don't stop. Do you hear me?" Otis shook Cheveyo's face.

Cheveyo tried his best to nod back.

"And you." Otis pointed at Oakie. "Don't go anywhere." Oakie frowned comically at Otis.

"I'll be back." With that, Otis dropped Cheveyo's face and charged toward his vulture. Without looking back, he mounted his feathery steed and raced off into the sky. In the blink of an eye he soared over a hill and disappeared from sight.

"Wow, he's really tamed down since I last saw him," Oakie said.

Cheveyo turned to his new friend with a look of confusion. "No ... no, he hasn't."

The two laughed.

"Well, what's it going to be? You just going to stand around staring at me all day, or are you going to dazzle him with your hole-digging abilities?"

"I would much rather just stand here and stare," Cheveyo sighed. "I sometimes regret saving him from that rattlesnake den. Minimal regret of course, but still, a hint of regret." Cheveyo smirked at Oakie as he walked toward the open field.

"By the way, what are you doing here with Otis?"

Cheveyo stopped and looked back. "Helping the great adventurer that risked his life for my tribe." Cheveyo looked at Oakie with eyes of gratitude, as though to say, *I have come face to face with losing all that I love and triumphed for one reason alone.* With that, he turned and hustled to the field, where he dug ravenously.

As the afternoon passed, hundreds, if not thousands, of holes had appeared all around Oakie. Cheveyo's shoulders now hung as he dragged himself, and his tail, slowly from hole to hole. Covered from head to toe in dirt, the last of his energy had all but run out. Like a mindless zombie, Cheveyo stumbled forward until he simply toppled over.

"I think it's probably a good time to quit," Oakie offered sympathetically.

Lying face down in the dirt, Cheveyo gave a thumbs-up, and then went limp with exhaustion.

Oakie admired Cheveyo's gratitude, faithfulness, and determination. If someone had saved the orchard, Oakie would have done anything in his power to let them know how much it meant to him. He had no trouble understanding why Cheveyo almost broke himself digging all those holes. Lost in thought, Oakie was startled by the hoots and hollers of his returning friend. He turned and watched as the vulture galloped through the sky toward him. Dangling behind the bird was some sort of branch covered in green needles.

Like a dive-bomber, Otis swooped down on the vulture, skimming above the earth. The needles combed the ground much like a broom, and dragged the acorns about. Otis made pass after pass, sweeping up the acorns behind him. The acorns rolled into open holes where they waited to be covered. Otis looked at Oakie, smiling from ear to ear.

"I told you I was a wise warrior!" Otis shouted as he soared past. Whizzing by Cheveyo, who still lay facedown in the dirt, Otis continued, "Hey Cheveyo, you sure dug a lot of holes, probably more than we needed."

Otis carried on innocently, "Don't worry though, you can just fill back in the ones we don't have acorns for. It's always easier filling 'em back in than it is diggin' 'em."

At that, Otis made a few more passes, knocking in the last of the acorns, and then landed his bird. "Well, that was a whole lot easier than I thought it was going to be," he commented as he dismounted. "Now all I have to do is get these babies buried. Hey, Cheveyo."

Cheveyo lay motionless.

"You look tired. Tell ya what, you take it easy and I'll

finish the rest of this up by myself. It's the least I can do for all your hard work."

Oakie laughed to himself as Otis went to work burying all the acorns. Before long, Otis had the field pretty well cleaned up. "Wow, that was hard work," Otis said as he walked toward Cheveyo, wiping sweat off his brow.

Cheveyo shook his head and rolled onto his back.

"Since you've been takin' it easy, you wouldn't mind getting some water from our supplies on the vulture, would you?" Cheveyo rolled his eyes, then dragged himself to his feet and slowly marched toward the vulture.

"You wanna grab me a slice of that desert fruit while you're at it?"

Cheveyo continued on, not acknowledging Otis.

"Great lizard, but a little bit lazy sometimes," Otis said casually as he sat and caught his breath.

As Otis and Cheveyo relaxed, Oakie shared with them the story of the orchard and the lessons he had learned through all of it. The two mourned for their friend and his loss, but not without celebrating what he had conquered.

"You remind me of Ituha." Cheveyo told Oakie after he had finished.

"What or who is Ituha?" Oakie inquired, hoping it was good.

"For many generations," Cheveyo began, "there has been an ancient legend passed down about a mighty tree my people call Ituha. Long ago, a great evil visited my people. This darkness enslaved them, leaving them bound and hopeless. During this time of slavery, a fearless warrior escaped. He scoured uncharted lands in search of a place free from the tyrants that was flowing with water and filled with cactus fruit, where he might lead his people into freedom. In his journey he faced many tests, but none so dangerous as those brought about by the spirit earth. He was led to the safety of a giant oak tree, where he took refuge in a hole that had been crafted by the tools of time.

"During the course of four suns and four moons, four trials visited the brave warrior. First came a very sad rain— its tears hoped to drown him. Then came a screaming wind—its voice sent to blow him away. After that, a mighty shaking came from the starving earth—its mouth opened wide, trying to swallow him alive. Lastly, there came an angry fire from the heavens, sent to consume him, leaving only ashes behind."

Oakie's eyes grew large as he thought about the fire.

"When all four tests had come and gone, the warrior still lived, as did Ituha, who had protected him throughout it all. While hidden away in the safety of the giant oak tree, a vision came to this warrior. Suddenly he understood that freedom for his people could never be truly found outside their homeland. There would always be threats and dangers 'out there.' Going away was not the answer. Finding freedom against their oppressors meant conquering the land they called home. With that, the brave warrior returned to his people and told them of Ituha and the wisdom it shared with him.

"Through many battles and much loss, my people eventually freed themselves. Though there have been those who have come to take this freedom away, desiring to shackle my people once again, they have had no success. Ituha gave my people a revelation of true freedom—one that cannot be stolen."

Oakie marveled at the story of the brave warrior and Ituha.

"You see, Ituha was mighty and strong. Immovable. No matter the forces around him, he stood as a safe refuge. Through his life, he brought wisdom and freedom. You have faced many challenges, yet you stand here. The words you speak are covered in wisdom, just as a baby is covered by a blanket. I believe you to be a spirit ancestor of this Ituha. It is a great honor to meet you. I will share with my people that I have met one of Ituha's own."

Oakie was speechless. Cheveyo's story of the brave warrior and Ituha made everything he had gone through feel so much more purposeful. Oakie felt great value for all that had happened. It was so much to think about. "Thank you for sharing that. It's very helpful."

Cheveyo nodded his head.

The three sat for a moment in silence before Otis chimed in and began sharing stories about his daring adventures in

Vulture Desert. The three celebrated Otis's many escapes from the clutches of death.

Even Cheveyo took time to honor Otis's bravery by sharing how he had saved the tribe from a giant night lizard known as Kokipa.

As the dust of the conversation began to settle, Oakie asked what he had been longing to know the whole time. "So why exactly did you come looking for me?"

"I told you I'd explore Vulture Dessert, tame me a vulture and make it back alive. Well I did just that, and I thought you might like to see it for yourself."

Oakie looked at the vulture for moment. "I'm really proud of you, Otis. You're very brave."

Otis looked at the ground for a moment before responding, "You know something? There were times I was so scared that I was going to die. So many times that I just wanted to turn back and quit. But you know what? The one thing that kept me going was you."

Otis's words caught Oakie off guard.

Otis looked around for a moment and then continued, "I would always think about the choice you made. Even though you wanted to stay buried above The Valley of Eagles, your gut told you differently. You knew deep down inside that your destiny was back in the orchard. It reminded me to follow what I believed, no matter what the consequences might be. I knew I would regret it if I didn't."

After all Otis had done for Oakie, it felt incredible hearing that somehow he had helped inspire Otis as well.

"So what happens next for all these acorns?" Cheveyo asked.

"Hopefully, after a very long wait, they grow up to be like me," Oakie said with a smile.

"Well, it's getting late and we need to head back to The Valley of Eagles." Otis jumped up, rubbing his belly. Hunger had kicked in and they were low on supplies.

"You can't stay a little longer?"

"Sorry, but adventure doesn't bend to meet my schedule. Besides, we have tons of supplies to gather."

Oakie's heart sank a little. His time with Otis had been so

good, but so short. He wanted Otis to stay forever. "Promise me you'll return," Oakie demanded.

"You couldn't keep me away, especially if you keep growing acorns!" Otis winked his wild eye and headed toward the vulture.

"Cheveyo, it was an honor to meet you. Please take good care of Sister Squirrel and make sure he doesn't get you killed."

Cheveyo chuckled. "It was equally an honor to meet you, Oakie." Cheveyo turned to walk away and then paused for one last thought. "There is a desert oasis of water near my tribe known as Waanaki. Waanaki is the source of all life for my kind. The elders tell of its story and its power to transform the desert almost over night. For many moons and many seasons, my tribe has gathered this water and used it on our crops, which always yield an abundant harvest. I carry a pouch on the vulture filled with it. May I have your permission to drizzle it over this field and speak an ancient blessing as we leave? I believe very strongly that it will do for these acorns what it has done for my tribe's crops."

"Of course. How could I say no?"

With that, Cheveyo walked away and mounted the vulture with Otis. After circling the field a few times and drizzling the water over the land, the two waved goodbye and set off for home, leaving Oakie with his thoughts and a field full of buried acorns.

CHAPTER

35

A FATHER OF MANY

35

After many seasons and many return visits from Otis, Oakie was no longer alone. Waanaki had done its job, and Oakie now stood tall in the center of a great forest, surrounded by sons and daughters.

Standing silently one night, he watched as a gust of wind started a tango with the fallen leaves below, twirling them in the air around him. As he watched the dancing symphony, the sun slowly faded into a family of gray clouds that were being carried toward the forest on the shoulders of a mighty wind. A hammering thunder billowed from the clouds as a tapestry of lightning painted the sky. The fingers of lightning tickled the ground as it combed through the forest.

A flash of lightning struck a bush that was growing before Oakie. The bush ignited into a blaze, burning like the midday sun. The flames, reminiscent of those that had taken his family long ago, consumed the bush. Oakie's heart began pounding with fear. Surely this had to be a nightmare. The soothing voice of a long-forgotten friend shook Oakie.

"Oakie, why are you afraid?"

"Morgan?" Oakie asked, befuddled.

"You make for such a wise and powerful tree. Why are you afraid of a simple fire?"

Oakie stood startled, yet oddly comforted by the nearly forgotten voice of his long-lost father. Whether this was a dream, his imagination, or an unexplainable miracle, it didn't matter. For one brief moment, Oakie seemingly had his father back.

"I'm afraid because fire destroyed everything I ever loved, and I fear it will do it again."

"Oakie, the fire never came to destroy or to kill," Morgan said gently. "The fire that spread throughout the orchard was no different than Amore. It came to cleanse and release life. It cleansed the land of all the dead, rotting trees. It's true, those trees that lived were burnt as well, but it wasn't unto death. All the years of our lives were left behind in the ashes of that field. It was our lives that made the ground fertile, and from that fertile ground of ashes, beauty rose. All the children that you see are the result of your presence in the orchard and the ashes of our lives. Without the fire, your children would have had no place to grow. Without the fire, you never could have fulfilled your destiny."

Oakie's eyes began to water as he listened to his father share the hopeful wisdom he had come to value so much.

"You see, Oakie, your destiny was never to be an apple tree—it was to be a mighty oak tree. Your destiny was to father many acorns and to be the father of a mighty forest. It's no coincidence that you were placed by my side. You were there to learn what it is to be a father so you could father a generation of your own children. I gave all that I had to you, loving you with the fullness of my heart, just as I did with my own son, Dakota. Through my love and friendship, you discovered that you were more than a tiny acorn.

"Now you're a father to many. It is a much greater destiny than growing apples like everyone else—a much greater destiny because it is unique to who you were made to be. No matter how hard you tried, you couldn't have dreamed of this destiny because it was deep within you from the very beginning. All you needed was something greater than you to carry you to a place that you couldn't get to on your own."

Oakie reflected nostalgically on the fateful day that Otis caught him and saved him from that gang of hungry squirrels.

"Now it's time to thrive and live out your destiny as a father, without remorse or regret. It's time to see your greatest loss as your greatest gain. The orchard isn't lost. We live on within you and through you. As you give yourself away to this forest, as I did, we will live on in your children, just as you will. And this, Oakie, is the beauty of life—that nothing has to be in vain. All things can be redeemed and used for a greater purpose than we could ever imagine."

The fire quickly faded out, leaving behind a bush that had been untouched by the flames. Oakie shook his head and squinted, gazing at the untarnished bush. What had just happened? Was it all in his mind? Had he imagined it? As the wonder and astonishment faded, Oakie found himself lost in reflection about his life.

Season after season, he had dreamed that one day he would grow up to make apples like the other trees. He dreamt that the peoples would come to climb him and collect the apples in his branches. He never could have foreseen that he would become the largest tree in the orchard or the magical base station to a little people who would dream the wildest dreams ever dreamt. He never could have imagined the fun he would have, or the tears he would cry. He never would have imagined that one day he would lose his family and be all alone with a people, and that through a people's touch he would create thousands of acorns. It had never even crossed Oakie's mind that the very thing he once was, he would create. It seemed as though it was in him all along.

As Oakie pondered the events of his life, the forest began to rumble. Birds flew from their perches to alert the world that intruders were near.

Squeak, squeak. Crick, crack. Squeak, crick crack, squeak—the sound grew louder as the invaders got closer.

"It's over here somewhere," a deep voice echoed in the distance.

"But Dad, they all look the same. How will you know which one it is?" The sound of a small boy's voice rang out over the noise.

"I told you, I left a tracking signal long ago in my early explorations. I'm using my manquest to follow the signal."

"Are there any ruins left of the ancient civilization like the ones I saw on TV?"

"The ruins were cleared away long ago by a famous archeologist. But I'm sure The Tree of Life must still be standing. It was indestructible, as far as I could tell when I discovered it."

"How old were you when you found it?" the little voice inquired.

"A few years older than you, I think. I was the only brave warrior that dared to venture out in search of The Tree of Life. It was said by many to be guarded by the spirits of past warriors who died trying to find it. All were scared to seek it out, fearing that the past warriors would kill them."

"Why did so many people want to find The Tree of Life, Dad?"

"I told you already—anyone who visits The Tree of Life stays young forever."

"Why would you want to stay young forever, Dad?"

"Because when you're young, life is fun and it can be anything you want it to be."

"How come it can't be like that when you're old?"

"It can. But most adults forget what it's like to be young, so they try hard to *look* young, but never figure out how to *be* young. Only time in The Tree of Life can make you young again."

"Will you transform into a little boy like me if we find it?"

"*When* we find it, I can become anything you want. Just dream it and I'll be it. The same goes for you."

Oakie listened curiously to the voices, hoping to catch a glimpse of the faces behind them. Through the trees, a man wearing glasses with gray-speckled red hair, stepped into view. In one hand, he carried a toolbox and in the other, he gripped the hand of a small red-headed boy. In the boy's other hand he pulled a rusty, dented red Radio Flyer wagon stacked high with lumber.

"Stop!" the man said abruptly, bringing the two to a halt. The boy looked around frantically, trying to under-stand what was happening.

"Dad, what—?"

"Shhhh!" the father demanded. Whispering, he contin-ued, "We're getting closer. I can feel it."

Frozen, the two glanced around, moving only their eyes, as they scanned the area. The sound of a twig breaking grabbed their attention. Without hesitation, the father dropped his toolbox and leaped on top of his son, knocking him to the ground. "Stay quiet and don't move. They're getting closer," the father demanded.

Oakie laughed delightedly. Hidden behind the large stature, wrinkles, glasses, tired eyes, and speckled gray hair was the imaginative little boy whose world was whatever he made of it.

"What's getting closer, Dad?" the boy squeaked under his breath.

"Hellhounds. They're the spirit dogs used by the dead explorers to hunt down trespassers. To my knowledge they're invincible. We have to stay low until we know they've passed."

"We can't just wait here all day, Dad."

"Well, Justus, do you have any better ideas?"

"Let me think." Grabbing his right ear, the boy revved up the gears in his head by quickly turning it back and forth. Letting go of his ear, he shook his head and went to work solving the problem. Nothing was invincible, not even Superman. These hellhounds certainly couldn't be more powerful than him.

Just out of the boy's reach he noticed a stick. Scattered around were dozens of acorns. His eyes began to cross as he mapped out an idea.

Oakie beamed with joy, watching his best friend play with this little people. It felt so reminiscent of Morgan's time with him.

"Dad, I think I have it!"

"Good, because they're getting closer, I'm sure of it."

"I was practicing some spells a couple of days ago. One was an electro-charge spell that could fill my toys with electricity so if anyone touched them besides me they would get shocked. And ..." Justus hesitated.

"And what? We've got to hurry! They're closing in on us."

"Promise not to be mad," Justus begged his dad.

Joshua seemed leery of what his son was about to say, but no matter what it was, it couldn't be worse than hellhounds. "Yes, I promise. Now make it quick!"

The sound of rustling paws drew closer through the woods.

"Okay, well, there's that boy down the street who's always making fun of me and calling me a 'ginger kid.'"

Joshua knew the boy and had wanted to exchange some strong words with his dad for quite some time. Knowing that the dad was much worse than the son, he had kept his cool and waited for the right time and way to do it. "I know the one. Go on."

"So I discovered a spell that could make a piece of dog poo smell like chocolate, and I put it in a Tootsie Roll wrapper and gave it to him." Justus smiled at his creative way of handling the bully.

Joshua frowned with disgust. "I'm guessing your smile means it worked?"

Justus nodded in satisfaction.

Joshua was torn between pride in his son's ingenuity and a parental sense of needing to say he shouldn't have done that. But this didn't seem like the time or place to address it. "Well then, hurry up and tell me how your spell can help us."

"If I can get my hands on that stick, I can use it as a wand. With a few adjustments to my candy-smell spell, I can make those acorns smell like dog treats. If I combine it all with my electro-charge spell ..."

"You can feed the acorns to the dogs and the acorns will shock the dogs and kill them! Brilliant!" Joshua rubbed Justus's hair in approval. "I'll grab your wand. Ready your spells." Joshua rolled off of Justus, grabbed the stick, and then rolled back. "Here, now make it happen." Joshua pushed his ear to the ground. "They're less than a minute away. Hurry!"

> "Stick to wand, magic turn on.
> Charge this acorn with an electro shock,
> One that will leave those dogs lying in chalk.
> In order for them to eat,
> This acorn must smell like a treat.
> I call this acorn tasty and good,
> Just like a doggy treat would.
> Zippity-zap, dippiddy-dee,
> These acorns will now turn as I tell them to be!"

Justus and his father watched in amazement as the acorns transformed before their very eyes. The smell of bacon acorns wafted into the air. No dog could resist that.

Without hesitation, the two grabbed handfuls of acorns and chucked them into the forest.

Oakie laughed as he watched the acorns rain down on the ground and roll around.

"You hear that!" Joshua shouted. "They're howling, it's working! They're eating them!"

Only Joshua and Justus could hear the wailing of the dying dogs. Leaping to their feet, the two danced around and pumped their fists in the air to celebrate the victory.

"My spells worked, Dad! I knew they would."

"So did I!" Joshua exclaimed, celebrating his son's triumph.

After a satisfying moment of celebration, the two grabbed the wagon and tools and headed on. Walking with their chests puffed out and heads held high, they navigated past the roots and rocks that would knock the wagon over.

Pausing for a moment, Joshua looked to examine the surrounding trees. There in front of him, staring him in the face, were the letters of his name etched years ago into Oakie's bark. Joshua marveled at the sight. A wealth of memories flooded his mind and filled his heart. Filled with nostalgia, Joshua pulled a rusty red Swiss Army knife from his pocket and turned to his son. "We've found it. This is the magnificent Tree of Life I told you about."

"How do you know, Dad?"

"Because this is the mark I made." Joshua brushed his hand over his name.

Justus looked at the carving and then at the knife in his father's hand.

"And now it's time to make yours."

EPILOGUE:
GENERATIONS

EPILOGUE: GENERATIONS

"The End."

"Grandpa, that can't be the end."

"Well it is the end, 'cause my thinker's tired," said the old gray-haired man as he rocked back and forth in his chair. "Besides, that's probably the best story you ever heard, or will ever hear for that matter. So quit complainin' and be satisfied." The old man smiled mischievously at his grandson.

"But what happened to Oakie? What about Otis, Houdini, and Smokey? What ended up happening to them? And what about Joshua?"

The old man sat for a moment, looking out from his chair on the porch. After years of being too busy to slow down and enjoy the simple things in life, the oranges, reds, and pinks painted by the setting sun received a moment of his attention.

"I'll tell you what happened to them," he said finally. "Joshua had a son named Justus. Justus eventually had a son named Jason. And Jason—" The little boy hung on the edge of his seat, ready for another epic story. "Well, Jason demanded that his grandpa tell him a never-ending story ..." The old man paused for another moment just to let his grandson hang on a bit longer. "And the rest of them lived happily ever after."

"Grandpa!" the boy exclaimed in dissatisfaction.

"Justus! Get your butt out here and tell Jason that everything turned out happily ever after and that's the end," the old man said.

Popping his head through the screen door, Justus came to referee the match happening on the porch.

"They lived happily ever after," he echoed. "Now get inside, little man, and get ready for bed."

"Dad, I am ready."

"Did you brush your teeth?" Justus inquired, already knowing the answer.

"Maybe ..." The boy answered hesitantly.

"Maybe always means, 'no.' Now hurry up and get in there or I'm calling the National Alien Patrol and telling them I found a Class One Zoid on my front porch. They'll be dragging you back to Mars kicking and screaming in no time." Justus winked at Joshua.

"Dad, I'm not a Zoid and there's no such thing as the National Alien Patrol."

"It's not up for discussion, you Zoid. Now march!" Justus demanded, pointing his finger inside.

"All right ..." Jason said reluctantly, getting out of his chair. "Hey, Grandpa?"

"Yes, Jason?"

"Thanks for the story. It was the best I've ever heard."

Joshua smiled at his grandson's satisfaction.

"But, just so you know, I tell better," Jason said pokingly as he smiled back at his grandpa and made his way inside.

Justus and Joshua looked at each other and laughed as Justus sat down in Jason's seat. From his pocket Justus pulled an old, dirty, rusty, red Swiss Army knife and a piece of wood. Quietly he sat with his father and whittled away, knowing everything really did turn out happily ever after.

UNWRAPPING
THE ALLEGORY:
MEANING OF NAMES

UNWRAPPING THE ALLEGORY:

MEANING OF NAMES

Within the pages of *The Tree of Life* exist eccentric names for characters. Every name is a key to unlocking the entirety of the allegory. Because of this I've created a short list to give the meaning of these names.

Verstand – German origin meaning mind or understand. An eagle owl represents Wisdom and freedom.
Morte – Italian origin meaning death.
Colpa – Italian origin meaning guilt.
Vergogna - Italian origin meaning shame.
Condanna – Italian origin meaning condemnation
Orfano - Italian origin meaning orphan.
Inganno - Italian origin meaning deception.
Verita - Italian meaning origin truth.
Speranza - Spanish origin meaning hope.
Amore - Italian origin meaning love.
Cheveyo - Native American Hopi origin meaning spirit warrior.
Numees - Algonquin origin meaning sister.
Salali - Cherokee origin meaning squirrel.
Ituha - Native American origin meaning sturdy oak.
Waanaki - Ojibwe origin meaning peace or inhabit.

ACKNOWLEDGEMENTS

ACKNOWLEDGEMENTS

My wife is a word of affirmation junkie! Affirming people is like breathing air for her. If she were writing these acknowledgements they would be a book entitled *The Tree of Life Part 2-The Thank Yous*! So let me begin by filling her "love tank" and saying this- Abi, none of this book would have happened, because I wouldn't be the man I am today without you! You are the most tangible expression of God's love that I may ever know.

Mom and Dad, you never cease to believe in me. Thank you for not allowing me to take over the family business. Thank you for demanding that I explore my heart and find out who I am and what it is that I really want to do. I'm still figuring that out, but it's much clearer every day.

Blair Reynolds, your faithful friendship and love has continually championed me and your word-smithing was key to the completion of this book.

William P. Young, your love and personal book journey inspired me to keep dreaming for Oakie's birth.

Noah Elias, your friendship has not only brought life to me, but also to the characters in this book. The visions in my mind found their place on these pages because of your artistic genius.

TT and PP, you are the extended family I didn't know I wanted, but always needed. Thank you for being a springboard for all the dreams I have had for this book.

Ryan Sprenger, I literally couldn't have launched this book without the faith journey of your own life. Thank you for walking arm in arm with me, especially after all the times I wailed on you in cribbage! Smells like a skunk in here and it isn't me!

To the One who took a broken little boy who was drowning in his own self-loathing; You introduced me to unconditional love and healed the shattered places inside of me that I didn't think I could ever put back together. Thank you Jesus, you are my all.